For Ilaria

# BUNYAN'S GUIDE TO THE GREAT AMERICAN WILDLIFE

QUENTIN CANTEREL

Acorn Independent Press

"Galeotto fu 'l libro e chi lo scrisse:
quel giorno piú non vi leggemmo avante"

                                                    - Dante

# 1

" **U** DRTY LIAR"

Even now, the words raise the faintest echoes of your voice. And I, poor scribe, continue to copy down your every dispatch, in disbelief that it is really you talking through the board. However incredible it might seem, I do perceive your presence here as you stalk among the guttering candles, guiding the shuttle through this dance of words, which can only be described as a sort of SMS of the afterlife.

"U PROMISSED"

So I did, as did you.

"BURN IT"

But I am powerless to do so. Did you ever believe I could?

"THEY WONT BELIVE U"

Perhaps, but push comes to shove, you, dog-eyed one, shall lead me through this dark forest.

"U LACK 4GIVNESS"

As do you, dear, dearest...

These scratches I put to paper are meant to be an invocation of the dead and indeed, I write by candlelight, hoping some of your ectoplasm will burnish these blank pages. Your little ark of flesh contained an unfulfilled promise, but never found its proper berth after being sucked into its self-obsessed whirlpool. John Bunyan, dead at 23. No doubt, you are flapping bat's wings in some ill-heated Purgatorio, surrounded by the decadent hiss of the unborn.

"I CULD USE SUM FIRE"

And even those sexless seraphs who hovercraft the clouds shall mourn your passing from here till the end of time. As I write, I can almost see your slender visitation as it threads the cypress choked clefts of an Uccello-like otherwhere. After all that has taken place, it is left to me to bring the hidden contents of your untethered vessel to shore. The great work you had intended, but had asked me to destroy all trace of.

*Bunyan's Guide to the Great American Wildlife*

I have pieced this ragged thing together from letters, correspondences, court testimonials and most of all your own work, the great *Guide*. Certain things I have had to change (large parts of Felicity's back story have been cleverly altered), making replacements, cuts and amendments to put it in a form that at least those around you could begin to understand. And finally, *mutatis mutandis*, I place it here, before you. Though we have had our differences and once competed, stupidly, for what we thought was some kind of literary supremacy, death, alas, has given you an easy victory and it is I, Zulfikar, writing this instead of you.

Presently, as I scribble these lines, I am reminded that Felicity, kind maiden, had supplied me the perfect piece of poetry to describe everything that could reasonably be summarized as your life. It is from no less than an English monk of an almost mythic vintage. Before I begin in earnest, I entomb here this little sprig of bitterness:

> *"The sparrow, flying in at one door and immediately out at another, whilst he is within, is safe from the wintry tempest; but after a short space of fair weather, he immediately vanishes out of your sight, passing from winter into winter again. So this life of man appears for a little while, but of what is to follow or what went before, we know nothing at all."*

Oh, how true, how true…

But, enough, let those tarts, the muses, have their way and allow us to trace the musical beginnings of our relationship that would one day culminate into that sad fugue of personalities, lifelines, and ultimately, bombs.

"ULTIMA CUMAY VENIT EYAAM CARMINIS 8AS"

You will (no doubt) remember how we first met: I responded to an ad in The Village Voice or perhaps it was that more sordid affair, the hardly mentionable Craig's List:

> Single, white male, seeking quiet,
> clean roommate. Small 1 bdrm
> apartment in the Diamond District.
> Professionals only need apply.

The ad was as terse as your little cartoon cave above the anonymous deli. Here, my New York salad days were largely misspent. In our brief time together, I was tossed between wrack and ruin, only to be disgorged months later like a soured piece of borsch in a rather unpleasant back alley of Alphabet City. But first, our Midtown idyll. It was there that we floated like Rajas, on air mattresses a hand's width above a rat-chewed carpet. It was there that we cartwheeled entire nights away in booze and barbiturates. It was there, alas, that amidst all this wasted wattage, we forgot that despite our pissing away our daily bread, time's inexorable clockwork still pounded on in the form of an old Jewish landlord (claiming Josephus' descent) who would invariably send up his golem-like thug to collect our rent when we'd trespassed his patience by mere days.

"MET HIM YSTRDAY. HE PAID IT BCK IN END"

You lived invisibly inside the little loft space, hardly larger than a coffin. Your first words to me…

"As they say, this ain't hell, but you can see it from here."

I didn't know what it meant then, but I do now.

Days, we watched an entire spectrum of thick smoke as it billowed from the black window across the alley. We both knew its menace and how it shortened our lifespans, invading our lungs with its prismatic poison. Despite this, our days were never lacking in color; even when the storm clouds gathered, they would needfully part before we had time to look up from our petty squabbles about the laundry, the rent, and most of all, lack of sex (the last being primarily my concern).

"Insanity is the sound of your own voice, whispering into no one else's ear." Another of your gleeful emissions, its crystal clarity cast in sepia tones, your darkening spirit.

Then, amidst our moans and sighs and lamentations, there suddenly emerged the Age of Felicity.

Oh Felicity, the irrepressible inconnu that supplanted sense with a strange obsession and haunted your constantly unfocused gaze. Long hours you peered in silence through the fern frost, her very likeness quickening your mind, astonishing your blood.

Winter, year zero.

It was in that season that Manhattan was transplanted by a magician's wand into some Hyperborean realm as if in a Russian ballet. She was just then suffering her usual moonsickness and in your almost infantile dysphoria, your ark was first sundered on some uncharted coast of Bohemia. I still remember your first meeting, at the Bethesda Fountain in Central Park, while she was still tugging round that sorry, little dog in tattered form: *The Cloud of Unknowing* (yes, the first mark of her medievalism). Taking the opportunity, you played your card.

"At least, let there be a silver lining to MY unknowing by letting me discover your name?"

Silence. Bad beginnings.

"My name is John."

"Ok, John."

"What is yours?"

"Felicity."

"Ah, then it was meant to be. I am yours and you are mine."

"What? What can you mean?"

"You would be a cruel soul indeed to deny my happiness, and I a rough one to refuse accepting it. Thus, we must give ourselves to each other, completely and entirely."

Confused eyes didn't deter you and simply bored a new emptiness into your life. Who spoke like that anyway?

"John, you're a funny guy, but I've got laundry to do. Sea-Monkeys to feed. Bubble wrap to pop." *La dame sans merci.*

For days afterward, weepy music filled our little cave constantly – *Le Vent* from Alkan's *Tres Morceux dans le Genre Pathetique,* Couperin's *Les Barricades Mysterieuses*, and at times, his barbarous *Passacaile*, then onto Joy Division and even Depeche Mode. Dark moods.

Another bit of kismet or arranged chance, or perhaps old-fashioned courtship (but, actually, and most probably, plain old stalking) brought about a more lasting bond. Naked after shipwreck, Nausicaa once again clothed you in a now defunct record store in the East Village.

After that, your meetings were mostly in the native darkness of the Natural History Museum, you showing her the stuffed wildlife, she following you in sheer wonderment, and perhaps in a little bit of fear. And what of this stuffed wildlife that in your eyes seemed so very alive? Indeed, at times, you appeared to stand enraptured in front of those twilighted dioramas.

Pronghorn... *Antilocapra Americana*

Antelope jackrabbit... *Leus Alleni*

Musk ox... *Ovibos moschatus*

Ooooooooooooooooh, he's a hairy one.

Common loon... *Gavia immer* ("The most prevalent species found around in the Meat Packing district at this hour.")

Bufflehead...

All characters, you identified amongst our circle of friends and loose associations.

"MANHATTEN ZOO"

It is with these same associations that I have tried over many moons to invoke your ghost on the board. At times, the shuttle was shared variously between Mr Great-Heart, Lord Hate-Good, Madame Bubble (who did it merely on condition that I attempt to contact a number of her dead pets), Mr Fucked-Brain (and can you believe, Much Afraid), and let us not forget rugous, little Mr Feeblemind and alas, the unforgettable Mr Sagacity. Of course, all this black magic could only but eventually tempt Mrs Bat-Eyes, the Bitch of Many Centuries, Mr Msason, and even that pitiful, little Demas. For completeness sake, I eventually tapped the feckless Old Honest and lastly, Felicity herself...

But we are getting ahead of ourselves and must return to that long courtship that changed everything.

Oh, trice crossed Felicity! You, John, became her Oklahoma whirlwind, consuming everything in your path, leaving her disoriented as you cleverly removed all her familiar landmarks and replaced them with a new set of transgressions. Your candle truly burned at both ends. And finally, at your wits' end, you took her to a late-night reshowing of Parajanov's *The Legend of the Suram Fortress* (Oh, what could you have had in mind?), and it was there that you first dared to clutch her hand.

"SHE SHOOK BRETH FRUM ME"

She liked to describe you as something straight out of the 18th century: impavid mien, old-world manners – top hat, tails and ridding crop at the Knitting Factory, the occasional (and always orgulous) "are you serious" cravat. Oh, Tolerance, you are a steadfast widow.

You spent gentle, poetic weeks in her slipstream, chasing her gentle spoor and then suddenly, amidst a foxes wedding atop Wave Hill, you were gone:

"Moving downtown, near McSorleys"

Oh, muses, what shall we say about Felicity: Church of England, slender, little beanpole, waxy pallor of a holy relic, blush of a broken rose, cupid bow lips, preternatural and possibly, yes probably, possessed.

And you, John, black raven-haired, androgynous locks, the faintest of crow's feet, fashionably skinny and, for a man, certainly heteroclite. Thin voice and long fingers, slender lips always a snide remark away from disaster.

"U ARE A SHITHEAD"

In those days (really the cigarette butts of nights snuffed out at 2 or 3a.m), your daily toil up Hill Lucre began at six crossing paths in the Financial District with By-ends and that unrestful gaggle of carbon suited I-bankers. In the fogs and snows of February, the city was given over to grisaille. Always late, you hopped on the R line. Arriving, at Rector Street, only to be met by "that Basilisk", your boss, the abdominous Mr Skill. For months, you toiled in that "slick glass dick", temping for $14.50 an hour. What prosperity!

"These shitheads are virtually throwing money out the windows. Bankers paying me for next to nothing."

It was then, while collecting rejection slips from small magazines, that you began *The Guide*. In between fits of all-nighters, you'd invite me round and we became a threesome, united by a common hatred of clubs, house music, and nouvelle French cafes. Building, by fits and starts, our own little mutual admiration society...

I remember us once being stuck uptown at an illegal rave, the Russians and Israelites taking turns spinning their trance, the base tones detonating like little depth charges through the low hum of gas generators. We swayed in the summer heat and leaned against a tree stump as a police boat cast its fiery eye through the surrounding trees, setting each branch aflame. You somehow managed to share a bitter pill of ecstasy with that tenderest of Felicities so that the world nudged against you like purest organza silk. It was still normal then for you two to have conversations consisting entirely of questions:

"Why do people need drugs to make them happy?"

And you.

"Why should people be happy without them?"

"Well, isn't that a very cynical way to view the world? What about love, poetry, children?"

"Well, I suppose it comes down to a person's capacity for happiness and what has the capacity to make him happy, doesn't it?"

"Well... and what makes you happy?"

"Well, it should be you, shouldn't it, little duck?"

"Do I make you happy?"

Chewing the insides of your gums as the drugs began to take hold.

"Do you feel anything yet?"

"What am I supposed to feel?"

"What do you want to feel?"

"Happiness?"

"Well, I suppose that is what you are supposed to feel."

Happy then, but the relationship would one day move into its endgame of declarative statements:

"You don't care about me."

"Of course I do."

"That is a lie."

"Of course it isn't."

But alas, we are once again, getting ahead of ourselves. Now that we have left you once more in the graceful arms of opportunity, it is only up to you, petty egoist, to ravish her amidst the Riverside gloaming. Ah Felicity, you finally kissed her hot swan's neck and for the first time, strangely (I think) purred. Another hour of oeillades, until unrestful dawn had at last spread her fiery wing tips across each end of the Hudson. Then, finally bored of seeing the dancing of shirtless, dreadlocked white boys and down-to-their-bras girls (whose

Fig. 9 "Felicity"

failing glow sticks tricked the air out in feints, which couldn't muster even the slightest interest), we three began our journey downtown. We would eventually walk well over 100 blocks in what felt afterward like a final bastinado. (Note to reader: We were, unfortunately, forced to do so as Felicity by that point was unable to stop rubbing herself against the cold, slick tiles of the subway walls.) In our state, the entire earth turned to thistledown and left us with the unanswerable question: What does it mean when one's own fingers touch, tip to tip, yet each one feels a stranger to the other, folded as they are in a knit of double-sided sensation? By mid-morning, we ended our stroll on an anonymous aluminum paint rooftop, watching the scarlet sun levitate over a denuded Soho, whose alleyways and rayless windows resembled the interior of an ornate columbarium. Felicity's eyes were then lashing out "GREEK FEYRE" as you started to tease her for her recently being "possessed". Whoever said you can't manufacture love had never taken a pill of ecstasy.

Even you, John, would agree that New York is a strange place at five in the morning. It's almost as if the place shouldn't exist. It is a city between two worlds. Ironic then, that when I looked into your distant, unforgiving eyes, I knew you too were living in between two worlds, not just at 5a.m., but at all times. On rare occasions, you would prick your flesh and allow yourself to move amongst us.

"What do you think of Felicity?" you sputtered out over coffee. As you *never* asked my opinion about anything regarding women, I thought it my duty to give a considered response:

"What do you mean?"

"She really queers the pitch?"

"'Queers the pitch'? What a strange and outmoded turn of phrase. What is your pretentious ass talking about now?"

"None of my spells seem to be working on her."

"She seems pretty taken by you, if you ask me."

"That's exactly the problem. She seems so, but really she is utterly bored by me. She's like a little Circe, no, rather a Siren, that is only trying to seduce me into shipwreck. She knows I like her, so she secretly thinks she can convert me."

"Convert you?"

"Yes, she is devoutly Christian, but not in any traditional way. She would say 'spiritual', but I think she sees something inside me, a tiny crack where she can stick her little, holy crowbar in and pry me open."

"Why do you think that? Aren't the English all atheists?"

"Her parents were Scottish or something, but settled in some little nowhere called Little Missenden, where she grew up. She is religious, all right. Her parents where missionaries at one point, but she doesn't want to admit this to herself. But she can't shake it."

"Well, what are you going to do about it?"

"Well, I've got to convert her before she converts me."

"Convert her to what? The devil?"

"Of course not, that would be ridiculous. I've got to convert her to me. I've got to trick her out of believing she can convert me and instead, make her try to find something here on this earth that she can hold on to. Something mythical enough to let her forget all that hidden religious mysticism."

"And what is that?"

"In my mind, I think she needs to grow more attached to the flesh. Not in any carnal way, but in a way that makes her attached to living in the religion of her body: the sensation that only another person can give her. The mystery that makes one even curse a god."

"Love, sex and rockets?"

"No, not love, nothing so tired and irresponsible as that, but awareness. Awareness of the moment, here and now and lost forever. She is always living for somewhere else, something else. So, I bore her, because I am only here in front of her. She can't understand that IS everything, the entire universe."

"And what will you do about it?"

"I need to do something to help her find the immediacy in anything, in everything. Experiences that will shake her out of her body and then, violently force her right back into it. She needs an itch, what Whitman called to 'urge and urge and urge'. She needs, in fact, to understand that we are not humans at all, but rather that underneath it all, we are nothing other than beasts."

"That all sounds mystical as well."

"Not if there is nothing else in it. She doesn't have that natural feral instinct. She is too holy for that. Ultimately, she has to understand real, biological craving, not for anything in particular, but for the very experience of craving. She craves, but doesn't enjoy it, the craving. She only wants what she craves for. "

"Which you want to be you?"

"That is secondary. My religion is craving. And I want her to crave like I crave. You see, then there is no me or her, just craving, just the endless feeling of dying while at the same time living. At that moment, when you feel like that, you feel you can do anything. I need to be with someone who at any moment can and will do anything. Once you don't have that, you can't live anymore."

"Like daredevils without a cliff."

"Yes, we need a precipice to want to jump off of."

Dear reader, it all sounded good enough to write down when blitzed, but now, well… these are in Eliot's words,

"Tears shaken from the wrath-bearing tree."

SHE NEVUR UNDRSTOOD. MAYB NOW. I STILL CRAVE. HEERE. ENDLESS CRAVING. HERR KIND UF CRAVING.

None of us ever knew what made you begin *The Guide* at that time, or by then completely understood your relationship to the shadowy Willow, the "other girl in your life". Yes, indeed, we knew, but the barest of details, gathered in your few moments of incoherent bathos. We knew that you two had grown up in proximity to each other in the "wilderness", that she, "electively mute" and a "child of the wild" (perhaps a little Mowgli), hadn't spoken since she was four years old. We also knew that you'd faithfully kept all the precious, little acorns she'd squirreled away in her diaries. Basically, these diaries were her only form of communication with the outside world. In a way, you said, it was Willow that was the original author of *The Guide*. For some reason, it was clear, you saw a part of yourself in her, but even then, it seemed rather peculiar, because ultimately, Willow was for you, the Tree in the Garden of your youth, the source and continued fount of all Guilt.

SHE SUFFRS AND I WAS HER SUFFERING

Some of what lies herein is taken from Willow's diary (another of the tragedies that seemed to harry you like a harpy's wings). The first mention of "WILO" occurred with Much Afraid, that spooked child of 33. No doubt with him, the shuttle shot straight out of his hands before we'd barely turned down the lights. But then, more and more her visitations came:

PA TOLD ME 2 STAY CLEAR OF THEM BOYS

Broken, short at first, then with more confidence until they became a virtual flood. And it was through this that we confirmed Willow's secret and your suffering. Oh, how silly we seem, dear Retrospect, in the ampleness of your arms.

# 2

Hidebehind – *Ursus dissimulans*

- *A normally nocturnal, fearsome critter that possesses the capacity to conceal itself behind a wide variety of objects. The critter's ability to hide itself is greatly aided by its facility in sucking in its stomach, rendering its total girth to that of a #2 pencil. The critter is known to stalk lumberjacks and attacks without warning. The creature is known to primarily subsist off the intestines of its prey and has a considerable aversion to alcohol.*

Hidebehind

Pappy always told me to stay away from them boys. They was always there on the hill. Always chasing the living and bringing back the dead. Possums, raccoons, squirrels and even otters. One of them had a twisted face. His name was Shane. I didn't like the looks of Shane and neither did Pappy.

My Grandpappy and I live alone in our little house in the woods. My Grandpappy's name is Paul (like Paul Bunyan) and he is the strongest man in the entire forest. He has a big, bushy beard and I like to pull it so that he makes all kind of faces. My name is Willow. I am nine years old. The school where I go is 40 miles away and Grandpappy has to drive me all the way there in his old beat-up pickup. Sometimes I don't go. I hate school. They think I'm stupid because I don't talk. They don't know I can talk, but I can. I haven't spoken to nobody in five years. Not a single word, not since I was four. Nobody knows why. They think I'm as slow as pond water, but I ain't. They think I lost my voice, but I ain't. I talk to all kinda things. Mostly the Fearsome Critters, especially my friend Hidebehind. When my granddaddy drinks white lightning, he said it's to keep the Hidebehind away. He thinks I'm scared of the Fearsome Critters, but I ain't. They is the only ones in this whole entire world I can talk to.

My Grandpappy took me to the doctor once and she made me write everything down. Every day, I write everything down. Everything I am thinking and everything I do. Sometimes my Grandpappy and the doctor want to read everything I write down, but I only show them some things. The doctor says it's not really important how I express myself but that I do. She said they shouldn't try to force me to talk as it would only make my condition worse, so they taught me and my Grandpappy to speak with our hands using sign language.

I remember how little I was when I first heard about them Fearsome Critters. My Grandpappy's friends when they drunk moonshine was always giving me a hard time. And one of them, my favorite, his name was Broady. He said "You know what I am, Willow?" I shook my head. He said he was a CRYPTO-ZO-OLOGIST and that's exactly what I want to be. A CRYPTO-ZO-OLOGIST finds Fearsome Critters that ain't been found before. They would always tell me like this: "Willow, you know what a Fillyloo is? No, you don't? Well I thought everyone knew what a Fillyloo is? A Fillyloo is a creature with giant wings, like a giant dinosaur-bird and it flies upside down. Why does it fly upside down? So it can see where all them little frogs is? You see, it eats frogs, lizards and all kinds of things that are mighty cold and slimy. Give you a bellyache, they will. Anyway, when the Fillyloo finishes eating, it flies upside down so the sun can warm up its belly and that way, it won't get no bellyache." Then Trigger would pipe in. "No, Birdie, I'd say you got it all wrong. A Fillyloo flies upside down so it can see all the little children that play in the forest by themselves. See a Fillyloo loves to eat little children, especially little girls that walk too far away from their homes." "I don't believe you. You're just trying to scare me." I'd shake my head and my finger. Then, Grandpappy would say, "No, you both got it wrong. A Fillyloo flies upside down because he wants to find his wife. He flies backwards because he only wants to see where he's been. You see, the Fillyloo lost his wife a long, long time ago. How did the Fillyloo lose his wife? It happened in a terrible storm one day when she disappeared and the only way he can find her is to fly backward and upside down. That is the only way he can go back to finding her in the past." "Paul," Broady would say, "you drunk, old skunk. Stop being so depressing now." Then they would hit each other on the back and drink another beer and sometimes, they would give me a sip. I don't like beer because it tastes and looks like wee-wee. Anyway, they wouldn't give me much, as they said it would prevent me from growing up big like Grandpappy. After that, they would say, "Willow, do you know what a Snalygaster is?" It would go on like this till they all started laughing up a mighty storm. Once it got really late, like midnight, they'd send me to bed while they'd go on drinking till the early morning and I would listen to them tell stories and sing to my Grandpappy's guitar. The way he played guitar, he could burn down a building. Everybody knew he could play bluegrass like a ten-engine fire alarm. After they was done drinking, my Grandpappy would always come in late at night or early in the morning to make sure I was still sleeping. He would always whisper in my ear, the same thing. "I hope you's gonna talk tomorrow. Tomorrow, you're gonna to say something. I know it. I'm gonna pray for God to give you back your tongue tomorrow. I know them Fearsome Critters took it, but we will find it one day."

It's because of Broady that I know all the names of all the Fearsome Critters. He told me to keep track of all the names of the ones I met out in the woods. Here are the all the names, though I haven't met them all yet:

Mangrove Killfish, Hoop snake, Hugag, Teakettler, Cactus cat, Agropelter, Hyampom, Hog bear, Squidgicum-squee, Tote-road shagamaw, Glawackus,

*Tripodero, Skunk ape, Dwayyo, Snoligoster, Santer, Rumtifusel, Squink, Argopelter, Billdad Dingmaul, Sidehill gouger, Slide-rock bolter, Gumberoo, Jackalope, Splinter cat, Axehandle hound Roperite, Lufferlang Handown, Fur-bearing trout, Flittericks, Goofus, Leprechaun, Hugag, Snow waste, Dungavenhooter, Swamp auger, Toteroad Shagamaw, Treesqueak, Ball-tailed cat, Snalygaster, Cactus cat, Hodag, Jersey devil, Snipe, Central American whintosser, Snife, Whiffenpoof, Funeral mountain terrashot, Joint snake, Splintercat, Wampus cat, Squonk, Wapaloosie, Whirling whimpus*

You name it, I know it. I done memorized all those names all by myself and I know how to draw pictures of them all too. That's because Brody drew me nice pictures of all them Critters. I always wanted to see a Squonk because they are the saddest creatures in all the forest. But I never managed to see a Squonk. Broady told me that only one person has ever seen a Squonk and he is the one who discovered it. The Squonk has a hard time living in the forest because he is sad and lonely. My Grandpappy always told me there was no place for weakness in the forest because it is full of wild things. He would take me out with him to go worm grunting. He was the best at worm grunting you done ever saw. When he'd grunt, those worms would come straight out of the ground. I love catching them worms and then we'd go fishing. Catfishing so we could eat catfish. In school, I heard that in India, they even have these giant catfish that eat little children. Gross! Anyway, before we could eat, Grandpappy would have to cut wood for the fire. Grandpappy is strong as an ox. He could lift an entire tree above his head. Grandpappy used to say, "I won't always be this strong and one day, you gonna have to take care of yourself. You think you can do that, Willow?"

Sometimes, Grandpappy and me would sit in the bathtub together and we'd smoke his corncob pipe and play gin rummy. Then he would tickle me all over and I would throw the daisies I'd picked all over him so they floated everywhere around us. I loved to see all those daisies swirling all around the bathtub. I love my Grandpappy too. He don't mind much if I don't say nothing as he doesn't say much either. He said if a man talks too much, he can't be up to nothing good. Talking is for layabouts. Anyway, me and my Grandpappy could talk with our hands whenever we like.

My Grandpappy had a glass eye. He said he lost his real eye in an accident when he was a logging man. Sometimes, he would let me play with his glass eye. Sometimes, I'd put it in the bottom of the bathtub and it would look up at me and Grandpappy would smile. I told him to cover his face and ask him if he could see what I was up to. No peeking. He could always see what I was up to because Grandpappy had a magic eye. He even showed me his eye on the back of a one-dollar bill. He said though he didn't have much money, he could see where all the money in the world was going and that was into the back pockets of the wicked.

# 3

I am an American. Let me rephrase that. I am called an American. In actuality, I am called many things. Some of which I actually am. For instance:

1. I am a white male.
2. I am healthy and middle class.
3. I am bad at chess.

Other things I am called (or referred to as doing), but might have reasons to debate:

1. I am rich.
2. I am lucky.
3. I love Jesus Christ.
4. I am an imperialist butcher and murderer of babies.
5. I am a slaver, a supporter of sweatshops and child labor.
6. I eat animals needlessly and starve others by doing so.
7. I talk loudly and out of turn and say things like, "Awesome" and "Holy shit".
8. I eat fast food all the time and have a waistline the size of a small mastodon.
9. I say exactly what I think.
10. I am an imposter.

Every American must have a guilty conscience. It is our birthright. Is there anyone who isn't born with blood on his or her hands (if even just the blood of their tortured mother)?

After all, what does it mean to be a self-hating American? A self-hating American, living after the end of the century, the end of the millennium, the supposed end of time. Two millenniums that together, began with the death of a Messiah and ended with my being drunk and puking into a paper bag at the back of a yellow cab (my first taste of what was to become somewhat of a leitmotif).

In reality, I have no idea what it means to be American. To be part of its fauna. I have a hard enough time even answering what it means to be human. No lie, in a high-school biology class, I filled out the following definition for myself as a representative of *homo sapiens*:

Kingdom – United States

Phylum – God knows, but I'm told it doesn't separate me from the common roach

Class – Hopelessly middle

Order – As you can see by my answers, I certainly could use some in my life

Family – None to speak of, but I'm still trying…

Genus – If you had at least left in the "I", I could have scored some points by answering a definitive "no"

Safe to say, it wasn't one of my finer academic moments. Fortunately, there were others to make up for it.

But in life and in university, I discovered one thing you can say for sure: some questions (at least the very important ones) are much like the humiliations brought on by poverty, in that they tend to spawn more want than any effective response. After all, if I can't even answer what it means to be a somewhat sentient human being, living in a rent-controlled apartment in lower Manhattan, how the hell can I answer what it means to be an American?

Everyone else around me seems to know what one is. Americans, after all, have a definite penchant for standardized tests (this much I know). So, perhaps if I phrase the question as such: Is an American:

A) An animal, born, raised and fed in a cage of a specific shape in a specific part of the world?
B) One possessed of a particular state of mind (a particular portion of insanity)?
C) One who has the right to a rather undistinguished passport?
D) All of the above?

I have posed similar questions to others. The butcher tells me, "I'm an American." The taxi driver: "I am an American." The banker, the President, all Americans. But what do they say about me, who feels a stranger in his own skin? I ask them, what does it mean to be an American? Does it mean being someone who loves his country? Someone who stands for its values?

The usual answer they give me is D), which always demands several more questions I never bother to air, like: are any of these "American values" we constantly speak of, uniquely ours? Do I even agree with these so-called values? How can you say we even share them if you don't know what my values are? Let it be known, I don't walk the streets sharing my "values" like a pack of cigarettes, or like a sexually-transmitted disease.

Exasperated, I usually come back again and repeat the question to myself: what is an American? I know America, but I don't know any Americans. I know its laws, but not why they should apply to me. I know its territory, its anthem, even its history, but don't see any of its stories reflected in my own? Day after day, I am spoken to by politicians as an American. We, the People, will do this. We, the People, will do that. What the hell is "The People"? A creation myth about "the father of our country" chopping down a cherry tree?

Pop quiz:

Did you know that the original American pledge of allegiance was supposed to last 15 seconds?

That it was supposed to contain the words "equality" and "fraternity", but didn't because the author understood that the state superintendents on education were against equality for women and African Americans?

Did you also know that the original salute to the flag was frighteningly similar to the Nazi salute?

I didn't, but I read in on Wikipedia. So, I ask you, what am I pledging if even the goddamned pledge of allegiance is born out of a lie? Where did I sign up for any of this? Can I ever cease to be an American, really?

Ultimately, having lived here so long (and nowhere else), I do know something about America. Primarily one thing: that its history has been completely defined by two important, countervailing forces: the spiritualistic and the animalistic. I can say without much doubt that every critical development in the history of this country has been the product of these two impulses. One might justifiably ask, what about the intellectual impulse? America's great, inventive history? The civilizing energy that has given us so much: the cotton gin, the Jacuzzi, peanut butter, sea monkeys, the microwave oven, a man on the moon, the internet? I could perhaps lamely answer, "intellectual spiritualism", but this would be a bit disingenuous. I now know (and for certain this time) that these "inventions" are nothing more than the maniacally refined result of a human being's fundamentally animal nature. The same nature that first put a flint hammer into an ape's hand. This is not the first step into a new kind of humanity, what we could quaintly call a "civilizing force", but rather the last step in a more organized form of bestiality, one that ends in holocausts, nuclear winters, and human manufactured death.

Put simply (and hardly originally), the American psyche can be broken into two distinct halves, its inscape dominated by two, very different contours: the self-ruling, but expansive curves of the spiritualist and the harder, acuter angles of the animalist. In a very real sense, the measure of man is hardly more than the hypotenuse between each of these diverging tendencies (some national histories have more of one, some more of the other, and I would argue that it is exactly this composite set of ratios that separates each from the other). Let it be said that while the spiritualist attempts with all his strength to leave the world behind, the animalist attempts with all his might to dominate it. Either way, it ends the same, in a depopulated planet. Ultimately, these two forces are part of one another, like an American kind of yin and yang, a separate but equal, a pacifying force, a passive aggressiveness. Oh, Lord above, let us not come unto contradiction, for truly, the hypocrite is indeed more hateful than the sinner. Amen.

Why is any of this important? Because I grew up in America. A small (need I say forgotten) part of America. A ropy backwater (my life's "warm, little pond") that most people would be glad to have never seen. What I want to do is to tell you a story that, as far as I can attest, occurred in America. It may even be a story about America and (if you will allow me some small bit of pretension) you might even call it an American parable.

Without further ado, let us begin the story in the manner that all of our private fictions (dare we call any of the stories involving our own lives true?) should begin: Once upon a time, there was a little girl. Her name was Willow. I had known of her existence my entire life, but I only started to become acquainted with her and her story when she turned nine years old. She lived on a hard piece of land, deep in the Georgia backwoods. Her family's property happened to be connected with that of my own. She was a peculiar little girl, particularly because she never, ever spoke. Not once. That kind of thing tends to get noticed in a place like where I grew up. The truth of the matter was that she had been diagnosed as being "electively mute" and had been that way since the age of four. Basically, her condition boiled down to her refusing (or rather being unable) to speak to anyone, whether out of a sense of deep anxiety or uncontrollable fear. However, some claimed she could and would talk in her sleep, especially when she had bad dreams. Some said she even spoke in tongues, reversing all the words that, if turned around, would reveal the dark secret to her muteness. Most people thought she was stupid, but in actuality, I suspected her muteness was the result of some kind of tragedy, the details of which were indubitably daubed by the exaggerated and somewhat false hues of the local colorists. As one might imagine, tall tales and the truth rub shoulders a great deal in that part of the country, and while they should be kept separate, one always suspects a large degree of incest (a suspicion born from a certain unhealthy pallor and naturally accentuated by the uncanny appendages that are the true hallmark of these types of stories).

Willow was certainly a lonely and troubled girl. Some women would turn their faces or walk to the other side of the street when they saw her on the street or in school. Her absolute silence haunted them. If you can believe it, many thought the devil himself had ripped out her tongue on one of his frequent sojourns in the town (his mischief was particularly known to occur on weekends or whenever the stills of Ma Pearl's moonshine were set a tippin'). They also thought that her guardian and grandfather, Paul Bunyan, was an evil man. That he did things to her and thus was the origin of her reluctance. For that reason, most people just left the pair alone and held to a time-honored tradition of non-interference. Interferers were people you saw on TV, people who lived in the cities. Here, you don't get involved in other people's business under any circumstances.

My friends and I, who were also young at the time, would see Willow playing in the woods by herself. We regarded the lime-green, plastic whistle tied around her neck with some unutterable measure of horror and lack of understanding. She presumably wore it just in case she ever got into trouble, but we as often saw her without it. She also went to my school, but was a few grades below my own. The teachers (some of whom incidentally referred to her by the more popular moniker of "Quietness") had to take especial care around her to prevent her being bullied. Much to her disadvantage, she also possessed another flaw almost fatal in surroundings like those: according to the accounts of all those in any position to judge, she was an incredibly bright student, which set her on the path to further ostracization. Needless to say, along with her native intelligence, she was (as frequently happens to those of her nature) endowed by an equal measure of wildness. She would, on an all too frequent basis, throw violent, unpredictable temper tantrums. Indeed, she was what the other kids referred to as a "spaz". Back then, our small part of the world didn't have access to drugs like Ritalin or Dexedrine (not that her grandfather could afford them in any case), which meant that to deal with these frightening "outbursts", the teachers would beat her or lock her in a closet until she quieted down. It is hardly worth mentioning that this foul treatment had the only result of making sure she ran away from school even more frequently.

By the time I'd got wind of her, I was dawdling beneath a hawthorn tree, huddling amidst a pride of boys who were taking the measure of a snotty-nosed nerd we'd wanted to beat up. I was usually that very snotty-nosed dork, but on this occasion, I was spared by my happenstance association with a much bigger and brasher nerd-beater than myself. As a group, we'd hear some pretty fell rumors; that someone had been casting aside their stained underwear in inappropriate nooks of the school property for weeks. It was a most disgusting and embarrassing problem haunting the smilingly sedate and otherwise senile headmaster. Of course, this was all quite normal for the faculty of the middle school across the street, but over here, it was fairly unheard of. It later turned out that Quietness was quite a bit more precocious in ways no one could have imagined. It all started one February afternoon when a rather daft gym teacher had found a girl's panties clogging the toilet in the female lavatory. For the life of all involved, no one could identify whose it was. A school gardener found yet another incarnadined pair, most inconveniently at the bottom of a potted plant. At the time, it was thought that it was the work of one of the younger, more uncouth teachers, or perhaps one of the older girls from the adjacent middle school. One who was either deliberately dropping red herrings to void her own guilt or otherwise making some kind of dirty protest. No one could quite untwine the mystery. But then again, no one quite noticed the subtle changes that were occurring inside of Willow. Changes that made sure she began to hide her legs and wore bigger and bigger shirts to mask what were scarcely moving beyond mosquito bites to become the tiniest of breasts. If they had, they would have no doubt put her erratic behavior down to the early onset of adolescence.

Quietness was always a disruptive student in more ways than one. I remember hearing that some of the teachers used to make her write her responses on the blackboard, which always prompted the other students to laughter. Indeed, even the teachers sometimes forgot that Willow was "dumb" but not deaf. On one particular occasion, the teacher had asked her, "What did the settlers and the Indians eat on Thanksgiving?"

Willow, having had enough, wrote down the following:

"Each other."

# 4

My name is Felicity Fawkler. I am aged 26 and a British citizen by birth, though I've lived in the United States for five years now. Specifically, I have lived in New York City, where I moved on little more than a whim, or perhaps it was to follow another man I was secretly in love with. Who knows? Who cares?

*Le cœur a ses raisons que la raison ne connaît point.*

To the best of my abilities, I promise what is written here is as true an account of my relationship with the deceased, John Bunyan, as I can possibly produce. Though this document was begun as a court testimonial, it became for me more, so much, much more. Every time I switch on the laptop and start tapping away, the memories just overwhelm me in a flood of disjointed images. These mental tapestries are of course all I have left of John, and I want to keep them close to warm my heart, to keep putting to paper each moment we ever shared together. Sadly, it is the only way I have left of being close to anybody.

I first met John on February 28th 2009 at the Bethesda Fountain in Manhattan's Central Park. At that time, the fountain was still one of my favorite places in Manhattan and, to some degree, it still is. It was one of my many retreats. Where I would go in all seasons to read under the cherry blossoms and watch the Terrace pulsate with the crowds like a living muscle, draining and filling its arteries as the day's rhythms progressed. Indeed, New York is a living organism like any other, and at a certain time of day, when the density of light thins out and the window beams seesaw toward the ceiling, one can feel it beginning to relax. One can literally feel the bridges, the buildings, the trees, every integral part of the city's anatomy, lengthen itself out toward the outer reaches of the evening, like a feline preparing itself for the fierce activities of another night. As people are often wont to say in one way or another: you can never really possess New York, it possesses you.

At daybreak, as bokeh reflections gather underneath the Bow Bridge, the Terrace affords, to those who would see it, a view of some of the best things New York has to offer. In the Bible, the Pool of Bethesda was where the angel stirred the waters by dipping in the merest fraction of its big toe. And it is true; here, one could find healing. John would mark down this reference as one more sign of my religiousness, but for me, it was more than that. Having grown up rural England, I needed a bit of a branch. John would teasingly describe my life like this:

*Born in Diss,*
*A thing amiss*
*Then bourn a babe*
*Sans astrolabe*
*To Missenden*
*Where dale and fen*
*Found her bourne*
*Of English corn*

I was used to being amongst wood and glade, but in Manhattan, I had none of that.

One thing I should mention before I go on (lest you refuse to forgive me for it later) is that I come from money and privilege. My family is an old one. The kind that almost had a stitch in the Bayeux Tapestry. In addition, it appeared they'd once hove a clove sachet on the Arabella, meaning I'm certainly not the first part of the line to put a print on the shores of New Amsterdam.

As almost everyone is aware, the English are very susceptible to class consciousness. And those of us fortunate enough to rank in its upper echelons spend too much time being either extremely ashamed or extremely chuffed about what we perceive to be our "place in society". It is true that for all our congenital maladies, the English upper classes have evolved a highly attuned and dangerously accurate sixth sense for this sort of thing. In a room full of anonymous, gray-clad persons, I bet you my inheritance that an English aristocrat, by mere observation alone, can part the seas in under a minute. We spend most of our lives torn between jealousy for those above us, and little less than sympathy for those below. This wasn't my world. I wanted to escape. It's (oh these dreadful American contractions) hard to explain to people not of this class why one might want to, but nonetheless, I did. Nevertheless, it's hard to argue with maths, and what do the maths say? In England, everything in your life boils down to a few factors: the postcode in which you were born, your father's occupation, and (I would hasten to add) how your grandmother pronounces the word "marvelous".

So, yes, I am what you call blue-blooded. John would say I spend too much time hiding this fact, so for his sake, I have decided to clear the air. My English nature still harbors some fear that my admission may alter the reader's impression of me in ways I can't possibly imagine. Needless to say, I am what Americans refer to as a "trust-fund baby". In this regard, I could have whiled away my time sipping martinis at Pastis, air-kissing the seasonal eurotrash, making sure I was at all the most fashionable art openings with the tiniest of canapés. But that is not what I wanted from the City. My ambitions led me elsewhere and how could they not? Here is a start: My father (of whom I am very proud) was almost a Lord Mayor of London. Furthermore:

1.   He attended Oxford (I dropped out);
2.   He went on to head a bank (I live like I'm bankrupt);

3.  He's listed as a Knight of Malta (I spent a few, extremely
    hazy nights in Malta).

That's where the similarity stops. If you can believe it, I came
here to New York to work in an animal shelter. Yes, you read it
correctly. That is what I do or did, until shortly after I met John.
So safe to say, for whatever reasons, I wasn't meant just yet to
follow in my father's otherwise outsize footsteps.

I lived on Roosevelt Island then (perhaps the most
unfashionable of Manhattan addresses) and would commute to
the City from my tiny flat, on most days, riding the funicular
tramway. At that time, my head was still spinning in an
outrageous axis between flipped bob and feathered bangs.
Indeed, I remained at the very fringes (excuse the bad pun, I
make a lot of them) of my krautrock phase. I listened to anything
from Can, Faust, Neu! and even Tangerine Dream. All this
was of course a carryover from an almost sexless relationship
(though redefining the word "intense") with a carbuncular
German who'd studied something called "General Systems" at
Cambridge (he also had the distinction of taking me to see *Das
Boot* on our first date). Then, once I'd contracted an incurable
case of "bleeding heart syndrome" and decided the manatees
and icebergs needed saving (as did other parts of my own
anatomy), I'd determined that the place to start my world-
rescuing project was in New York. By happenstance, it turned
out that a particularly handsome boy named Angel, a DJ I had
met on a weekend in Malta, had just attained a booth residency
and moved only weeks before. However, not long after the first
touch on the tarmac at JFK, I got swooped up/hijacked by a tribe
of media and fashion types from the L.E.S. It was certainly in
New York that I discovered the combined art of being completely
self-conscious, self-absorbed and ostensibly selfless (remember
the manatees), all at the same time. Living in the City, you are

in some ways under a microscope; not allowed entry unless you wore the right clothes, listened to the right music, and eventually knew the right people so that your name was on all the right lists (by the way, why are all clubs in New York invariably guarded by some bitchy-looking metrosexual?). Essentially, you had to possess the right code. And if you did, Manhattan became an oyster bed, a place for suspended adolescence and exploration. However, one had to make sure one was current and therefore relevant. For a brief time, it seemed I'd been pushed back into sixth form, where everything revolved around what bands you listened to, what books you read, and what television shows you were and were not watching. Previously, I'd tried to explore, listening to the entire history of the City from Gershwin, Ellington and Sinatra, through to the Velvet Underground, the Ramones, and Blondie, finally hitting a breaker with UTFO, Big Daddy Kane, and Afrika Bambaataa. I would eventually arrive all the way up to The Kraven and Cannibal Ox. How else was I to fit in this city's patchwork fabric? I tried the clothes, all the right restaurants, all the most talked about trance, house, and jungle DJs, until finally, gutted after a year's time, I finally gave up. I was never going to properly fit in. The velvet rope cut too hard and despite wearing blue jeans instead of wings, my Angel invariably flew away.

The next time I "ran into" John (after that unfortunate initial meeting at the Fountain) was at a record shop in the East Village called the Wax Werks. He didn't have much "room" for "modern music". Whilst leaving the store, I spotted him walking his fingers across the dull jewel cases of the classical CD corner. Despite my previous reservations, I thought I'd go up and say hello. He was wearing a black fedora hat and, without even looking up, his first words to me were, "Are you still following me around?" To which I replied, with some surprise, "Me? What makes you think I'm..."

"Two is a coincidence, but three…"

"Three, where did we meet the second…"

Finally looking me in the eyes, he mumbled through a wry smile,

"Perhaps in my dreams…"

"Oh, God…"

"Or perhaps you were just pretending not to see me the other day outside the Blue Elephant Tea House."

"You were there?"

"Of course, it's only my favorite… Ah, ha! I finally found it. You into Mehul? No, I bet you prefer Kalivoda."

"Kali…who?"

Without missing a beat, and entirely unprompted, he began running me through his manifold musical tastes and the relevant justifications for them. He wasn't anything, if not confident. Not one for pissing about, he established right away that his favorite music was taken from the *Sturm und Drag* era, a musically-forgotten non-sequitur that existed ever so briefly as a sort of "proto-Romantic warm-up act". Thus, his masters were a host of names I'd never even heard of: Dussek, C.P.E. Bach, Vanhal, Muthel, Kraus, etc. His other favorite composers were either from the Mannheim School or the reform operatists like Vogel, Gluck and Jommelli. In particular, he thought the latter composers were "dreadfully underrepresented in the Lincoln Center repertoire". It all sounded so utterly pretentious and off-putting, but he convinced me he wasn't deliberately being an obscurantist, but rather that he had a deep interest in transitional periods, when the beginnings and endings of things were all mixed. He saw the entirety of music history as one gigantic sonata, whose boundless music was so full of quaint codas and odd, little repeats, it made one forget which way and at what pace the story was resolving itself. "You wake up one day and realize there had to be something between Handel and

Beethoven." Quite frankly, I had gotten so bored of the New York lads trying to impress me that I didn't bat an eye. Their idea of being "cool" was dragging me to see the latest underground DJ or some hopelessly esoteric, modern, experimental piece. John's approach at least had the benefit of being original, if not honest. It could have been worse, I guess. He could have been into The Carpenters or Celine Dion. After some further discussion, and not a little arm-twisting, I finally coerced him to the "modern" section, where he finally conceded a liking for Cole Porter, Amelia Rodriquez and Al Bowlly, of all sins. In regard to anything later than that, he confessed to being "lost". For weeks after this fateful meeting, I had always wondered how he tracked me down to the East Village. He would later admit that our "second" and "third" meetings weren't exactly "accidental", however, he would never reveal his method (leaving it up to "strange, dark powers at work"). My theory? I think I must have somehow let it slip that I worked in the area. He would one day concede that his approach to women was that of a "persistence hunter"; "You chase one a hundred miles and eventually, they have to give in."

So there we were, stuck in that record store in the East Village, having the quasi-first date of indie dreams. That was where I first noticed a very peculiar thing about John. His scent. Strangely (and perhaps embarrassingly), when he came close to me, one of the first things that attracted me to him was his scent. Call it whatever you want, pheromones, musk, but there was definitely something about John that always smelled good, something that drew me towards him with an animal-like magnetism. But, beneath all that, there was something else more important. Something that even now, I have a hard time putting my finger on. Indeed, it didn't take me long until I suddenly felt extremely comfortable in his presence. Even at the record shop, I couldn't quite believe it. Could I actually be falling for this bloke? Though I was initially put off by his rather strange manner, it didn't take me long to notice that there was a quality inside him that separated him from other men. He possessed a certain kind of patience, a tenderness even. Indeed, unlike your typical Manhattanite hipster male, he would listen to me, as if he reveled in everything I said, smart, stupid or otherwise. There was also something slightly, otherworldly about him, even effeminate, but incredibly manly at the same time. I should also say that he was exceptionally clever, a trait shared by many of the men in my life. However, he was younger than me, and had graduated NYU at the tender age of 19.

Once we emerged from the record store, he immediately lit and started sucking on an apple-bowled meerschaum pipe. In retrospect, it shouldn't have been so surprising, but I couldn't really understand what century this bloke was from. In secret, I suspected a monocle was on its way. But ultimately, this was John at core. In many ways, he was old before his age. Before we had made more than five steps together, he immediately went into a long monologue about medieval printing techniques and the purgative virtues of reading Ficino and Pico della Mirandola.

Later that week, we met for the first of what would later prove to be many trips to the Natural History Museum. Though I had been there before, I had never seen it in the same light as when I went with John. John clearly knew a lot about animals and wildlife. Furthermore, he seemed to care a great deal about them, though not initially in a PETA-Nazi kinda way. I guess that's what we shared, what in a sense initially brought us together. In "animal circles", you meet a lot of awkward people who form incredibly intense bonds with animals, because they are either unable or unwilling to form those same connections with human beings. In my experience, it is usually for the former reason. Essentially, these are the type of people who become animal hoarders or jump in swim tanks to befriend killer whales. But John and I were both different. We grew up in the wilderness and had been around animals all the time. He would tell me fascinating stories about living in the woods. John said he particularly liked the museum because of how dark and intimate it was in many sections ("must be the darkest museum in the world"). The Hall of Minerals and the Asian Ethnographic wing were particular favorites, and perfect for stolen moments of intimacy. He also appreciated the sheer scale of some of the exhibitions, and we would always stagger beneath the life-sized blue whale as it swam through the diaphanous net of our combined imaginations.

John often dreamt of finding a forgotten corner behind one of the displays so he could get himself locked in overnight. Needless to say, out of everything else, his favorite part of the museum was the North American Mammal Hall. He always stood enraptured in front of the dioramas. And out of all of these, he always lingered longest before the one containing the humble raccoon. On many occasions, he repeated the notion that if he was embodied by any animal, it would probably be the twilight-dappled raccoon, a smarmy creature of the night. I never understood why he saw himself in that raccoon, or why he considered me "a medieval-looking pangolin". In any case, he said the nature depicted in the diorama reminded him very much of where he grew up. Furthermore, he also said the Aztecs believed raccoons had spiritual powers.

Another of my favorite places on the Island was the Cloisters museum in Fort Tryon Park. John would wave this away as another sign of my "medievalism", and that my "spirituality" was nothing more than a "recrudescence of a late Antiquity form of proto-Christianity". It was just like him to come up with these odd associations. As spring began to light its fuses, John and I went rowing in the Central Park Lake, where John captured a now framed picture of my hair being blown back like a windsock. I cannot think of the occasion now without hearing Liszt's *Au lac de Wallenstadt* in my head, a song he played through earphones as we floated listlessly (I warned you of these puns) on the stilled lake. After meeting at our usual place and being serenaded by a street performer named Thoth, we went walking in the Ramble (referred to by John as the "gay forest"). He joked that some ecologists described the Ramble as a "climax forest", and despite their being occasionally refuted, there were many obvious examples between the tree trunks of their being patently correct. At this point, John had decided to ask me if I thought he was odd, to which I replied:

"You are certainly unconventional."

"The English always fall for a decent eccentric, don't they? Byron took a bear to university and Jeremy Bentham carried a pair of eyes in his pocket. These he wanted to be inserted inside his mummified head, which I'm told still attends faculty meetings."

I couldn't help but laugh at such statements, and he knew it. I usually brushed off his normally lurid shock tactics.

"Is that what you're trying to do? To be eccentric?"

"On the contrary, it's clear I'm just trying to 'fit in', it's just not clear exactly what it is I'm trying to fit in to."

"Cheeky monkey. Well, if that's what your trying to do, please stop, as you're making a horrible mess of it, unless it is your intention to fit into an insane asylum."

"Aha! You know, Tasso pretended to be insane so he could get free rent. Think they have an asylum in lower Manhattan for starving writers who want to inspire global-scale religious warfare?"

"Frankly, if they did, I couldn't tell the difference."

After hours of getting lost and retracing our steps, we finally found our way to the Belvedere Castle, just in time to avoid a stealthy summer's cloudburst. For the entire journey, I had

Van Morrison's *Sweet Thing* in the back of my head, adjoining the *camera obscura* images of van Coninxloo's forest paintings. We had coincidentally seen a display of Coninxloo's works the previous week, which had the sole purpose of rendering some small bit of my art history degree useful. My reverie was quickly obliterated when I heard a pair of dizzy Liverpudlian slappers talking in a plastered Scouse accent. They were seemingly in their natural habitat, huddled over a packet of fags and half-consumed cans of Belgian "wife beater". It wasn't exactly surprising that they were reading a version of *OK!* magazine taken straight off the plane, giggling in a terribly American way and brandishing their lack of class like a passport back to hell. In two years, I could see them as pale petrels, sporting prams and "scrape backs", down some desperate Special Brew-strewn alleyway in Liverpool, fags dangling half out of their mouths and their crotch-crimping skirts stained in chip grease and HP sauce. A third rain-soaked chav, wearing a "Princess" hoodie, tracksuit trousers and a tight shirt, through which her two-pence strawberry creams were already beginning to show (obviously pushed out to compensate her for her "boat race"), joined them, spitting grime and tagging along her Cockney-haired "innits" and "luuvs" like little Pomeranian puppies. "Dodging the filth? Been around the block more times than a Sherbet, more used than a Tesco bag, huh, girls!?" Fortunately, the Americans still love our accents.

Once the girls had left, it was there that John began to quiver, as a first embryonic kiss grew forth from his lips. It is a moment I will always remember. When I opened my eyes, I saw that his were open too. This is when I learned that John was an open-eyed kisser. In my book, this important fact indicated his either being one of those non-trusting types or perhaps one of those that was a close observer of others. In John's case, it was a part of both.

As I keep saying, John was definitely of a different sort. To entertain me, he would sometimes read to me the naughtier bits of Francesco Colonna's *Hypnerotomachia Poliphili* (a strange, almost mystical, book he referred to as a "painful paean to blue balls") or Aretino's *The Secret Life of Nuns*. He had mentioned the fact that his father was an antiquarian art dealer of some repute, specializing in maps and various medieval texts. John had reproductions of some of the more famous maps in his room, including the "Red Line" map of North America, Ptolemy's *Geography*, the *Tabula Rogeriana*, a world map by Petrus Kaerius, and the Evesham map. He also has had a beautiful red-spined, Morocco leather-bound version of *Très Riches Heures du Duc de Berry*, and a lesser version of Gossuin's *Imago Mundi*. John used to wax philosophical about the changes wrought in medieval cartography. When opened, these old books revealed a bouquet of vanilla flowers and almonds, a smell that sent both John and myself into raptures. With some pride, he mentioned his father specialized in Bestiaries and one of his most prized possessions was a copy of the *Physiologus* of Isidore of Seville. He also had rare copies of the *Aviarium* of Hugh of Fouilloy, the Bestiaries of Guillaume le Clerc, Gervaise, Philippe de Thaon, Ashmole, Aberdeen, Rochester, Pierre de Beauvais, the *De Naturis Rerum* of Hrabanus Maurus and the *De Propretatibus Rerum* of Bartholomaeus Anglicus. We would spend hours flipping through those pages, observing those splendidly reproduced miniatures, as we practically breathed in the gold-leaf, framed pictures that sprung open to us like caskets of delightful oddities. Amazingly, John could differentiate between all the colors delineated in *Art d'Illuminer*, every blue from *azur d'outremer* to *azur d'Allemagne*, each green from *vert de Hongrie* to *vert de flambé*, the reds of cinnabar, ocher, *mine* and *rose de Paris*, even the yellows of massicot and orpiment, and finally, the ormolu-based golds that insufflated us with so much joy.

John did all the things for me a girl wishes: he cooked amazing food, gave me massages, pretended to like all my bad poetry, left roses for me at odd times in odd places… everything a girl wanted after a series of bad, unrewarding relationships. No surprise, we soon became quite attached to one other. However, we certainly didn't retire from the scene. As budding and bosom friends in the City, we, in our little tribe, pretended to know everything about one another, but in reality, we knew next to nothing except for names, faces and job titles (sometimes, even the rent you paid). No one wanted to get too close. That was fine, because in this city, you could destroy and recreate yourself almost every day. You could push aside the past to become something entirely new. That was the refreshing thing about John, we didn't have to pretend and we really did want to know one another. As all new couples, we felt compelled to put ourselves in social situations, to spice our relationship with the usual excitements of going out and meeting friends. Largely, he seemed to endure all these nights out on my behalf, wearing earplugs in every club we attended. However, there was some small element in all this going out he enjoyed. In fact, he insisted that the night always had to have some degree of danger or unpredictability to it. We were still in the delicate phase were we felt anxious about any such inertia, as if a moment of staleness spelt doom to a relationship we both wanted to work (though he constantly mumbled something about my "trying to convert him"). We had had a good amount of momentum gathering about us. Furthermore, we both wanted to blow through each successive night like a cannonball. Put simply, we ached and ached endlessly to get utterly wrecked in each other's company. In these situations, there was only one man to call. In fact, to completely ensure we were nothing but absolutely plastered on a variety of substances, we needed "The Colonel". The Colonel – immortal one, diamond geezer – became the avatar of our meaning, the sheer manifestation of New York's nightlife. He was always dragging us to all kinds of parties we utterly detested, but which served the very important purpose of keeping us entertained. Each location had its own season; P.S.1 and the Czech Beer Garden in the summer, winter nights spent hoovering coke at the Milk Bar or chugging down the dark funk at Nublu, in the spring, dancing through Twilo Fridays or the Donkey Show, autumn became awash with cyberpunk losers in that Meatpacking dive, The Vault, and finally, in all seasons, climbing down the night and its airless altitudes at The Void, Bedroom Bar or Welcome to the Johnsons, and so it went, on and on. And it would go on forever, until we'd finally get our wings clipped at that abysmal "club" on the rusty tug boat ('The Frying Pan"), where I thought I'd contracted tetanus and The Colonel spazzed out on e's and vodka Red Bull. On one particularly epic night, we decided to go a bit off-piste. After the normal turn at Twilos, we moved on to a nameless hardcore Latin club in which we clearly didn't belong. My apathetic wardrobe could, in theory, get me into most places, but it did nothing to help me fit in here. Once there, The Colonel sent me up to the DJ booth to get a phone number of a drug dealer named "Mr Smiles". In the booth, there was an improbable black man from another decade with a Jheri curl, shutter shades, a fishnet shirt and leather trousers with far too many zippers. We were instantly decoded as imposters. After politely requesting the presence of Mr Smiles, he came up to me and said, "You tryin' to jive me, girl?"

I replied, "Sir, I'm in no way trying to 'jive' you, but really would appreciate it if you could give me the mobile number of Mr Smiles."

"Mobile number? You sure you get down and wet like that? Where you from, girl?"

Flummoxed, I thought I was certainly out of my depth and merely said, "England."

To which he responded, "Oh, like the UK? How's the Queen then? She still livin' up in Versailles."

"Versailles is in France, sir."

"Bitch, I know where Versailles is. You sure you're not Five-0?"

"Sorry, sir. I'm certainly not up to date, but I'm not as unfashionable as a 50 year old, I hope."

"Git the fuck outta here."

And there it was. Two countries divided by a common language. Coming down from the booth, I accidentally stepped on another women's high-heels, to which she coarsely responded, "What the f… Watch where the fuck you goin'. I oughta cut you, bitch."

"Excuse me, I'm sorry."

"Sorry don't cut it here, Wonder Bread. These shoes are brand new Louboutin, bitch," she screamed, while showing me the expected red underside of her heels.

Staring into the abyss of her eyes, I had nothing to say. At this point, John came up and kindly interceded, "Sorry, my friend here is a bit drunk. Can I buy you a drink?"

"A drink, punk… how 'bout a new pair of shoes?" At that point, the girl pulled a switchblade out of her pocket. "I oughta cut you. I keep it real, bitch. You betta ax somebody before I put a shiv yo' ass. My boo will put you both up in Belvue."

Fortunately, her friend pulled her away by the arm and said, "C'mon, girl. You crazy. It's just some shoes."

Her friend, Damsel of the Crooked Weave, shouted back, "Just some shoes! These are La Bou—"

"Ca'mon, girl. Don't think I know that. You're already on probation. Just leave it. No use messin' with these…"

"It took me six months…"

"I know. I know, but we gotta get home and pick up your daughters anyway. It's late…"

"Damn, those little bitches always gettin' in the way of me havin' a good night. You lucky this night, bitch."

It was definitely time to go home and lay low for a while. John spirited me out of there. Despite our both being shaken, our spirits survived on a previously split "dove" and we accordingly managed an enjoyable trip downtown, exploring each other's tonsils with our tongues. The driver put on some Sinatra, quietly endorsing us as we found our little corner of oblivion. The ride of course ended too soon. An old-fashioned type, John left me at the door with a farewell kiss and a good night.

"Hey, I got some work to do tomorrow…"

"Well, you can stay over. Don't leave just yet."

"As much as I'd like to, I think it's best I just leave."

I pulled him close and he gave me one final kiss. I've never been so painfully let down in my entire life. My privates were practically screaming out for restitution. Just as I was trying to put myself to sleep, I began to start thinking about John and what I imagined he'd be like in the sack. I realize that after three months, we hadn't spoken much about sex yet. It was actually John who didn't want to rush into it and to be honest, the issue seldom came up. He half joked that it was to protect my religious sensibilities and my no doubt unblemished hymen that he refrained. His lack of pushing me toward sex was certainly a surprising enough fact in modern Manhattan. It was usually on the menu after the cursory two or three dates. What was perhaps even more surprising was that outside of a few awkward fondlings, I hadn't had sex myself for well over a year (maybe the carbuncular German had ruined it for me). There was something about the smell of certain men, of most men, that made sex in the majority of cases impossible (merely thinking of England didn't seem to do the trick). I was highly sensitive to smell, and the smell of arousal and armpits made me want to puke. In addition, most of the men had an awkward way about things and always seemed to be poking about in the darkness into all the most inhospitable places. Though I had thought about it on many occasions, I concluded the suggestion of an anatomical map and a Maglite wouldn't have gone over well with any of them. In general, I'd had surprisingly little experience myself, and John took a straight edge attitude, in that he didn't want sex to interfere in our relationship at so early a stage. Furthermore, in addition to my issues with smells, I had other more physical problems. It is a medical fact that I was frequently dry. Therefore, sex wasn't always on top of my list of things to do, and when it was, it was frequently unpleasant. It had made some of my relationships difficult. Fun fact: they say female pandas are only up for it 3 days a year and that was becoming generous for me. In fact, John joked about the precise dates of my "panda season", which he likened to a "movable Christmas". As sex is at the center of so much of the world, it was refreshing to see that it wasn't the barycenter of our somewhat lopsided relationship. In fact, I've always wondered why we dress ourselves up so much, just to get ourselves dressed down again. Anyway, we had plenty of other things to be talking about. He was writing movie script about an abandoned ship full of cannibal rats that drifted inexorably toward Manhattan. He had other peculiar hobbies: besides going to the gym and the opera, he liked to frequent lower Manhattan's only firing range. It didn't take me long to realize that John had another, more secret part of his life and personality. I remember once, outside of the Amato Opera, where we were smoking during the intermission of *The Marriage of Figaro*, John was waxing philosophical about the similarities between Beaumarchais' Cherubino and Cervantes' Persiles. Cutting himself off mid-sentence, John asked me a rather peculiar question out of nowhere:

"You're not one of those nosey types, are you?"

"What... what do you mean?"

"I mean the type to go snooping around in garbage bins or through one's mail, are you?"

"No... no. Why would you say something like that?"

"How should I put it? You know that when Franz Mesmer cured Maria Theresia von Paradis of her blindness, he cured her no doubt by playing the glass harmonica. She hadn't been able to see since when she was a very young child and when she finally regained her sight, she used to laugh uncontrollably at people's noses, never having recalled seeing them before. She thought noses were about the strangest, most absurd thing one could have. She ended up going crazy and had to bandage her eyes for the rest of her life just to retain what remained of her sanity and her pension. I bet you didn't know that and it's all true."

"Ok. What does that have to do with the price of tea in China?"

"Of course, it means one shouldn't be too nosey, doesn't it?"

"Ok..."

"You know I'm a very private person... I don't like nosey people."

"Ok..."

"Shall we change the subject?"

"Well you brought it up."

"Yes, you're right. I guess I did."

Ironically, it was I who would eventually introduce John to a fractious, fat bitch (apologies to whoever might read this) whom he would one day dub Miss Light-Mind and who would one day succeed in turning me into a snoop. I introduced him to her through a mutual friend who worked with me at the animal shelter. Little did I know then that it was this seemingly innocuous introduction that would ultimately cause all our future problems and his untimely death. Before we get to this point, we have to rewind through a long dispersed cloud of hangover-wielding Saturdays. It was a particularly non-eventful night out and we had gone to Sweet and Vicious to meet some of Alessio's friends. As usual, Alessio (last name Dappertutto), that smarmiest of gits, was half-blitzed, with a sloe-eyed beauty's arms draped around his neck. The only notable thing about this "bi-coastal babe" was that she had a beautiful blue Glaucus tattooed between her all-too-evident shoulder blades. An actress, she was one of those siliconed bimbos who believed every silence must be filled in order to avoid the breathless terror of a vacuum. Words, if nothing else, served to give her an acknowledged existence, and she was absolutely desperate for an existence. The alternative of course was literally to be "a nobody". Unfortunately, she never got it through her head that no bunch of nobodies could ever give her the existence, the sheer relevance she so powerfully craved. Thus, it wasn't long until she was completely ignored and flitted off into the night like a fading spark, never to be seen again.

Upon touchdown at Rudy's Bar and Grill, we were a little worse for wear. Afterward, we decided to go around the corner to Hell's Kitchen to pay a visit to another notorious dive. After being chatted up by a swarm of ex-frat, I-banker knobs who were trying it on more than I could take, I went outside to smoke a fag, with one of them yelling after me, "What's wrong luv, don't fancy a shag? Plate-glass cunt!"

It was a cold night, so I could only smoke half a cigarette outside in my short skirt. After I ventured again into the interior, I made a beeline for the bathroom, where there was at least one fake blonde spilling her guts into the porcelain sink hung below a shattered lipstick heart, drawn on an even more shattered mirror. She looked right at me through the mirror and said, "What are you lookin' at, you little waif? Stick bitch, don't pretend like you haven't been on a diet before."

Running out of the bathroom, I received a call from Shinkirō. He instructed us to meet him at Sakagura in midtown, but it was all a bit touch and go, as John was presently off his head on acid. Shinkirō, a petite *mondain* in his early 20s, wore women's clothes almost exclusively ("I'm a gay-cisgendered-transvestite, girl! Keep up!"), though he did stop at dresses, which he thought "dreadfully camp". I had recently met him at a Whistler exhibition at the Met. After a couple of shots of sake, he led us on to Pony, a Japanese gentlemen's bar one floor up, where a rather plump Japanese transvestite named Yoshizawa Ayame entertained whiskey-drinking businessmen with karaoke, whilst rail-thin hostesses giggled into their ears, talking about stocks, bonds, and Tourbillon complications. We were there because Hiroko, one of his female friends, worked as a hostess. While the quite beautiful Hiroko perched on a man's lap like a swallow, we went to the bar and ordered a round of drinks. We could clearly see many of the robotic-looking salarymen were already lashed; whilst their faces bore the mooniest of smiles, their physical gestures were becoming even more exaggerated and violent than usual. Shinkirō had told us that in Japanese strip clubs, it was common for strippers to dance in schoolgirl outfits, sporting candy cane smiles for an audience of devoted men. It was also common once the show was done for the men to take photographs with their favorite strippers, giving two-fingered "victory" gestures. People in Japan normally shrugged their shoulders. The *mizu shōbai* (or "water trade", a reference to the impermanence of much in life) had gone all the way back to the Edo period, and it was only our Western, moralistic hang-ups that put us in a position of constantly suffering from false pretenses.

After a short while, the hostess came out in a wonderful white kimono and sang what I was later told was *Shura no Hana* by Meiko Kaji, a song I found utterly and heartbreakingly beautiful. It wasn't long until some of the middle-aged Japanese men (who by this point were barely able to stand) noticed my singular height and blonde hair. With gruff gestures, they insisted I also sing, shoving a microphone and a thick, well-worn karaoke book below my face. Because the book lacked many English language songs, I first sang *Non, je ne regrette rien*. Much to my surprise, it went off with a bang so that all the men and women clapped with overwhelming enthusiasm. Feeling slightly more confident, I was surprised to find a version of *Brûlure* by Françoise Hardy, which I sang after another stern shot of sake, zapped with a bit of Rohypnol for equal measure. Soon, they were requesting all kinds of songs that I was forced to sing (rather incompetently), until Hiroko dragged me out at the insistence of the other working girls, as it was decided my continued presence potentially threatened their own interests. The hostess couldn't have been more pleased. Whilst handing me her business card, she give me a kiss on the cheek and whispered in my ear, "You are welcome back anytime."

Indeed, there are some strange corners in Manhattan you would have never realized existed, except by a mere chance occasion with a parallel universe.

After moving on to another nameless haunt, we met a real tool named Billy Rubino, who insisted we venture downtown to some dyke bar that might still be serving at 3a.m. Once there, we spent a few awkward minutes. John was noticeably uncomfortable, whilst Billy leered in every direction with a pompous smirk on his face. Just the look on his face made me want to vomit. This was another provocation I didn't need, given I was already sick to the gills, courtesy of what was becoming a minor case of alcohol poisoning. Indeed, when I finally made it to the bathroom, it was my own turn to empty out the contents of my stomach. I closed myself in the stall. I was more than a bit dizzy and was profoundly wishing the night would end, despite Billy's wanting to go to some upstairs club in Chinatown. As I looked at the black metal walls of the stall, I noticed that they were absolutely rife with graffiti. Only in a downtown dyke bar could one find the following les latrinalia written in silver, indelible ink:

*Were die werlt alle min*
*Von deme mere unxe an den Rin*
*Des diu chunegin von Engellant*
*Lege an minem armen.*
And next to it...
*Mary, Mary quite contrary*
*All flushed in red, so sick of head*
*Keeps her lips all sanitary*
*A pillow queen to wet your bed*

Americans are strange animals indeed. Soon after emerging from the stall, I was chatted up by a few of the more butch types with buzz cuts. It didn't take them long at all to suss I was damaged goods. I left. Across the street was a queue into a very high-end dance club we couldn't have hoped to get into: outside, in the sub-zero temperatures, bitchy tigers crouched and trembled in this coldest of urban jungles – short skirts, cat-fight claws and lipstick smiles that broadcast the luxurious beauty of a perfect set of perfectly white fangs. *Homo sapiens Americanus.*

It was that night that John took me home and spent his first night at my place. He spent it watching over me like some guardian angel, as I made sick all over the floors. It is ironic that as many times as I wanted him to stay over, the first was in my worst of states. It was indeed the very first night we spent together and John (bless his strong stomach) spent the entirety with his arms draped around me.

It was the next morning that John had the bright idea of moving down to the East Village so we could live closer together. Fortune must have shined on us because a couple of propitious events occurred at the same time. John got a regular job editing a new arts magazine and simultaneously, one of his connections told him about a rent-controlled flat coming open next to McSorley's on the ground floor. It was then that we got our little puppy together and named him Titus. All the girls at the shelter particularly loved this little black ball of fur, and when I showed it to John, the first time he came to my office, he fell in love. John's flat was littered with, amongst other things, old *Journey into Mystery* comic books, and when Titus had reason one day to pee on a particularly favored issue, John became initially furious, but that fury quickly subsided as he increasingly bonded with the dog. It was through one of my colleagues, Much Afraid, that I was introduced to the dog run mafia, ruled ostensibly by Ms Light-Mind, a strange, middle-aged woman with a sailor's mouth and a wooden leg. This little clique never took well to strangers, not even allowing other dog run members' pets to play with theirs. At first, they were very suspicious of John, as he claimed to not have had a dog before, despite being in Manhattan for over five years. Furthermore, Ms Light-Mind would never have anything to do with me. In fact, she constitutionally hated me because she thought I was some dozy, posh bird from England. However, the ice gradually thawed between John and her, due solely to the fact that one of her many mutts, Queen Telosia, took an immediate liking to Titus despite her distemper. This had the unfortunate consequence that the two dogs were required to go on "play dates" every weekend. Whilst John was moving up in her estimation, I continued to descend to new depths. This was primarily because her other bantam mongrel, Laika (named after the first dog to enter orbit on Sputnik 2), had a less than charitable opinion of me, usually reserving his aggression for anyone who wore hats.

By that time, John had started to give me assigned reading. The first book he asked me to read was *Satan came to Eden* by Dora Strauch, an account of the Galapagos Affair. John had always been intrigued by Friedrich Ritter, a Nietzsche-loving doctor who had surgically removed his own teeth and that of his newly betrothed wife of one week. The extractions were conducted to avoid the consequences of their teeth rotting once they'd begun to live at the ends of the earth. Incredibly, Dr Ritter discovered his wife via newspaper advertisement. Even more incredibly, the marriage lasted well beyond the duration of most Manhattan relationships. The next book he recommended was surprisingly more pedestrian, *White Fang* by Jack London. John said if he didn't aspire to be a writer, he'd be a naturalist. To live out in Alaska in the middle of nowhere where in the winter, the stark, architectural landscapes blessed one with a sense of timelessness. Where the entirety of history could be grasped in a single, geological moment. He would draw in his pixilated mind those castles of ice, magnificent palace-like glaciers, each glass-etched with the fractal-like precision of an intelligent design. A great fan of color, he said these silent, imaginary cities were possessed of the identical bluish hue called upon to render the distant, mountain perched conurbations glanced in the canvas corners of Patinir, Bosch and nameless, placeless others who all sat on the outermost edges of a vitreous unreality. I imagine this was what was going through his head when he'd space out in front of that family of Alaskan Dall sheep behind glass at the Natural History Museum. That stranded pack, enviably safe from any hint of extinction, hermetically sealed as they were inside their own ice cube diorama. Without fear, they would no doubt stand at a cliff's edge until the end of days. In an hour's time, all this would melt away as we were once again forced to confront the summer blowtorch, crying fury out of the end of a maxed-out blow drier.

Later that week, after a particularly sticky August day occupied in Spanish Harlem, we spent the entire night in each other's arms, listening to The Doors' *Indian Summer* over and over again until we fell into a trance. Ultimately, it was to become our song. It was there that another very important moment in our relationship occurred. It was there and then that I finally felt John began to open up to me about his private life and his past. Indeed, it was then that John first started telling me about Willow and showing me snippets of her diary. In almost hushed tones, he told me he was working on his first full-length novel, what was to become *Bunyan's Guide to the Great American Wildlife*.

# 5

Rumtifusel – *Villosus sumptuosus*

- *A rare animal that "plays on man's greed". Resembling the expensive pelt of a mink, it lays itself across tree trunks in sight of logger outposts. When a victim approaches, the Rumtifusel jumps with "lightning-fast" quickness to envelope its prey within its mass of sucking pores that line its inner ventral surface. It is these same pores that the creature uses to digest its meals.*

Rumtifusel

didn't want to be no lady.

Grandpappy told me that in a few years, I wouldn't be a little girl no more but would turn into a lady, and that sooner or later, them boys would come sniffing around me. He told me there weren't no other girls around these parts for miles around. He said all the other little girls lived in the city, and said I should have other little girls to play with. He said that people in the city didn't understand us and the way we lived so we should just ignore them and the nasty things they always said about us because they wasn't true at all. They always looked at me with them eyes dogs have when they is angry or when they is scared. I didn't like any of them people, especially Shane. He had an ugly scar on his face. He was an evil boy and always wanted to be the biggest tadpole in his puddle. All the Fearsome Critters was scared of him 'cause he was always shooting and killing all kinds of creatures over on his land. One day, I saw him come over on our property. He come right up to me and said, "Is it true you can't talk?"

I just sat there and waited.

"What, you stupid or something?"

I just sat there and waited.

"Is it true your Grandaddy's a rapist?"

One of the boys, he was picking his nose and looked at me all cross-eyed. I could smell them boys and they all smelled of earth and rain and rotten apples. Shane then come up to me and grabbed me by the arm and said to me in an angry voice, "Why won't you say nothing? Cat got your tongue? Don't worry, we won't say nothing?"

I just sat there and waited.

"What, you think we're stupid or something?"

He began to squeeze hard. So hard I felt the tears begin to swell in my eyes. Then my Grandpappy was coming around to fetch me so those boys hightailed it off, laughing at me. When Grandpappy came round the corner, he asked me, "Them boys been bothering you?"

I shook my head and Grandpappy looked deep inside me to see if I was lying. Him and his magic eye probably knew I wasn't telling the truth, but he didn't say nothing. He told me to come on to lunch. Most days, we ate bologna or maple syrup sandwiches, corndogs and yummy tater tots. In summer, watermelon and Slim Jims. When the fishing was good, we'd eat catfish and crawdads, all washed down with loads of RC Cola, Gatorade and moon pies. For Christmas, Grandpappy would deep-fry a turkey and the whole thing would go up in a big flame. Whoosh!

Grandpappy and I would do everything together and he would teach me all kinda things. How to bait a line, how to fix a carburetor, even how to shoot at thermite cans and track deer. In the back of the house, we had an old junk pile with all kinds of things in it. You name it, we had it. My Grandpappy could fix anything. My favorite thing was an old blue welding helmet. When I put it on, I liked to take a metal trashcan lid and pretend I was a knight, or maybe even a deep-sea diver. In the summer, it got so hot, we could barely put any clothes on. Some days, Grandpappy and I would go down to the lake and swim when there weren't nobody around. Then we'd go to the still part of the river where the water spiders would jump about the pond scum and try to catch some dragonflies. We hardly ever managed one, but it was lots of fun. I like the summer the best, 'cause I'm outta school and at night, I can listen to all the crickets and toads singing all hours of the night. Sometimes, I'd go out and catch lightning bugs and let them go in my room. I'd watch them fly around all night until the morning, when I'd find them all dead. In the fall, when the wind would blow, we'd catch all the helicopters the maple trees could throw at us. Whenever there was a big storm or hurricane, we used to count the seconds to see how far the lightning was away. In the winter, Grandpappy and I would have to sleep together as it was so cold. We only had a single heater in the entire house and it was broken most of the time. We'd listen to bluegrass and he'd play his guitar most nights to keep us company. He made me hum along and then we would have prayers before we went to sleep. We always asked Jesus for two things: first, to give me my voice back and second, to help me catch a Squonk one day. Once a week, Grandpappy always used to take me to the library because he knew I liked to read. I could read five books in one week! The lady doctor said I was precocious and the nice woman at the library would always leave some books out for me. She always said, "Don't worry about them kids' books. You are smart enough to read some grown-up books."

In the spring, we'd sometimes cook around a fire. Grandpappy was always full of stories and when he sat on a log, I'd love to sit between his knees while he told them to me. They were even better than the ones I read in the books. My favorite ones were the ones he told me about the Indians and living in the wilderness. He told me all about the skinwalkers and their magic spells. The skinwalkers were these scary Indians who could change into any type of animal just by taking an animal skin and using some black magic. He said when he was logging out west, he saw a Navajo witch turn into a raccoon one night. Scariest thing he ever did see. He said there were skinwalkers all around us and that is why we needed to protect and have respect for the animals because you never know, they might really be people. He said the skinwalkers could even read our thoughts, and animals knew better than to mess with no people. He said people like us killed all the Indians and all the bison. He said the Indians used to kill bison by chasing them off a cliff. I didn't know why they did that and it made me very sad because the bison is so beautiful and strong like my Grandpappy. He told me people have to live some ways and only God could judge others. He said man is both part of nature and outside of nature. Nature is man's best friend and his worst enemy. When man puts himself above nature, he doesn't recognize himself anymore. In the Bible, man and nature used to be in harmony, but because of original sin, God turned nature against man and threw him into the wilderness. Ever since Cain and Abel, man has been fighting against nature. Only people who live in nature can understand this. You take man out of nature, he forgets what he is, forgets what he needs to do to survive.

Grandpappy had gone out West when he was 14. He was completely on his own. He walked by himself across the entire country. That is how he came to know everything. He walked and walked every day until one day, his feet just stopped walking. He had nowhere else to walk to so he started wildcatting in Montana and Wyoming. After that, he eventually made his way to California where he started logging. He told me plenty of stories about his time out in Oregon and California, where the trees were a mile high and the mountains and rivers were bigger than anything you could ever imagine. My Grandpappy made some of them roads, rivers and canyons out there with his bare hands. I even heard about it at school. He said when he used to be a logger the men would go out drinking moonshine and run in the woods at night, naked as dogs. They would rub themselves all over with black grease, beat their chests and howl at the moon to get the dark spirits out. He said a man needs sometimes to get his dark spirits out; otherwise, he'd turn into a beast himself like Cain in the Bible. He said they used to have the best of times and everything was good until people told them they had to stop cutting down the trees as they was killing all the salmon and spotted owls. He said the spotted owl was a sacred animal to the Indians and he thinks the skinwalkers put a curse on all of them. It got really bad for him and the rest of the loggers. The protesters began spiking the trees and it all became real dangerous so the loggers were getting hurt and angry. Grandpappy said it only takes one drop of blood in the air to bring the vultures out. He said in nature, blood is always exchanged for blood. No day in nature goes by when something's blood isn't spilt. No one could talk to one another anymore 'cause the winter was so cold it froze all their words. He knew what was coming down the pipe so he wanted to leave before the spring released all the shouts that were still left hanging in the air. They wouldn't let him so he stayed on till summer. It was July 1987, the year before I was born.

Sure enough, the heat made everybody's head boil over like a teakettle. Then, all of a sudden, everything went BANG! The protesters were angry and came out in a big crowd to stop the loggers from cutting down more trees. The loggers was angry and didn't want to stop so they shot one of the protesters in the back with a gun. He was a young man. Grandpappy was sad and angry and he didn't want anyone else to die. He had no choice. His sad feet started walking him again and took him all the way across the country back to Georgia where I was born. He had been logging for nearly 20 years and when he come back, he was dirt poor with not even a pot to piss in.

Grandpappy had very rough hands. After our bath, he would turn the lights off and light a candle so everything was really dark. All you could hear was the crickets outside. They made a sound like a band saw. Sometimes, the sound was really low, like a Norelco electric razor, then it would get louder and louder until the noise filled the entire room. Grandpappy said they was calling for each other. They was singing love songs. It didn't sound like love songs to me, but like a band saw cutting the whole forest into pieces. After I dried myself with the towel, he would tell me to lie down on the long white table we had in the kitchen. In the winter, it would feel real cold because I had no clothes on. I felt like I was lying on a bed of hard snow. In the winter, there were no crickets and no lightning bugs. I especially didn't like it when I couldn't hear the crickets and toads singing their love songs. It made me feel real sad and lonely. Almost like I was dead. I could only smell the wax of the candle. I liked to watch it melt slowly into nothing. Grandpappy always wanted to hear me hum while I waited for him to get everything prepared. Sometimes, I would get goose bumps all over. When he came in the kitchen, he would sing to me while he put Johnson's baby powder on me everywhere. He said the talc gave me the smell of babies and made my bottom soft. He said that in the woods, a person's bottom is the only part of one's body that should be soft because out here, there was no time to sit down. I used to love the smell of the baby powder. He would always tell me to close my eyes and he would put the candle out so there was only the light of the moon. Then he would take a handful of the powder and throw it up in the air. I would count to five and open my eyes just as I felt the cloud of dust sprinkle all over my body. For a few seconds, everything would sparkle and I felt like I was flying on moonbeams all the way to heaven. After that, he would tickle me all over and give me the giggles. Sometimes I laughed so hard it made me hurt. Then he would put on my nightgown. We would stay up and play gin rummy. I loved my Grandpappy.

# 6

You counted amongst your dreams fishing for piranha on the Oxbow Lake in Peru, *hanan pacha* reflected in its moveless glass. *Oh, Hylas! Dreadest thou my fate without you? The manliest heart criest out with voice like that of the sickliest babe. Wouldest thou then have given into temptation and easeful death?* To be devoured there beneath the placid surface. Like Empedocles, leaving to posterity only a pair of secondhand flip-flops.

"LEEV OF ME NOTHING MORE. ERASE. ERASE."

Two charmed years is all we had: a circular dream of running and never being caught. One learns to believe in daily reincarnation. In our vacated vision of a normal life, we spotted the remains of our mummified bodies, tattooed with a shower of golden scarabs. There is a recurring undertow that sweeps Manhattan, the gray-blue atmosphere that sinks one into endless nights of drugs and drunkenness, purified only in the lustral waters of mid-morning Bloody Marys.

"HERE YRS MOOV LIKE SECONDS"

Days we watched entire complex systems fall apart, modalities shift into contradictions beyond repair, borders and their geographies slither away like frightened snakes, water turn into wine, goats fly into volcanoes, crowds leaving their traffic jams to run and embrace each other, casting cell phones into the melt, while sharks swim backward…this is how it was in our little part of the world. That is how it was.

"LIFE BLINKED B4 WE DID"

St Patrick's Day on Staten Island and Jägerbombs brought visions of Purgatory. The week after, you spent in an almost personified darkness. You shivered like a Nubian child, tortured by the quartan fever. Submerged under a timeless ocean, your room was a dark pocket of air, reeking of sweat and stale urine. At times you raved and were given visions, the hours and days knitted together by the strains of Hildegard von Bingen. We thought your end was certainly nigh. Upon your salvation, we decided to celebrate outdoors. However, chill Boreas had his way and refused us respite. Dark days still lay ahead, prowling each corner and rusty gangway, until spring's bright curvet into summer. That Eastertide, you only came in glances as your life became increasingly occupied with Felicity. Then, in a bolt out of the blue, a geosynchronous angel reemerged and delivered your tidings:

"Time to get out of our minds."

We spent a summer's day swilling. On a suggestion or perhaps a hunch, we went to the Bohemian Beer Garden in Astoria. Awaiting us on flagstones and patches of AstroTurf were a dread litter of drunken "sods"[1], a soupçon of Brooklyn-looking "scummers" we unfortunately called "friends". Our smallish group was gobbled up by a much larger cell of gangly shoegazers, some of which sported neon-bright Mohawks, others proudly displayed nightmare menageries of badly-done tramp stamps. It turned out we had come just in time to witness the last reverberations of a hardly listened to drone metal concert. The performing band was evocatively named "Yellow Piss". It was well after the smoking laws, nonetheless, one could still easily find oneself under the silvery thread of chain-smoke. It was there that we found that odd odalisque, a curvaceous Greek encased in ruched dress (except for the dress, she shared some large degree of resemblance with Titian's *Venus of Urbino*), who by one of those great ironies of betrayed hope, was christened Chastity. There she stood, imperiously stamping her high-heels

---

[1]   I am reliant on Felicity and her 'Southampton English Dictionary' (SED) for these terms.

at the bar, berating the besotted bartender about "running dry". At close intervals, she air-kissed that other delible girl, Katie, who forked out wrist-fulls of glimmering trumpery, hugging seemingly everyone who came into the bar with loud peels of "Oh, my God, what are you doing here?" Once the music began, the wallflowers started their seizures (what might be generously referred to as "arseholed" dancing to gypsy cimbaloms). It was then that Chastity stole away our poor, unassuming Felicity. After a sexualized fit of hip swaying and being pushed with some force into an ever-closing gyre of berserk, foot-stomping metal heads, Chastity gave her the most salacious of kisses that got all the boys chanting in another language in another time:

> *Swaz hie gat umbe*
> *Daz sint allez megede,*
> *Die wellent an man*
> *Alle disen summer gan.*

Amidst all the hand clapping and bacchanalian shouts, you, John, stood there mystified and slightly put out. Your only question to Felicity:

"I didn't know you liked girls."

And Felicity:

"Never had that happen to me before."

Once back on the Island, we met with Colonel Kurtz (the "E"-addicted "hedge-fund guy"), a last graft purloined from the *Semi Gotha*. The "Colonel" (as he was known to his close friends and associates) had long sailed down the river to a new morality: stuffing Asian girls full with ketamine until they worshiped him. Part party animal, part would-be cult leader, he barely managed to stride the fine line between his life as Stat Arb quant and that of a quasi-club demigod. At one of his more infamous loft parties, his bearded likeness was raised on a living room wall.

The constituents of this simple yet powerfully-realized icon were a king-sized bed sheet and black bits of patched together electrical tape. His present girlfriend was a six-foot, steel-thighed Valkyrie who worked as a management consultant. Almost singlehandedly, she laid waste to entire divisions with one fell swoop of her ballpoint pen. In talking to her, it seemed inefficiencies were rife everywhere and that she was constantly rooting them out with a six-sigma-like clarity. In her world, PowerPoint arrows had a way of confining entire factory floors to the dustbins of history, all for the sake of progress and general prosperity. Her body was built such that in a long dress, she looked like the thrust chamber of a Vulcain rocket. She had a passion for swimming, biking, and S&M (evidently, forking people to the sharks wasn't enough to move her resting heart rate beyond that of a blue whale). It had taken her mere seconds to metabolize me. The Colonel was trying to improve his VO2 max, just to keep up with the exertions involved in bedding this Laestrygonian maid. He'd heard from a reliable source that in her relentless climb to the top, she'd already resigned two of her weak-hearted managers to the dustbins of corporate history. The Colonel would soon have to give way after a few nights on her vomit comet. New York invariably has its casualties.

Why should she be mentioned? If only for writing down on a piece of paper for me the Dannemiller formula for change management on a soiled napkin:

Dissatisfaction x Vision of what is possible x First concrete steps taken toward the vision > resistance

Not to be confused incorrectly with the Beckhard and Harris version of the same equation:

Dissatisfaction x Desirability x Practicality
> resistance to change

She explained in clear terms that if any of the values on the left-hand side of the formula were zero, any form of significant or meaningful change was impossible. In fact, her entire career was based on reversing the equation so that it was made eminently clear to all that by removing dissatisfaction, vision and practical alternatives, it was easy to obliterate any resistance to change. What was her magic? Simply this: to reverse the formula by making one simple addition to the left-hand side of the equation: F.E.A.R. (in her terminology, "False Expectations Appearing Real"). It was soon clear to her that my life had always been ruled by two simple forces: fear and a resistance to change. As she put it, "while many maintained that to achieve success, one shouldn't be afraid to fail..."; in fact, "it was exactly those who weren't afraid enough of failure, who were on the lowest rungs of society" (i.e. their parents hadn't take them to enough prisons or heroin rehab centers). Thus, by implication, my failure was entirely due to my "not being afraid enough of becoming a loser", which I obviously was in her eyes.

It took me over an hour to escape my Brunhilde's clutches, after which I was subjected to yet another pointless conversation about the death penalty and the potential benefits of legalizing drugs (evidently a favorite topic of drug users other than myself). After unrecoverable minutes, we strode onto higher ground and shared everyone's opinion about the best way to consume ecstasy. While Kurtz vanished to make his point, we began chatting to one of his entourage, a good-looking Italian derivatives trader named Alessio. Alessio, rather colorfully went on and on about the merits of his foremost wingman, the also impossibly good-looking Blimp Pilot ("more sex than you've had hot dinners"). The Blimp Pilot was a blonde-haired, blue-eyed gigolo who enjoyed nothing more than bragging about his conquests and then complaining about almost everything else. His basic complaint with the world was his having to endure the numerous jokes aimed at him by his "real" pilot friends, who claimed he did nothing more than sit in the cockpit all day, "clubbing his seal". "Actually, flying a blimp is really difficult, you know." He also lamented his "not being taken seriously by women," a point that sealed for us the perfect resemblance between the man's mental capacity and that of his craft. Amongst his long-cherished dreams was to start an airline called "Happy Landings,' its only route being between Tokyo and LA, its entertainment only confined to international airspace. "As for stewardesses, Asians on the way there, blondes on the way back. Loads of roulette. Brilliant, ain't it?"

It so happens that the phrase always at the tip of Alessio's tongue was "the fire station's burned down". For him, it seemed this singular phrase held the key to everything untoward in life. He seemed to injudiciously apply the statement to everything from the Mets losing the playoffs to his brother-in-law's hair replacement procedure. Alessio's girlfriend was a Japanese ex-hooker (Natsuki, I seem to remember), who had also come under the Colonel's sway. Within our constantly flexing and expanding group, she reintroduced us to the impish Shinkirō, who came with a gaggle of waifish-looking Gaultier models straight off the catwalk. The non-waifs quickly unbuttoned their shirts, eager to bare a set of bronzed plastrons for all to admire (all except Shinkirō, who chided them to "stop showing off" and in turn, re-buttoned their shirts and zippers). Exiting the bathroom, Colonel Kurtz made us all aware that he had just decided to put a pill of ecstasy up his anus, convinced it would aid absorption (exeunt sense being chased by a bear). His predilection for being a high-mettled empiricist made sure he would attempt to win our argument by example.

## "XPECT I WIL SEE HIM SOOON"

A bad voyage ensued downtown. After a quick jaunt to the L.E.S. (for us, a Bermuda Triangle where on every occasion, we would lose a number of our party), we invariably ended up at The Void in Soho at 3a.m. The Void was one of the Colonel's many *terrae incognitae.* The elusive bar had the sole distinction of serving those dreadfully troubled souls who believed it wasn't worth killing a night if it hadn't killed you first. Prior to The Void, we had to pick up Alessio's other thug of a friend, the slithering and rupicolous Billy Rubino, who went on and on, comparing the relative cinematic merits between an unheard of film with the inauspicious name of *Café Flesh* and another Yugoslavian one (even more unheard of) called *Sweet Movie.* By this point, the ecstasy was proving too much for the Colonel. We wouldn't see him again until the following weekend on Fire Island, where you were gossiping about the changing light, sand over half your body as we buried you like Priam along the beach. Though you had a minor sun allergy and had to cover up like a devout Muslim, you didn't regret your time. Unfortunately, just before he had melted away into a cesspool of incomprehensible gibberish, the Colonel brought us to our Ultima Thule, Red Hook Brooklyn, where we met yet another troop of ravers on their way to a party at the Freedom Tunnel. Fortunately, these borderline cro-magnons were too messed up to speak to us much (the Lord tempers the wind to the shorn lamb). However, here, a very important event occurred: Felicity came upon the bright idea that you two should have a puppy together.

"We should get a dog."

"And when you say 'we', my dear Felicity, are you once again invoking the royal 'we'"?

"No, silly, you and I."

To which you responded, "We haven't even moved in together." Felicity's basic line of argument was the following:

that she missed having a dog and her apartment was too small to contain another life (it was banned on her tiny, little island anyway). In fact, she had just seen the cutest puppy at the shelter and had arrived at the mistaken understanding that according to some apocryphal New York myth, if you kept a dog in an apartment for over a year without it being discovered, the landlord couldn't throw you or the dog out.

"What do we do to get it in and out of the building? Mail it to ourselves? From what I've heard, the post office won't take boxes with air holes."

"HAPPY CULD DO A GUD SET OF PUPPY EYES AND SO I FELL"

You, John, held up little resistance and two weeks later, you both had got your little puppy, Titus. It was through Titus, that she was introduced to Much Afraid, who then in turn introduced you to the hardcore fringe at the dog run – the members of the shadowy Ota Benga society, whose lieutenant was an overweight woman to which we will henceforth apply the sobriquet, Ms Light-Mind. This disgusting harpy was deathly afraid of ceiling fans (they gave her vertigo) and wore a neck brace most of the time due to the vertigo induced by ceiling fans. Her master and sometimes lover, Lord Hate-Good, was a rather sad, old man, an expert in evolutionary game theory, but embittered by life and, it seemed, logic. His time was mostly spent casting his reality distortion field ever wider, an event horizon through which logic enters, but seldom ever escapes. In my mind, it was certain that by sheer perseverance, a smattering of guile and the aid of a heedless form of entropy, his efforts would succeed until all of New York became a mass of broken thoughts and orphaned bits of misinformation. The Ota Benga society was really nothing more than a bunch of unimaginative anarchists and arch animal lovers, who even PETA-freaks were scared off by. Their name was derived from Ota Benga, a

Congolese pygmy who was actually displayed in the Bronx Zoo at the beginning of the last century. You, John, would ultimately give them their motto, *Novus ordo Selorum*. To add a sense of seriousness (if not ridiculousness), each meeting would begin with everyone slowly intoning the words:

*Magnus ab integro saeclorum nascitur ordo*

It was there that you gave "code names" to the various members of the society, which I still use to refer to the mentioned affiliates, for obvious reasons (especially considering the investigation is still ongoing and I too must sign these words under an assumed name). It was, of course, Willow's last name that gave you the idea to use characters from John Bunyan's Pilgrim's Progress. Furthermore, you and Felicity had discussed the 17th century Christian allegory a number of times (something you considered to be little more than a shameless Protestant rip off of the insomnia destroying Piers Plowman). It was a book her father had held dear. The other immediate members of the burgeoning Society were as follows: the uliginous Giant Maul (a fat and disgusting oaf of a man with a kind heart), Old Honest (a septuagenarian crook who made his money peddling life settlements to homeless people, repurchasing them for cents on the dollar), Mr Fearing (nerd, computer programmer and suspected child pornographer with an inordinate fear of a nameless authority), Mr Feeblemind (dumb enough to have lost a large portion of his small wealth to persons imitating expropriated African millionaires), Mr Msason (lawyer who had 60 cats, yet couldn't fetch a wife if his life depended on it), Madame Bubble (a whale of a women who had successfully trained her dogs to give her cunnilingus by smothering liver between her legs), and even Ms Bat-Eyes (an Iranian slumlord and suspected witch who knew everything about everybody).

## "SHUDDER PAST THE WICKED G8 THEY SHUDUV CLOSED"

Other parts of the allegory were filled in as the need suited. Thus, various locations were given names such as the "Wicket Gate" (your default headquarters), Slough of Despond (the Brooklyn Zoo), Doubting Castle (City Hall), Gaius Inn (a local vegan bar and restaurant), Vanity Fair (the many Madison Avenue boutiques that sold mink coats), By Ends, etc. Then there were the "Ill-Favored Ones", represented variously by cut-throats, meat-eaters, butchers, zoo-keepers, fur-coat owners, dam-builders, loggers, whale-fishers, hunters, poachers, circus-operators, bull-fighters, and anyone else in the general population who didn't love animals, etc.

For all their shortcomings, the Society was particularly well organized and daring. In terms of ambition, they had nothing less than the complete demolition of a system that imposed an "unfair" human-led hegemony over the animal kingdom. To their credit, they worked ceaselessly and single-mindedly towards this dubious goal. To achieve their ends, they had a number of clandestine meeting points and a close network of crypto-anarchic cells, all working more or less toward the common goal of overturning the status quo. With impressive foresight and admirable perspicacity, these societies had long ago agreed that it was innately impossible for them to ever agree on any one vision of the future. Therefore, they implicitly agreed to disagree about almost everything. Propitiously, they found one common denominator that they could all concur upon, the desire for complete anarchy. It was an unspoken rule that if any one group could achieve ascendency, the others would fall in line and help where they could to dismantle the present society's framework. What wasn't exactly clear was what would happen if one of the groups did indeed manage to come to power. Would the others by definition have to topple the topplers?

It didn't really matter in the end. What did matter was how much the wider world underestimated their capabilities. These societies had an incredible reach and it would frighten one to learn the types of instruments of mass destruction they could procure if need required it (not to mention the hidden cabal of fifth columnist they could and did draw upon if the proverbial shit hit the proverbial fan). One particular example of their wide span was embodied by the exotic location used for the final preparations of the "Great Work" that would eventually lead to your dissolution. It was the haunted hospital on the abandoned and off-limits North Brother Island (referred to as the "The Land of Beulah") that housed the revenant Typhoid Mary, chef extraordinaire with a brand of bouillabaisse you literally had to die for.

"MY BLOOD IS MY POISON THEY WATCH ALL WATCHING WONT LET ME LEEVE MY MELLON IS SICK MY BLOOD MY POISON DYING 2 LEEVE THEY TRAP ME MY BLOOD THEY SAY QUITE CONTRARY LONELY SO LONELY 2 WATCH SO MANY DYING RIVER GOD RISES AND TAKES AWAY SO MANY NEVER 2 RETURN NILE RIVER TAKES THE SOULS WEST 2 WHERE THE SUN WILL SET AND WHERE DRESSED IN GOLD I SHALL MEET OSIRIS WHERE IS THE LIGHT WHERE IS THE LIFE"

There, Lord Hate-Good and his renegades began a pirate radio station stupidly close to New York's largest prison. The radio station in question broadcasted an amazing array of gibberish, including amongst other things, recounting the story of a king blinded by grief and the horrors of the Battle of Clidium (which occurred a mere 900 years ago, but for Lord Hate-Good, it was reoccurring every day in every facet of life – "The King, your President, will fall from sorrow, for only one man in 10,000 can see"). It had been purported that Lord Hate-Good was one of the original founding members of the Weather Underground and had actually been injured in the Greenwich Village bombing (the purported source of a curious and unexplained burn mark on this left hand where he was also missing half a digit). Many-Eyed Rumor had indeed gained him a dubious reputation. He was a tall, thin man, most distinguished by his being a sufferer of cat-eye syndrome, a deformity that haunted most whoever looked him in the eyes. He was also disturbingly possessed of Vulcan-like eyebrows and a Beckettesque widow's peak. In person, he was gruff and verbally parsimonious, but in the cyber-world, his retiary nature was incredibly capable, seducing via Tor a veritable rogue's gallery of hucksters to his malign causes.

Lord Hate-Good had his own lexicon. He referred to all Jews as "Green beards". "Women", he spelt "w.o.m.e.n." ("what other men engage needlessly"). Police, he referred to as "Offsidesmen". Though he claimed he was inspired by the "green anarchism" and the anarcho-primitivism of the Élisée Reclus, it wasn't even clear he really liked animals. Rather, he just wanted people around him crazy enough to do his bidding, and these animal fanatics were his easiest port of call. Originally, he dreamed of founding a new group of Pythagorean worshipers and wanted to base his cult around the twin pillars of Euler's identity and transcendental meditation. Unfortunately, none of his would-be disciples had even mastered the basics of long division, much less trigonometry.

Personally, I don't think you cared about those idiotic losers or their stupid plots; what you ultimately wanted was one thing, your shot at real anarchy, immediacy, a vent for whatever anger it was you held pent up inside you. I distinctly remember you dragging me to one of these meetings that seemed a cross between a satanic cult and a Methodist revival. The attendants were all dressed in black nylon robes with deep hoods, under which the bourdon note (similar in character to the buzzing of an old dehumidifier) of indistinguishable Latin was intoned. Lord Hate-Good stood before them in his position as Hierophant. They all began shouting:

"Down with Apollyon!"

"Down with Apollyon!"

Apollyon was of course another of your inventions to add "spice" to the meetings. It was certainly better than "Down with Big Brother" or "Down with The Man". It is undeniable that after the chants, I was waiting for the obligatory ritualistic sex or at least a vivisection of a Union Square squirrel, until out of the spelean shade of the anteroom, there would appear our *Là-Bas* worthy Lord Hate-Good. Incidentally, Lord Hate-Good was possessed of an interesting pedigree. His great-grandfather was purportedly a Skoptsy moneylender and taxi driver, persecuted under the Russians at the end of the last century (a breed of men who after siring children, relinquished their manhood). His brother, who lived on Carpenter Avenue in the Bronx, still sold old telephones, radios and women's hosiery from the back of a truck at the Aqueduct Flea Market in Ozone Park.

Post meetings, John would get all psyched up and ready to attack any around him who were unfortunate enough to be possessed by slightly more balanced views. Felicity, of course, was deliberately held far from all this. Her views were more or less straightforward and typical of her breed. One typical conversation went as follows:

John:     "Do you not think it is impossible to escape the consequences of revolutionary socialism?"

Felicity: "Whilst I believe things need to change, violence is never justified under any circumstance. Violent revolution is just as wrong-headed as war or the death penalty. Man is not a god after all, and we are not running around in the woods like savages anymore."

John:       "Do they not teach you history anymore in the UK? I
            really despise you English royalists and your professed
            egalitarianism. You and those foolish Octoberists are
            just two peas in a pod. It really sickens me how you
            adhere like midges to the dirty flypaper of a simpering
            brand of socialism. A bourgeoisie construct jerry-
            rigged for shopkeepers. Wake up and realize the world
            needs changing and you won't accomplish that by
            sitting by the sea and making salt."

Felicity:   "History would say otherwise. And why do you have
            to be so insulting and aggressive anyway? It won't
            make your point any truer. I mean, why don't you read
            about the Dalai Lama, Mother Theresa and..."

John:       "Only because we define history by its exceptions. Read
            Bakunin. Read Proudhon. We need praxis! Praxis, not
            social-justice warrior rhetoric or tugging at the heart
            strings. Praxis, you hear!?"


And so it went on and on. Alas, after a few hours' relentless
interrogation and the mental equivalent of mortal combat,
Felicity would force an "inhaler" between her now trembling
fingers, a last ditch attempt to calm her nerves. Removed from
your withering presence, she would tell herself that your
increasingly more radical views were just that, views and
not actionable ideas. I remember at one such point, she came
under the spell of a moonlit window drape, embowered by a
cascade of zinnias. It was then that she assumed a dreamlike
unreality. In that instant, as I peered through my Vaselined
lenses, she became for me a pre-Raphelite study in the aetherial.
What grace? What profound patience all wasted on you? And
how could you not see it? I couldn't take my eyes off her as
she sat there smoking her menthol (by now more hanging ash
than cigarette). She seemed to me to possess the coeval traits of

coquettishness and vulnerability, which in combination were so attractive. I was simply desperate to absorb her radiance as she held the skeleton key to every recess of my darkness. Indeed, I felt she could measure with her mere sighing the small size of a soul. Even now, I could see how you, John, had broken your tender ark upon her rocks. As my heart ached and the small rain down came, she once asked me in a half-laughing manner:

"You ever think John has lost the plot?"

"I think he just needs to get laid."

She would always laugh a laugh of quiet insurrection against the perceived seriousness of our little *tête-à-têtes*, but secretly, I wondered at you two. I was always taught that people talked about sex for lack of having it, but strangely, you two never talked about sex, despite strangely, never having it. It was like an awkward piece of furniture in an otherwise beautiful room that had to be tiptoed around for fear of breaking the china and other domestic delicacies. So many times, I fantasized about her... so many times, I only had myself to comfort after being ravaged by her quiet beauty. Driven by instinct alone, I became a skulking wolf, left to roam the streets, looking in the darkest corners for any form of warm contact. I needed a new language to express my increasingly unformed and unutterable thoughts. Like Mowgli, I was in wont of an alphabet to explain my brutal lack of success. Unfortunately, that day's alphabet returned me reluctantly to the arms of Brunhilde, the Type-A, "always a plan B", C-suite exec who spoke in acronyms. On our second (and thankfully final meeting), she instructed me to employ the no doubt patented "A.B.C. model" of behavior (Activating Event, Beliefs, Consequences), as it would help me to achieve better and more predictable results "through positive reinforcement and the consequent reduction in negative thinking patterns". After drawing a number of schematics on countless paper napkins, she went on about life being "a contact sport". As for my own "lack of play", she recommended that I just go out there and "play ball". My weak retort: in a city like New York, one gets bruised too quickly, so that eventually, one ceases to appreciate anything approaching real contact. Unfeeling, unfocused, we, the battered wives of lofty expectations are constantly left to seek out the most unsatisfactory of interactions, replacing the sought for thing by the all too savory means. John, more than any of us, needed that contact and he would eventually find it in ways we never could have imagined.

# 7

**S**quonk – *Lacrimacorpus dissolvens*

- *A quadruped, a squonk is a very shy and unhappy animal that only comes out at night. The animal's unhappiness is entirely due to its perception of its own ugliness. The squonk has exceptionally large eyes. Its body is almost completely covered in warts and moles. It is said that would-be hunters can easily track the squonk due to its perpetual weeping, which has the effect of occasionally leaving a visible trail of tears. Furthermore, it is said that the squonk's lachrymose tendencies are significantly heightened if the beast is cornered, which can cause it to dissolve itself in its own tears. Hunters have been said on many occasions to hear the animal's weeping in the forest, which "has been compared to a Cross-feathered Snee". It is thought better to hunt the animal on colder, moonlit nights where it is more hesitant to move about and the flow of its tears is inhibited by the cold.*

The Squonk

Sometimes, I'd ask Grandpappy where my mommy and daddy was…

Whenever I asked, he would shake his head and say, "the Lord was taking care of them".

Sometimes, Grandpappy could be mean…

Like when I did something wrong, he'd give me a mighty whupping. Sometimes, I would run away and he'd have to chase me and give me an even bigger whupping. Sometimes, me and Grandpappy just couldn't be in the same house together.

He didn't like it when I took out my momma's old dresses. He didn't like it neither when I put on her makeup. One day, when he was all fed up, he burned them in the front yard. He said now I couldn't have them no more and I shouldn't go around dressing like a slut at my age. He said there would be plenty of time for that. He said God didn't like women who dressed themselves up for other men but not for him. I hated him then. I wrote "I hate you" all over his shed with white paint when he wasn't looking. He gave me a mighty big whupping for that. But sometimes, I was smart. Like a raccoon, I had hidden some of the lipstick under my bed. I had to hope his magic eye didn't find it. Some days, I would take it out and put on a little bit. One day, I put on a bit too much and went to go look at myself in the mirror. When I came out, Grandpappy was standing there with his shovel, about to go worm grunting. He told me:

"Willow, where did you get that stuff? Didn't I tell you never to put that stuff on?"

Grandpappy was furious and came at me to give me a big old slap, but I ran straight to the door and got outside. Grandpappy chased me for a bit and gave up once I'd got into the woods. I thought I would sit by a tree and rest my heels until Grandpappy cooled down. Then, I suddenly saw something hiding behind the bushes. I looked and looked and couldn't see what it was. I saw its head and thought to myself, well, if that isn't a squonk. When I got up close, he started to run a little farther away and then I figured out I'd have to sneak up behind him. He ran and ran in the wrong direction. I told him not to go on the neighbor's property as he might get hurt if they caught him. Shane and the other boys was shooting and trapping all kinds of animals over there. But he must have been hardheaded like me and he wouldn't listen none. He just kept running and running. I knew I would have to catch him so them evil boys couldn't get at him. When I was almost out of breath, he stopped behind a tree. I counted to three and then ran round that old trunk just as fast as I could. When I got back round to the other side, I suddenly saw Shane and the two other boys right in front of me. I could smell the gunpowder on them from when they was lighting bottle rockets and cherry bombs. Shane told me to come with him. He asked me if I wanted to see what the big boys do. I shook my head.

He said "Why not? You afraid?" I shook my head. He said "Come on then. We ain't going far." I started to follow him but I was walking real slow.

Shane had a mean look on his face. He was not as big as his best friend but he was the boss of the other two. One of the boys was real quiet and thin. He was weaker than the other two and almost looked like a girl. He had dark hair and was always looking behind him like he was scared of something. Maybe he had seen the squonk too.

Shane looked at me with a funny face as we were walking and said "How come you wearing that lipstick?"

I shrugged my shoulders. Shane then stopped with the other boys near some big honeysuckle bushes.

"Well, you ain't no girl, is you?"

I nodded my head.

"Well show us you is a girl then. Let's see you pull down your pants."

I shook my head.

"Why not? Is you scared?"

I shook my head.

"C'mon then. Show us you is a girl."

I shook my head.

"You're a whore like your momma."

Shane started to get angry. He grabbed me and pushed me down. He smelled like a rotten possum. I tried to get up but he kept pushing me down. Then he started taking off my shirt. I tried to stop him but he was too strong. I then reached for my whistle but he tore it away from me and threw it into the honeysuckle bushes where I couldn't reach it no more. He then yelled back to his other friends.

"Don't just stand there. Come and help me out."

The other boy then run over and started to help Shane take off my shirt.

"No man, just hold her hands down."

Shane then started to take my pants off me too. He pulled them clean off me. I tried to kick him but he punched me in my stomach so hard all the wind came out of me.

"Stop squirming. And you, listen. Hold her mouth shut now."

Shane then pulled off my underwear and threw it in the mud.

"Lookie here. I told you. So she was a girl after all."

Shane looked at me with an angry look and started laughing.

"You hold still now, you hear? We ain't gonna hurt you none. We just want to play a game with you. Just hold still now. Keep her still."

Shane then started taking off his pants.

"I'm gonna show you what the boys do to the girls. What your mommy and your daddy did to make you."

I finally got my hand free and hit him square in the mouth so he started bleeding. Shane stared cussing up a storm and holding his lip as the blood started pouring out.

"You stupid girl, you busted my lip."

After that, Shane got down on his knees and started choking me until I couldn't breathe no more. My head started to tingle and I knew I must be turning blue. Then, he stopped choking me and started slapping me in the face. He again took the wind out of me with his knee so I couldn't fight back no more. He then sat on my stomach and hurt me inside. I could hear him breathing all heavy, but couldn't see anything because one boy was still pinning my hands down. Shane started bouncing up and down on my stomach and then he started moaning like he was in pain. He was hurting me something mighty. Then I saw him get up and he had blood on him.

"Shit. Look at this. You nasty girl. I hope you don't have no AIDS. Hey man, it's your turn. I'll hold her hands."

The other boy looked afraid and shook his head.

"C'mon. What you scared of? Don't you want to be a man?"

The boy looked at me then at Shane.

"Listen, I'm gonna tell everybody you chickened out if you don't."

The other boy stood up and then started taking off his pants too. Shane grabbed my arms, but now I was too tired to fight anymore. I didn't cry but I couldn't breathe none. Shane was sitting on my chest and holding my hands. The other boy then started sitting on me but nothing was happening at first. Then I started feeling the pain again. The other boy started screaming too like Shane. When he was done, he got up and zipped his pants up. Shane and the other boy then looked at the last kid, the one with dark hair.

"Come on now. Don't be afraid. It's your turn."

The boy shook his head like he was scared.

"No. No."

"Come on now. We done it, now you have to do it. Why you always got to be a pussy."

The boy shook his head and started to move back. Shane jumped up off the ground and went and grabbed the boy by his two arms. He started shaking and his eyes were as wide as plates and bobbing out of his head. Shane was real angry and grabbed him by the neck. That made him cry. I still didn't cry though. Shane pushed him to the ground and kicked him. The boy still didn't want to sit on me, but they made him. When he sat on me, I didn't feel nothing. I didn't cry. He cried. He kept crying and didn't stop. Shane then yelled at him,

"Come on and finish up. We can't hear you? We gotta get outta here. Don't you know what you're doing?"

The boy started making the sounds but I didn't feel nothing. Then they pulled him off of me.

"That's enough."

Shane then come up and put his face in mine. His face was all red and angry. He had dirt and twigs in his hair. His lip still had some blood on it.

"And listen. You better not tell anybody, you hear? You tell somebody, we gonna come back and burn your house down while your asleep with your rapist granddaddy, you hear? You hear?"

I nodded my head.

"What am I saying? You can't speak none anyhows. You're too stupid to say nothing. Serves you right for busting my lip."

After that, they put mud in my face and spit on me. Then I closed my eyes real tight. Next thing I knowed, I felt warm water all over my body. I opened my eyes and I seen Shane was spraying me with his wee-wee. He told me again I was stupid and couldn't talk no how. They all walked away and left me all by myself. Even when they was far away, I could still hear Shane laughing. I hated his laugh. I hated him.

After half an hour, the bottle flies started to smell my blood and after that, they started feeding on me. I wanted to say something. I wanted to scream, but I couldn't. I felt like I was just a piece of road kill, lying in the road to hell. Just like those dead opossums we find here in the summer. I didn't move for a long, long time. I couldn't. I just sat there lying in the dirt and looked up at the top of the trees. I was listening to all the creatures and all the animals as they was screaming. It was like the whole forest was screaming. Everything: the trees, the birds, the crickets, the dogs, even Grandpappy. Everything but me was screaming. The world was screaming.

My Grandpappy done told me that when an old wolf dies, he does it all by himself. He just goes and finds a little corner in the woods and lies there and waits until he is ready. When he finds his little place, he just closes his eyes and stays there until he is dead. I had felt something like that inside me for months. It was inside my ribcage. That is where that old wolf that was looking for a little place to crawl up inside me and die. All this time, he was the one making me bleed. I could feel his hairs at the back of my throat. I could feel his teeth on the inside of my leg. My whole body hurt. Now, I felt he was gonna eat me from the inside.

# 8

Dear John,

There is something rather old-fashioned and pleasant about writing letters to one another. I must say, your handwriting is absolutely wonderful and the stationery you chose was exquisite. You are really a man of the 18th century! :)

Right now, my head still feels a bit numb. Still feeling the comedown from those Mitsubishis. I must really have been rolling hard last night. Did I really avoid making a fool of myself? Oh well, plenty more time for that. I'm having some dreadful flashbacks. I hope I didn't really mess up and tell you I loved you? Alas, I'm spending this rainy day reading the papers and thinking of you almost (I stress almost) constantly. Random, but somewhere I read they found water on Mars. I don't know why, but it seems that should be important. I also saw a news clip about an inflatable hijab-wearing sex doll that floated onto a remote island in Indonesia. If you can believe it, it was actually worshiped as an angel until the authorities confiscated it. The world has indeed become a strange place.

Anyway, before I keep babbling on, I wanted to respond to some of the questions you posed in your last letter. I have been thinking about them a lot. Amongst other things, you asked me:

A. To describe what ecstasy feels like.
B. What I feel like it when I'm on it.

You also asked me why I refused to give into the sheer feeling of the drug and somehow release myself to this endless craving you imagine yourself to feel. That I somehow needed to "let myself go" in order to understand what desire really means.

What can I say? Where should I begin? Maybe in typical Fawker fashion, I'll answer a question you didn't even ask. For instance...

When I was a teenager, I loved biology and possessed this crazy imagination. I had this sixth-form teacher named Mr Stokes, who I had developed a mild crush on (bookish, brunet hair, horn-rimmed glasses and a very serious tone). Anyway, we used to talk after class and I couldn't help but to tell him my theories about life and the origin of the species. I had one theory in particular I used to call the Fawkler Fuzzy Fork Theory. It was called "fuzzy" for obvious reasons. The "ork" part, I never quite understood, but I think it sounded vaguely intelligent to me at the time. Anyway, in this theory, I used to imagine the brain was a kind of gray coral, made up of all these little cell-looking creatures from all over the ocean. Each had its own singular memory of a different past, a different depth, perhaps even a completely different ocean. These were simple enough automata, yet somehow, when these little things came together, they figured out en mass (and perhaps rather democratically) how to create an entity much larger and more advanced than themselves. In essence, despite obvious limitations, these mighty cells managed to convert their chosen tribe into beautiful, unique forms we all recognize as looking like trees, flowers, or, well, funky brain-looking things. The Fuzzy Fork theory states that each of us is not really an individual at all, but rather the sum total of an entire galaxy of people. In fact, we are the deliberate result of a million holocausts occurring secretly within ourselves. Why? Because as individuals, we occupy a living form made possible only by the decimation of trillions of other potential forms (here, you may read personalities). Ultimately, we are what is left over at the end of a long process of elimination. Indeed, perhaps I could have been born with webbed feet or even been made a mermaid? One day, maybe I will be. We are all special human beings, chosen by nature to be who we are.

Alas, despite what I thought to be a thing of great promise, my theory met with a sad demise. Unfortunately (and notwithstanding of all my eager efforts to explain it), the Felicity Fuzzy Fork Theory was summarily discredited, even alas by my beloved Mr Stokes, who ended up almost giving me a fail (not stopping at the rather humiliating grade, he went so far as to suggest to my parents that I perhaps switch to a more imaginative subject for my A-levels). Oh, well... seems I always fall for guys I'm biologically incompatible with.

Fortunately for you, I have a different theory about all this (the Revised Fawkler Fuzzy Fork Theory), formed at a random point between two years and two minutes ago: I remember reading somewhere that when you're an infant, you really have no personality, no individuality at all. In fact, your personality is somewhat akin to a kind of mysterious lava-like goo. One that spills forth from a primeval source older than us, perhaps even older than the universe itself. As I see it, this semi-sentient goo, before it knows any better, runs in all directions and adheres to any object that gets in its way. In doing this, it attempts to glob onto any form that will give it shape. In most cases, during late infancy, this goop (which will eventually come to be called an individual identity) begins to harden. It does this once it has managed to find what it thinks to be its singular channel. Ultimately, it discovers this "channel" only by encountering the proper forms through which it can be molded: persons, events, even a specific object (a toy train, for instance, that made you want to be a train conductor). However, in rare cases, the soul never finds its proper channel and this sentient goo continues to spill forth throughout a number of different directions, never really finding a singular shape at all. Depressingly, a person who finds herself in this position becomes within herself a source of constant reincarnation, an unmade thing.

From what I could gather from the abovementioned article, it appeared to suggest a number of fascinating theories about infant psychology (if that isn't a contradiction in terms). For one, it suggests that an infant cannot separate its own actions from those of others. Indeed, from the child's perspective, its existence and that of its mother are still bound up within a single entity. What we might quaintly describe as a single personality, or perhaps more philosophically as a single point of consciousness. Why am I explaining all this to you (assuming you're still even reading my letter)? It's because this theory describes the exact way in which I understand love. It has nothing to do with drugs, desire or anything of that loose category of elements. When you tell me I should find myself, I honestly believe that a person can only find oneself within love. And when I say love, I mean love in its most profound manifestation as a deep, spiritual connection. This can only occur when one finally realizes that our perceptions of self are just a fiction. That they are just a drab piece of clothing we wear every day to make sure people act towards us the way we expect them to. We must ultimately realize that the mind is nothing more than a coat tree full of pegs on which we hang our various habits, habits we sometimes mistake in the darkness for a person stealing into our empty homes. It is then we can really appreciate the profundity of a true spiritual essence that encompasses everything. After all, what is there left in cracks between our thoughts? This wonderfully fictitious glass palace we've constructed for ourselves.

Blah, blah, blah...

Needless to say, you will always go on and accuse me of being some type of unregenerate Christian spiritualist, but indeed, it was how I grew up. You'll be delighted to learn that my nanny was a nice, old Catholic lady from Sassi di Matera. Indeed, she was a wonderful old woman: deeply religious, of course. How she used to speak to me when I still could understand some Italian:

> Eh Felicity, le dici le tue preghiere? No? Ma perché? Dio ascolta solo coloro che parlano a Lui. Lo devi ringraziare ogni mattina per averti dato un nasino all'insù così carino altrimenti ti potresti svegliare senza.

Then afterward, we would kneel together in the darkness before the window and pray together:

Angelus Domini nuntiavit Mariae
Et concepit de Spiritu Sancto

Ecce ancilla Domini
Fiat mihi secundum verbum tuum

After she died, I went through a short period of hating God for taking her away. Then afterward, an intensely religious stretch where I wore all black and prayed almost constantly to a painting of the Virgin Mary she had once given me. It was this very painting, which, with her help, I hung next to my bed to form a small "shrine". As it were, this shrine consisted of a small wall-hung shelf on which I would light candles and could (upon my choosing to do so) leave the dear Virgin all the flowers of the field. In my pagan simplicity, I left her all manner of things: seashells, bottle caps, dead mice I hoped to return to life (in the end, I'm not sure she quite appreciated all my offerings). I even made private confessions for all the spiders I'd ever washed down the drain. In some sense, I imagined the Virgin was my dear Nanny of a much younger age. To complete the illusion, I put colored films over my windows to mimic stained-glass windows. Indeed, my parents were becoming concerned that my room was looking increasingly like the ambulatory of Bourges Cathedral (always candlelit, always smelling of frankincense and myrrh) than a pre-adolescent's bedroom (perhaps they wouldn't have preferred me to hang the typical teen sensation on my wall?). They were, bless them, concerned, not because they thought I might burn the house down, but because I might convert to being a Catholic. Ultimately, it got worse.

When I was an early teen, I started to read Teresa of Avila and Catherine di Siena. I remember feeling incredibly inspired when they spoke about their visions, about their becoming one with something outside of oneself. I remember how it made me feel as a child. I remember feeling every atom of my body vibrating furiously outward. I hadn't felt the same since until, well... I'm too embarrassed to say, until we started dropping & together. I think much of my life has been spent trying to find that feeling of intimacy (or should I say infancy), before there was this ME to hate with all the acne, with all the pretentiousness, with all these remontant worries. Now I feel sure that it is only through love of someone else that we can approach the majesty of God, the majesty of uniting with another of his creations.

You always say I believe in fairytales. In some sense, I do. In some sense, I took that "leap of faith" because, unlike you, I have to have faith in something. I need to feel there is a point to anything in life. Is that so wrong? My father always believed that once you've felt the absurdity of love, you could understand and appreciate the absurdity of faith and resign yourself to its infinite possibilities. You ask me to feel, to be alive, to crave, and I do. I do crave the idea that love could be infinite. When I asked my father why I should believe, he explained to me the flawed logic of Pascal's Wager. Despite its obvious defects, something always stuck for me. It made me ask myself that if for a second, I could believe that God's love can be infinite, then I should also believe in an infinite capacity to be loved and love another. If I am allowed one certainty in life, it is this: one's life and wellbeing <u>will</u> be improved by the mere possibility of something rather than the certainty of nothing. We are only human after all, and therefore, we can never possess any real certainties, so why not learn to open oneself to the transcendent, to the radiant corridor of one's spiritual self? Once one gets the handle and opens this door, one will instantly appreciate the fact that one stands at the long end of a never-ending corridor. This corridor is one's existence, one's self. Just as any corridor can be filled with beautiful objects and comforting baubles, one's existence can also be filled with the trophies and obsessions of this world. However, once one learns that it is better to empty this corridor of everything, to remove all distractions from true vision, one can begin to perceive a radiant light that extends from its opposite end. One begins to feel the infinite tug of love, drawing the entirety of existence through oneself like an eternal golden thread. Some would call this the Holy Spirit. Once one feels that, one doesn't need to crave love, one has it within oneself, always. It is at this point that one will forever be open to another's love, which is the greatest gift in this otherwise lonely world.

When I was a child, my father used to read me Bunyan's Pilgrim's Progress. I loved it then and still have a special place in my heart for it now. It was my first introduction to what a spiritual journey could be. The fact that some of the most amazing odysseys can occur completely inside of oneself blew my mind. Indeed, I might have come hundreds of miles to New York to find adventure, but I know that in my heart, I will have traveled millions more. I hope to continue on this journey with you. Ultimately, I'm not sure what I believe and I don't want to sound naive, but love, forgiveness, pity... They can and will save the world.

P.S. Though he is certainly an awkward one, I had the most interesting conversation with Lord Hate-Good (who I must admit, I'm slightly afraid of). He told me that even the story of Christ feeding the multitudes with two fish and seven loaves could be explained mathematically by something called the Banach-Tarski paradox. Go figure, maybe there is some hope at the end of faith.

# 9

**Luferlang** – *Soinacaerulea tresarticulosus*

- *A Luferlang is an extremely dangerous animal that only attacks once a year, yet its attack always proves fatal. In regards to appearance, the animal is described as follows: "a dark blue stripe down the spine, a bushy, swivel-jointed tail set in the middle of the back (this appendage is most useful in keeping off the flies), and all four legs triple-jointed." The animal is reported to be extremely quick and able to move in all four directions with equal dexterity. The only known method with which to defend oneself against a Luferlang attack is to hold up a large mirror in front of the creature, as "the double image will so confuse the beast that he will rush off in disgust."*

Luferlang

Grandpappy had a million questions.

He asked me why I wasn't eating none. Not banana popsicles or even ice-cream sandwiches. He asked me why I was always staying in my room and didn't go out in the forest no more. He asked why I didn't like humming when he was playing banjo. He asked me why I was always following him round like a six o' clock shadow when he left the house. He asked why I didn't hardly want to take baths with him no more. He asked why I didn't want to go to school or to the library. He asked me why I didn't have no answers and why I was so silent, even for me.

I didn't say nothing about them boys and he didn't know no hows. Them boys went real quiet and we didn't see them around for nothing.

Sometimes, I sat inside all day, picking scabs off my knees. Grandpappy thought it was strange. I didn't even want to go fishing no more. I didn't want to go for long walks or call the birds down from the trees. I didn't want to trap otters. I didn't want to go worm-grunting or looking for moles. I didn't even look for the Fearsome Critters no more. Most of all, I didn't want to be away from my Grandpappy, not even for a second. I didn't want to be afraid. I didn't want no one to see me.

One of the girls at school told me that if I stuck pins in the electrical socket, I could kill myself and go and see my mommy. I told her my momma wasn't dead. She asked me where she was, but I couldn't tell her.

I had my own questions too. About a billion of them.

I wanted to write to my mommy, but when I gave the letters to Grandpappy, he never sent them. He said he didn't know where she was nowadays, but every month, she'd send a check. I asked him why she never came back and why she didn't want to see me if I was her only daughter. Didn't she love me? He said yes, she did, but that she was sick and couldn't really see me till she was well. I only saw one picture of her. She was beautiful. She had long, dark hair. Big eyes. She looked like me.

She was in a picture with my pappy when he was dressed in his military uniform. He died in the war, the one in Afghanistan. I asked my Grandpappy where Afghanistan was on a map and he couldn't tell me. I could tell from the picture that my mom and dad was so happy. Grandpappy said that when he got killed in the war, my mommy went over to find him, but she ended up losing her way. She became all turned upside down like the Fillyloo bird that flew backwards and upside down. She was sick in the head and what made her more sick was the fact that she couldn't see me. She sent money though. Lots and lots of money, but we never used none. One day, we would have enough to get on a big old airplane and go see her. That's what Grandpappy said.

Fall was coming and we needed to cut wood for the winter. Grandpappy could split logs like no one else's business. He would sweat up a mighty storm when he cut up the wood and sometimes, he would get to wheezing and he'd have to sit down. Sometimes, he got so sick, I felt he might die. That made me scared.

Then one day, when he was putting powder on me, he notices my belly is getting all swolled up and he says, "Willow, you feeling alright? Your stomach has been swelling up like a watermelon."

I nodded my head, but he looked at me all deep with this eye. He said "We haven't seen them boys around these parts for months. Seems strange all of a sudden, they would disappear. Well, good riddance to them anyway."

One day, one of the boys' moms done come over to the house all in a tizzy. She was the mom of the quiet boy and her and Grandpappy were talking a long time over in the corner by the front door next to the refrigerator. Grandpappy kept shaking his head. He had an angry look on his face. So angry I was afeared. She looked at me and I could see she was crying. She finally left and Grandpappy come over to me and said "Listen Willow, you sure them boys didn't do nothing to you?"

I shook my head.

"Now listen, Willow, don't go lying to me now."

He grabbed my arm really tightly. So tight, it began to hurt, and I could feel he was squeezing the hot tears out of me as he shook me like a little rag doll. Then he gave me a big ole slap.

"Listen, Willow, you have to tell me now. This is important."

When he finally set me down, I could see his eye looking at me. The hot tears kept squirting out of my eyes. I could see his magic eye looking through me like an X-ray. I could see what he saw. He saw the creature locked up inside my ribcage. He saw him eating the insides of me. I was scared. I turned around and ran. I ran and ran as fast as I could and he come all hollering after me, mad as hornets. He couldn't catch me though and I hid in the woods were I was very sad. I was hiding myself, like when we used to play Ghost in the Graveyard at school and nobody could ever find me until they all gave up looking for me. Then, I saw something behind the trees. It moved so fast, I didn't know what it was. I thought it might be another Critter so I went to go follow it. It was dark and narrow and moved real slow. When I finally come up behind it, I could not believe my own eyes. I had finally seen it. It was nothing else but a Hidebehind. Though I couldn't exactly see him, he would whisper to me inside my head even though his mouth wasn't moving none. I could see his eyes was burning red like coals in a fire. He had a scary voice, like one a monster would have. He would say:

"Willow, what you hiding from? Don't you want to come play with me?"

I said no.

He said "Why not? I am your friend and I want to play with you?"

I said no.

The Hidebehind said "Are you afraid of them boys? Is that what it is?"

I said no.

He said "You don't like them boys, do you?"

I said no.

"He said would you like me to go get them boys and eat them up?"

I said yes.

"You want them dead as road kill?"

I said yes.

"You want your mommy and daddy back?"

I couldn't see nothing then and everything went dark. Next thing I knowed Grandpappy was carrying me back to the house in his arms. Grandpappy gave me some honey mixed with whiskey so I would fall asleep again. Just when everything was going dark, I felt him pull my shirt up and he put his ear against my tummy. Then he took off my underwear and I could feel his cold hands down there where the boys had hurt me.

Next morning, Grandpappy was in a bad, bad mood. He said he had business to take care of and was going to go visit them boys.

"Willow, you don't worry none. I know what them boys done did and I gonna make sure it don't happen again. There's gonna be a reckoning, you hear? You don't worry none about that. You stay here."

He walked out of the house and he done took his shotgun with him.

# 10

dear jayna,

i know we haven't spoken in years and i know we never really met eye to eye. lord knows, i wouldn't contact you unless i had to. but i write to you today with a heavy heart as god's judgment weighs heavy upon me.

there are no two ways about it. willow needs you and there is no one who can help her down here. i tried my darndest to take care of her the same way i tried my darndest to take care of brice, but something's happened i can't fix.

after all these years, i don't know where to begin to say i'm sorry. i don't mean to dig up all what should stay buried, but it can't be helped as something has come up that's bringing all our history back to haunt us. you know when it all started, i had lost two already. bishop drove himself off the ridge, josiah shot down in kandahar, and brice... well, brice, when he come back from afghanistan, he certainly wasn't the same man we knew before he left. you don't know what it's like to lose two sons and a third halfway down to hades. i couldn't lose another. i would do anything to keep him. he was like his mamma. he wasn't meant for no war. he was the weak one and the war took him away from us long before the lord did.

you guys were too young. too young to deal with all that. i know you missed him during all those years in the service and two tours. i know you worked hard

to try to get through college. you was driving 70 miles
a day. you didn't deserve none of the way we treated you.
i should have stopped it.

but we should never have done what we did. i live
every day regretting it. the lord has punished us for our
sins. but he is forgiving too.

i keep praying he will have mercy on us all.
willow most of all, who didn't deserve one bit of this,
poor child. i know a lot of things was forced on you.
even willow was forced on you and you had your
reasons for leaving. god gave me the willingness not
to blame you for what happened that day. i know the
redeemer has the power to forgive my part in it too.
even a poor sinner like myself. i keep praying every
night.

i'm sorry god didn't give me the gift of writing or
saying much in the way of words, but i ain't heard
nothing still. this is the second letter i am sending
you. we keep getting the checks all regular, but i am
a fearing i only have your old address. i'm still
guessing you're living in new york by the address on
the checks. if you get this message, please write back.
there ain't much time now to save her.

# 11

Dear Felicity,

You devilish little syncretist!

Will I never be able to change your mind? To make you see? To make you live?

YOUR WAY OF LOOKING AT THE WORLD IS PREPOSTEROUS! Corals and Corridors!? Peace, Love and Harmony!? WTF!!!!!!!!! Hello!!!!! Epic fail!!!!!!! Put simply: your life is based around NOTHING ELSE BUT PITY: pity for dolphins, pity for the manatees, pity for faggots, for blacks, for American Indians, for everyone you have pity! It is a sensation that drives a LARGE portion of your life. YOU WORK AT AN ANIMAL SHELTER, FOR GOD'S SAKE! But have you ever asked yourself why? Why do you feel so much pity for the world? ARE YOU EVEN PRIVILEGED ENOUGH to feel pity for anyone else outside yourself?

I have my own thoughts anent the subject of your pity. GET OVER YOURSELF ALREADY!!!! Your pity is merely the SOUR AFTERTASTE left by the bitter pill of virtuous guilt. A pill, which quite frankly, is even hard for me to swallow. You wear your guilt like a badge of honor. It's so boring, all this guilt of being privileged, wringing the tears from your silk handkerchiefs. GIVE ME A BREAK! You! You! You! GUILT IS THE MOST SOLIPSISTIC FEELING OF THEM ALL. The most self-indulgent. The most condescending. I bet you just enjoy wallowing in all your guilt. DROWNING IN THE SORROW of being allowed to live the life you live while others suffer - STOCKHOLM SYNDROME CHRISTIANITY!

I have been reading A LOT of Nietzsche recently. I am smart enough to realize that this is NEVER A GOOD THING. However, he saw everything years before everyone else did. UPON HIS DEATH, THE 20TH CENTURY WAS BORN. Now, let me give you a few morsels to chew on while you choke down the remainder of your virtuous guilt. So what does he have to say about your pity?

107

*That however – namely, pity – is called virtue itself at present by all petty people: – they have no reverence for great misfortune, great ugliness, great failure.*

Indeed, I would say so. Christianity, ESPECIALLY THE ARISTOCRATIC BRAND, is the balm you use to cure the trance of your self-induced guilt. It is the basis of your morality and, without a doubt, the ultimate foundation of your bourgeoisie brand of Christianity. Pity is certainly a natural human emotion and, as a result, WE ARE INCREASINGLY LIVING IN A COUNTRY OF VICTIMS. An America in which NO ONE WANTS TO BE OFFENDED. Jews, blacks, homos, freaks. WE HAVE FINALLY REACHED A LOWEST COMMON DENOMINATOR! Thus, instead of pity being a feeling of sympathy, IT HAS BECOME AN OVERRIDING FEELING OF EMPATHY, A NATIONAL ANTHEM. Empathy? Empathy among the weak, downtrodden people of America! THE RICHEST, MOST POWERFUL COUNTRY IN THE WORLD! America will change, you see. One day, it will be overrun by the TARANTULAS, who will put forth a GREAT TYRANT. But this tyrant won't look like some clichéd, mustachioed third-world caricature. NO, he will be the splitting image of us all, because we too will expect him to be THE FOREMOST SLAVE IN OUR SOCIETY OF SLAVES. This person, we will call a President, but he will be nothing else but a populist bully. One that that will destroy WHAT LITTLE FREEDOMS WE HAVE LEFT, all for the sake of our great DESIRE TO BE EQUAL – EQUALLY IMPOVERISHED.

"*And 'Will to Equality' – that itself shall henceforth be the name of virtue; and against all that hath power will we raise an outcry! Ye preachers of equality, the tyrant-frenzy of impotence crieth thus in you for 'equality': your most secret tyrant-longings disguise themselves thus in virtue-words!*"

Do you begin to see, Felicity? In this tyranny of the Gadarene swine, we have become our own slave masters! And why exactly is this? BECAUSE WE ARE ASHAMED OF OUR OWN WEAKNESS! It is a COUNTERFEIT PRIDE we submit to. Mercy is a preserve only of the powerful, for only they can be "above the law". To Nietzsche, PITY IS MERELY A FORM OF SELF-LOVE. A feeling that allows us to FEEL GOOD ABOUT OURSELVES, but ultimately, will BREED ILL WILL AND WEAKEN THE RACE. For a long time (TOO LONG), the world has been infected with this "God virus". I STRONGLY subscribe to the idea that we force all high school students to read Nietzsche's On the Genealogy of Morals. In this book (Nietzsche's masterpiece, if you ask me), pity is defined as NOTHING LESS THAN THE TRIUMPH OF A SLAVE MORALITY. Thus, it is my firm belief that if we are to survive in this wild land, this America, we CANNOT BE WEAK. We have to do EVERYTHING WE CAN TO RESIST PITY! Read Zarathustra and the chapter entitled "The Pitiful", where Nietzsche proclaims:

> "Behold Zarathustra! Walketh he not amongst us as if amongst animals? ... So be ye warned against pity: from thence there yet cometh unto men a heavy cloud! Verily, I understand weather-signs!"

Why do I know him to be speaking the truth? Because I HAVE SEEN WHAT HAPPENS IN THE WILD. I have seen what happens to people like Willow. The Wild teaches one lesson and one lesson only: STRENGTH PREVAILS. Indeed, WE LIVE IN A WORLD OF HAWKS AND DOVES! One has to fight. One has no choice. ONLY A CHOICE OF WEAPONS! If I was stronger, I could have stopped it. I wish I were stronger!

I've been spending a lot of time with Lord Hate-Good recently. Indeed, I think we share a great deal of intellectual common ground. He also reads Nietzsche and was delighted to hear about Dr Ritter (another big Nietzsche fanboy). Not only does he read Nietzsche, but he gets him as well. In some sense, we are truly kindred spirits. I wish so dearly we could bring you to our side and show you all the things we are trying to build. Bar anything else, I want desperately to shock you into a state of wakefulness. I know you have had your reservations, but he is, in reality, a profound man. Like myself, he is a keen student of zoology and evolutionary theory. Incidentally, I took him to the National History Museum. Can you believe it was his first time there? You would be amazed at how much he knows. Not just about animals, but about history, about culture, and why the world is the way it is. He explained it all to me like no one else has. He opened my eyes and taught me that evolutionary theory shares a lot in common with the thought of Nietzsche. Ultimately, they both teach us that THE BASIS OF OUR SOCIETY IS BUILT ON A DEEP FALLACY. It teaches us that the very existence of altruism in nature represents a fundamental problem, one that can only be justified as a means to an end. But I do stress MEANS TO AN END, because one cannot escape the vicious laws of this world. Thus, Zarathustra chides us:

> "Verily, I have often laughed at the weaklings, who
> think themselves good because they have crippled paws!"

Don't worry, I know exactly what the voice inside your head is saying to you. You may think I'm crazy or that I've gone completely off the rails. You may think I don't have the capacity for human love or emotion, but you would be VERY WRONG. In fact, if you really thought about it (and if you bothered to read the book I enclosed with this letter), you would realize how much I am trying to help you by means of revealing to you the nature of your character. I'm afraid your character is stock and has ALREADY BEEN COMMITTED TO PAPER. It has been dreamt up a hundred years ago in the Great Philosopher's mind. If you dare to open the book, you will clearly see your own reflection in the character of the "conscientious one" that so angers Zarathustra. Indeed, I can almost hear you saying these exact same words to me,

> ". . . you lust for the worst, most dangerous life, that
> which terrifies me the most, for the life of wild animals,
> for forests, caves, steep mountains and blind abysses.

And not those leaders who lead you out of harm's way please you the most, but those who lead you away from all ways, the misleaders. But if even such lusts in you are real, they still seem impossible to me.

For fear – this is man's primary and primordial feeling; fear explains everything, original sin and original virtue. Out of fear grew even my virtue, which is called: science.

The fear namely before a wild animal – this fear has been bred the longest in man, including the animal he hides inside himself and fears: – Zarathustra calls it 'the inner beast.'

Such long ancient fear, at last grown refined, spiritualized, intellectualized – today, methinks, it goes by the name of: science."

"Thus spake the conscientious one; but Zarathustra, who had returned to his cave and had heard and surmised this last speech, threw a handful of roses at the conscientious one and laughed at his 'truths.' 'What!' he cried, 'What did I hear just now? Verily, methinks you are a fool or I myself am one: and your "truth" I turn lickety-split on its head.

For fear – is the exception with us. Courage, however, and joy and adventure in the uncertain, in the unventured – courage seems to me man's whole pre-history.

The wildest, bravest animals he envied and robbed of all their virtues: only thus did he become – man."

Finally, I will say this, before you equate me to Hitler. It's not that I don't appreciate that people do truly suffer, that people are needlessly hurt every day, but IF WE ARE TO SAVE THEM, we need to save them from themselves. By giving into this culture of poverty, we only prolong their misery as they, the masses, will never act of themselves to CURE THE SICK OF THEIR SPIRITUAL BANKRUPTCY. Thus, it is up to us (and us only) TO RID OURSELVES OF THIS SLAVE'S PITY and AWAKE TO THE REALITIES OF THIS WORLD. Ultimately, pity was the LAST TEMPTATION that Zarathustra had to overcome.

"Unto your distress did he want to seduce and tempt me: 'O Zarathustra,' said he to me, 'I come to seduce thee to thy last sin.'

'To my last sin?' cried Zarathustra, and laughed angrily at his own words: 'WHAT hath been reserved for me as my last sin?'

– And once more Zarathustra became absorbed in himself, and sat down again on the big stone and meditated. Suddenly he sprang up, –

'FELLOW-SUFFERING! FELLOW-SUFFERING WITH THE HIGHER MEN!' he cried out, and his countenance changed into brass. 'Well! THAT – hath had its time!

My suffering and my fellow-suffering – what matter about them! Do I then strive after HAPPINESS? I strive after my WORK!'"

Thus, if you see things clearly, you will understand that life is not about suffering. No, indeed, it is in no way about suffering oneself or suffering the weak multitudes. On the contrary, it is about living, a new way of living. We MUST CHANGE THE WORLD otherwise, we will PERISH AS A SPECIES. Evolution teaches that WE HAVE TO GO BACK TO BEING WILD THINGS.

Only out of anarchy can the seeds of a new morality grow. ONLY THEN CAN THE TRULY POWERFUL COME TO RISE AND SAVE THE HUMAN RACE. We have come up with a solution together. Actually, as I write this, we are working out the final details of our plans to initiate the very first stages of our great master plan. I am to lead one of the parties. I can't tell you the details of what we're about to do, but IT IS GOING TO BE BIG. VERY BIG! New York will NEVER BE THE SAME AGAIN! At last, I've finally found something that I was meant to do.

Manhattan... no, all America is going to change once we're finished! I promise you that.

P.S. Please, don't hate me for all of this. Trust me, it's for the good of both of us.

Still craving you,

John

# 12

I could have killed him…

I really could have…

By the end of that night, I should have killed him…

It was then, after dating for about seven months, that John and I began to become more distant from one other. Besides the crazy, aggressive letters (some of which I will include alongside this testimony), he had joined some strange, secret society he patently refused to tell me anything about. Partly because of this, and partly because of the general disintegration within our lines of communication, I began to see him less and less. Even when I did manage to see him, he was always disturbed, anxious and distant. He kept mumbling under his breath, like an insane man. Occasionally, I could catch a word here and there: the "Wicket Gate", the "Gaius Inn", the "Land of Beulah". Words I thought were meant to mock me, given I recognized them as nothing more than encoded references to Bunyan's *The Pilgrim's Progress* (a book he would never let me live down). In his more lucid moments, he would occasionally mention his headway on *The Guide*, but in the same breath, would also hint at his having to work intensely and with great concentration (i.e. manspeak for "don't call me, I'll call you"). In sum, these were all given as reasons why he couldn't see me a great deal. He was also complaining of strange dreams containing, amongst other things, babies with snakeheads and chicken tikka masala demons chasing him whilst eating parts of themselves. Needless to say, John began to bring out the martyr instinct in me. I thought if I tried hard enough, I could ultimately save him like some bruised puppy brought into the shelter. I couldn't bear to watch him self-destruct before my very eyes (probably because I had seen it happen before and I felt some irrational level of responsibility). I never knew what was going through his dark, cavernous mind and somehow, I thought he needed me more than I needed him. I was willing to bear any amount of pain and humiliation on his behalf, if only I could save him. In ringing my own leper's bell, I really believed I could. How wrong I eventually was. You may justifiably ask why I loved him so much. Was it because I had a desperate "thing" for strays or "projects"? Maybe so. Though I hadn't known him for very long, he proved early on he could really read my mind. Spiritually speaking, I know for certain, we have been together a thousand years.

How did it start? Innocently, at first. It began as just another quiet night. One spent on the couch watching a movie. I forgot which one. During the course of the film, we'd become intimate and I put my hand on his crotch. In previous times, he'd move it away and I respected that, but this time, I was feeling particularly excited and wanted to be closer to him. As I started to put my hand down his drainpipe trousers, he recoiled with a lightning swiftness and slapped me in the face. At first, I didn't understand. I had suspected there might be something wrong with him sexually, but I didn't know for sure. Though we had been dating for months, I hadn't so much as seen him naked. It was clear he generally didn't like being touched or having his personal space invaded, but with me, he was different. He clearly enjoyed our kissing and being intimate. It was the only thing that convinced me he wasn't autistic. I never wanted to force things, but I was more than a little taken aback by this sudden show of violence. From that moment, I knew we were long overdue in broaching the dreaded subject that had hallowed out several moments of awkward silence that followed upon our abandoned sallies into each other's netherworld.

For some reason, my initial instinct was to apologize to him. However, he quickly insisted that everything was entirely his fault and that he never should have hit me. He seemed honestly contrite and shocked by his behavior, especially as the slap appeared to be more of a reflex than anything else. Once we'd kissed and made up, I went straight in:

"Listen, I know I shouldn't have tried to force you into something you are uncomfortable with, but you can open up to me. What is wrong?"

At this point, John stood up with an annoyed grunt and reverted back to his grumpy self. "Wrong with what? Because I don't want to have sex? Not everyone is constantly in heat like you?"

"Excuse me, but we've been dating for months and I haven't even seen you so much as with your shirt off."

"You never had a problem with it before. Now, you're suddenly all hot and bothered. What has changed?"

"John, that's pretty unkind and unfair as well."

"What do you want from me anyway? You know I'm under a great deal of stress and..."

"I know, John, I know, but I thought we could just... I thought it might help."

Again, with an unexpected violence, he shoved his face into my own, his eyes looking daggers.

"Help? You actually think you're going to help ME? I didn't realize I needed help, especially from a trust-fund baby like yourself."

With a mocking smirk on his face, he retired to a far corner of a room where a villainous laugh ascended the entire column of his body like a dark smoke.

"Oh, I know. I finally know what this is about. It's about power, isn't it? You've been a spoiled brat your entire life and gotten everything you've ever wanted and now you're bored and want nothing more than for me to put you in your place. You want me to prove to you that I'm a man, a knight worthy of tilting on your field of pleasures. You want me to prove to you that I can ravage you, don't you? You want me to split you in half."

"John, what are you saying?"

"Don't pretend you don't know, you little bitch. For someone who couldn't satisfy themselves for two years, you're sure hot and saucy now."

"What? What are you talking about, John? It's me. Why are you addressing me this way?"

"Well, if you want to act like a little whore."

"Whore? John, I was just trying to be intimate with you. I think it's normal."

"Normal. Normal. Is that what 'normal' is for you?"

"Well... yes."

John's head revolved with that awful smirk he always used, that maddeningly, arrogant smirk that greeted me as if I was something worthy of pity. I saw things were quickly getting out of hand. Thus, in a futile effort to achieve some form of détente, I tried to grab his hand, thinking my touch would bring him back to me. Make him remember who I was.

"John, listen. If you have a problem and Lord knows I do, we can talk about it. It's me, after all, not some stranger. I've lived with issues my entire life and I don't think it's such a big deal. Many couples face this all the time and we just have to get through it."

John jerked his hand away from my own with such a violence that he slammed his elbow into the nearby cupboard. This only served to make him even more angry.

"You have no idea what you are talking about."

"Look, maybe we can see a therapist. I don't know. I'm willing to try anything to make it work. Don't hate me for trying. We've never discussed it before and..."

"Oh God, are we really having this conversation? You want me to pull out right now and give you a good time just to prove to you that I can?"

"John, no, that's..."

Without missing a beat, death-ray eyes in his sockets, John started to unzip his trousers.

"Ok, since you so kindly asked for it, I'm going give you want you want so you won't go away disappointed."

At his point, John began to violently fondle himself in front of me.

"John. John. What are you doing? That is disgusting."

"It's what you wanted, isn't it? Look, I'm making it hard for you."

"No, it isn't. It isn't at all. I can't... I can't breathe... I'm... I'm leaving."

As I made for the door, he tried to pull me back. He grabbed my wrist with a fury I didn't think him capable of.

"Where are you going? Back to the Nile with your crocodile tears? Well take a bite out of this. Make sure you know how to swallow."

Suddenly, I felt something hard throb against my torso. I made every effort not to look and turned around in a wild fury, but he kept insisting.

"Hey, where are you going? Here it is."

In my wild confusion, I broke free of his grip and struggled toward his front door. Once I had opened it, I fled the flat and, without looking back, started down the stairs. I ran as fast as I could, all the while swallowing the bitterest of tears until something quite peculiar happened. It was as if a thunderclap had snapped inside my head. Then, all at once, my feet left the ground and I felt myself begin to float. My body resisted all force and whatever was left of me sailed through the now opened hallway window. Everything came and went in waves. I felt the present weight of all my vagrant emotions cascade through me until I was completely inured within the ink of a summer's sky. As the waves of a transient existence broke around me, I scaled that great tangle of the stars and sensed my skin being torn away by the night's invisible thorns. Below me, the city burned in thousand points of light. I thought this must be the feeling one has when one dies. In an instant (one which may have occurred a thousand years in the future or perhaps the past), the plates inside my head became unhinged and my soul oozed forth in a silent eruption of my inner self. Like a pubescent glowworm, I inched out of my nacreous shell and climbed a celestial branch toward the furthest corner of Night, leaving behind the dread manacles of all sub-lunar things. Finally, I was free. Free at last to be everywhere and nowhere all at the same time. I multiplied myself internally as though through an insect's holoptic eye. I understood myself to be in a million places, doing a million different things all at once. I watched the world blur into nothing more than colors and faint shapes, what became the mascara-blotted aquarelle of a stranger's face – one so strange that it could only have been my own. Feeling the urge, I took this all-too-familiar alien by the hand as she looked at me from her parallel dimension full of a sorrowless antimatter. I kissed her and stroked her hair into flame. Then I folded her into an origami crane of pure light. Our disembodied eyes revolved around one another, as would a swarm of misfit planets. Wanting ultimate release from my mimicry, I plunged my head into one of the icy, blue-green seas of Neptune. When the night air finally let me go, I was 40 blocks away and so upset that I put my lunch down on the pavement. I couldn't breathe. I couldn't believe John could be so cruel. I had been to the ends of the universe and back.

The next time John and I met was no better. Disgusted, we could no longer speak to each other. Our zero-decibel conversation went as follows (excerpted from my diary):

We stood warily eying one another like a pair of gunslingers in a Texas showdown. The stage was set for our little, silent Western. With the dawn sunrise frozen into frame, he looked at me with those wary slits as if to say, I know you are sick of me and will go on being sick of me and want to make sure I know you're sick of me. Sucking my teeth, I looked down at the floor as he wriggled his bare toes, still shriveled after a cold shower, from which he emerged completely dressed. He started to scratch his elbow and then firmly put both his hands down on the chair as if to say, I'm not fidgeting. So I shook my head and exhaled in an exaggerated fashion, making it clear I knew he was fidgeting, and picked a scab. Another 15 heartbeats would not so innocently pass. Then, he turned away and looked for something to read, almost confessing defeat until, at the last minute, he recoiled and gave me a quick snicker, cutting further his gimlet eyes in my direction, to which I guffawed and scratched my eyebrows, making the clearest of statements. One that said, "I hope you don't think that I don't know you almost gave in." An erratic pulse, the heart making a puddle inside of my palm, a stifling heat beneath the neck. Roving head stalks shoot a thousand, badly-aimed glances, each caroming off the walls, their trillions of vectors never quite intersecting. He then looked at me with *a look of pure seduction, one that sent shivers down my spine. At first, I let my granite eyes do the talking: "Don't even think you can..." Then his look switched to one of horror, causing my own wounded eyes to wax. I was paralyzed and blinked. Then blinked again. I finally asked "What?" I had clearly lost our silly game.*

It was another week before I came to John's flat again. I had been missing him and was absolutely knackered from work. He had begged me to come over, but when I arrived at his place, he barely spoke to me. He merely sat sulking in the dark, listening to the Talking Heads' *Wild, Wild Life* over and over again at an ear-bleeding volume. When I asked him what was wrong, he simply said, "Nothing", and wouldn't go on much past that.

I told him he seemed to have changed and he merely responded, "Change is good."

So much had been welling up inside me over the last week, I started to blurt senselessly, "Whatever it is you are involved in, you need to get out of it. Just understand one thing, if you want me to enter your personal hell, I will. If you want me to descend into your underworld, I will. You know I will. Just let me in. That's all I ask. Please. I know I can help."

"Oh, how romantic. You clearly suffer from what some dead, white guy referred to as a 'dangerous prevalence of imagination'. Whatever are you are you talking about Mistress Fawkler?"

Whilst saying this, John had a very pensive and ironic look on his face. One that came surprisingly without malice as he was busy listening to his music. He continued to rock back and forth, like a child trying to put himself to sleep. His face then screwed up into a question mark, dotted by his opened mouth.

"Speaking of dead, white men, you know, Mesmer believed that animals exude this force... He called it 'animal magnetism'.

He imagined it was some kind of dark influence that permeated the entire universe. In fact, it was this invisible liquid that he used to control people, to literally hypnotize them like some kind of proto-Rasputin. You ever think that is what we have between us? Draws us to do stupid things like fall in love and go crazy about it."

"What?"

All of a sudden, John stopped rocking back and forth and his eyes began to fill with tears.

"See, all I want is your spirit. All I want is you."

At this point, John jumped up and began kissing me furiously. He dragged me to the carpet and kept caressing me in a wild, almost bestial fashion. Wolf-like, he literally began ripping the clothes from me. At first, I tried to fend him off gently, but he wouldn't stop. He just kept going. Eventually, I resorted to giving him a powerful slap across the face. This finally went some way in breaking the wicked spell he had come under. He simply froze. Sitting stock-still, he just stared at me through those flying saucer eyes, reddened by the tears still streaking his face. The trance slowly faded, though it was clear that the moment of recognition was still some distance off. He remained uncertain, not quite in full possession of what he had just done. It was really awkward. Finally, as the veils of confusion parted, so did his lips. From that dark sliver, there emerged a rare bird of mystery, his heart's thumping conundrum.

"Why… why did I do that?"

The angel of recognition had finally dipped its toe into the sordid air. As her wings buffeted the curtains of the opened windows, he kept blankly staring at his hands as if they'd been dripping Duncan's blood. Without a word, he walked out of the room. I tried to stop him, but he continued on with the dead look of a zombie in his eyes. I tried to pull him back but he jerked away from me, his errant elbow hitting me in the eye with great force. Surprisingly, the impact didn't stop him. He just left.

After that, I wouldn't see him again for almost two days. This time, he showed up to my flat bearing hound-dog eyes and gifts of propitiation. However, I couldn't escape the thought of what had occurred. Now, it appeared that none of our meetings were destined to go well and usually ended in some form of violence, whether intentional or not. I felt like Sisyphus on the hillside. Like the battered wife who tells her friends, "He loves me deep inside, he just gets angry sometimes. He doesn't mean it really."

Though I tried to avoid seeing anyone, I went out with Shinkirō the next day for tea. Our meeting had been anticipated by the hopeful might of arnica. As soon as we had sat down, he did something he had never done with me before. He reached across the table and held my hand. With a concerned voice, he asked, "Felicity, are you taking care of yourself?

"Yes, why?"

"You don't look so good. And John doesn't either. I've been hearing things…"

"What things?"

"Nothing really. It's just… well, I just think he may be getting mixed up in some silly stuff. That's it…"

"You mean the animal rights crowd?"

"Yeah, sounds stupid, but I heard they're really crazy. You know, John told me the other day that you were like ultra-religious and that you hate faggots."

"What? Why would he say something like that?

"Ca'mon, Felicity… like duh. You know I'm only pulling your leg. You're too gullible. Anyway, do you love him?"

For my part, I couldn't believe how hard it had become for me to say it. My tongue stiffened under the toil of a new vocabulary: one of lies, cover-up and arnica.

"Yes, I am. But sometimes…"

"Oh my God, I just noticed it. Is that a black eye you have?"

"No, it's nothing..."

"Did John hit you?"

"C'mon, Shinkirō, shhhhhh... Please don't make a scene. Everyone will look. Hey, listen... it wasn't his fault really?" (Yes, I actually said that.)

Shinkirō squeezed my hand again, even tighter.

"C'mon, Felicity. You know better than that. You know what you're sounding like? I can't believe John would do anything like that, but..."

"I know. I know. Please don't preach to me now. It is really not what you think. An accident, really. And yes, he loves me. He really does."

Sensing things were getting a bit tense, I tried to laugh it off and put on a forced smile, despite my feeling utterly rubbish. Shinkirō didn't have to say anything. He looked at me with such disapproval as if to say, I've seen a million cases just like you. Maybe it was my British upper lip, maybe it was sheer denial, but I wasn't quite equipped to respond to him. To open up in such an American fashion about this facet of my relationship with John. So, dears, in a manner typical of my Scottish blood, I tried a dram full of bad humor.

"What did Burns say? Perhaps he just wanted to 'charm me with the magic of a switch'. Or, perhaps, yes, perhaps (sigh), we just love each other too much."

"You know what they say, sometimes love like this can be too much for both parties. Sometimes, love can be dangerous."

"I know."

"Ah, so madly in love. You know, both weeds and chrysanthemums tend to share the same earth. You put two people like that together and they will rip each other's hearts out just because they don't have the strength to rip out their own."

"C'mon, Shinkirō. Respect the copyright. Did you get that off a soap opera? Yes, an interesting piece of analysis, I suppose..."

As the minutes crept by, the ever-perceptive Shinkirō began to acknowledge my flagging interest in the conversation. I really was in no mood to rehash all this stuff that I had been going over in my mind a thousand times. I just sat there looking out the window, absently stirring my tea. After five minutes of silence (utter death for Shinkirō), he grabbed my hand resolutely.

"Ca'mon honey, the cream's all in. You're not listening. You have this wonderful, amazing guy in front of you and you're too busy thinking of John and what you may have done wrong to deserve this. Am I right? Look me in the eye and tell me I'm not right."

"Yes, Shinkirō. You are right."

"Listen, pumpkin, you just better be glad I'm a fag. Anyway, I know about these things. You have to be very careful in these types of relationships. These are the dangerous ones: the really meaningful ones (and I've had enough un-meaningful ones to know). I'll tell you why it's dangerous for you in particular. Because you are a sacrificer. You are one of those people who will take their own personality off the shelf just to make room for another person's dirty, old sneakers. But you forget, it's your personality that should have attracted the other person to begin with."

"Thanks for inviting me on your talk show, Dr Freud. Can I please wave to my family over there?"

"C'mon, I pay good money to have another homo-therapist tell me this stuff every week. Hey, you know what a parasitic twin is?"

"Yes, I guess."

"It's like this show I saw on TV... this poor girl in China was born with her dead sister still attached. It was only her head and teeth that were there on her back and they had to remove the entire thing. It was awful. Yuuuk!"

"Are you just trying to gross me out? What are we talking about parasitic twins for? I hope you're not going to say John and I are parasitic twins. That's just plain daft."

"C'mon, pumpkin, just listen... there was a point in here somewhere until you knocked it right off the table. Oh yes, here it is, right under your nose. You should know, my little pumpkin, that often, in these really intense love affairs, the weaker party's personality loses out and is subsumed into that of the dominant person's. Usually, it is only a small part of the other that survives. Believe me, I know from experience... if you keep going on in this way, you will be able to fit snuggly into his shirt pocket."

At this remark, I was slightly offended. It hit too close to home.

"Are you saying this because you think I don't have any personality and you do?"

"Of course not, I've had to fight off the lint too just to make enough space for myself in someone else's shirt pocket, girl. That IS something I know about. Sometimes, I still think I'm fighting. Maybe that's why I try to inflate my personality to a size way beyond its actual proportions. But people just think I'm putting on a show. That's why they don't take me seriously."

"C'mon. That's not true."

"Yes, but it is, dear. I'm smart enough to see that. I'm not as superficial and gorgeous a fashion bimbo as I seem."

"I know that. I listen to you and I think..."

"Take a chill pill, dear. Just hear me out for a second. Do you know why I do this? Try to have this outsize, over the top personality? Do you really understand why I act this way and live the life of a walking stereotype? Tell me. Because you think I'm insecure and overcompensating by being a diva? By living life out loud."

"No, it never really crossed my mind..."

"Listen, Felicity, you don't give me any credit. No one ever does. The reason I act the way I do is because I don't want to lose out like that again. I don't want someone to even begin to think they can just use me up like a wet bar of soap. Rub me between their fingers until I disappear into nothing but a puddle of dishwater."

"Aren't you afraid that is exactly what you've succeeded in doing to yourself? That you're just being someone you aren't?"

"Listen, dear, you're looking at this all the wrong way. This IS enabling me to be whomever I want to be. That is a powerful thing. It's about not limiting yourself."

"I want to be with John. WE are meant to be together. You understand? I haven't loved anyone like him before and I want so much for us to be together."

"Listen, Felicity, there is a part of you that remains outside this relationship. Don't let the relationship define everything you are."

"You know, to a certain extent, it is true... it is sometimes difficult to determine where he ends and I begin. For example, it sounds stupid and corny, but we sometimes complete each other's sentences. We even call each other at the same time. I've never had that before and I want to enjoy it. We mean everything to each other. We are different, but sometimes, we are just so in sync that it's like we're one and the same person."

"But it shouldn't be like that."

"Shouldn't it? Sure, you find yourself doing things you never thought you would. At times, you don't even recognize yourself in the mirror, because you only see the other person. But..."

"Yes, exactly..."

"But that is love. Love is sacrifice. Even if it means sacrificing every part of yourself."

"God, John was right about you and this religious thing... Are you actually saying you want to be some kind of martyr or something? (Laughing) A martyr to love... God, if that isn't ridiculous."

"Yes, exactly. It's not funny. I'm completely serious. I don't understand how it could be any different. Maybe I'm not as confident as I thought I was. Maybe I'm just an emotional sponge. But, for me, this IS love. The highest representation of love. Self-sacrifice. But for you... you think I'm being erased? Erasing myself, right?"

"Yes, well, sort of... especially if the other person is not reciprocating. Listen, I know there is more of you than meets the eye, but I'm seeing even less of that nowadays."

"I guess…"

Here, I began to run out of steam and didn't want to fight the good fight anymore. Conceding defeat, I gave in.

"Yeah, well maybe there is some truth in what you say. Maybe I am dissolving into nothing… maybe the colors are just fading out of me. I'm yesterday's Polaroid. Maybe that's why he doesn't fancy me anymore."

"C'mon now. Stop blaming yourself. Just make sure you take better care of the most important person in your life, you. Be the person you want to be. That's all I ask."

That was it. I finally had to admit it to myself: Shinkirō was right. Indeed, he was often wise beyond his years (though there was informed speculation that he wasn't as young as many suspected). After a very long pause, in which I continued to stare into the haze of thoughtless recognition, he forced eye contact on me again. With a look of anticipation in his eyes, he sought some sign of resolution. "So?"

"A moment of clarity?"

"Yes."

I thought I should say something profound, but there was nothing inside of me. At least, nothing I could verbalize. Before I realized what I was doing, I found myself speaking out loud, half to myself, half to Christ knows who. Something had welled up inside me from a plantation too distant to recall, its harvest too exotic to call my own.

"'His burden loosed from off his shoulders, and fell from off his back, and began to tumble; and so continued to do till it came to the mouth of the sepulcher, where it fell in, and I saw it no more.'"

"What? What are you mumbling about?"

"Nothing, just something I remember from my childhood. Thanks, Shinkirō, you really are a dear. It may sound really cheesy, but thanks for letting me remember who I am."

"Anytime, pumpkin. Remember, respect all copyrights. What would any of us be without each other?"

Shinkirō and I parted.

Ultimately, it was a pyrrhic victory I had won over myself. By now, it didn't really matter what I wanted to change between John and myself. He was spending most of his time at meetings with the Ota Benga society and repeating the utterly unhygienic rubbish spewed forth from that nutter, Lord Hate-Good. John had mentioned to me several times in passing that those desperate plonkers were planning "something big", but he couldn't tell me what it was. It all sounded extremely dodgy and I had a bad feeling about it. Every time I brought it up, he would always chide me to put a stop to my whinging. The only assurance he gave me was that everything would be revealed on July 4th, when all their plans would come into fruition.

It wasn't more than a couple weeks later that John came over to my flat at midnight, dressed something like a fourth-grade ninja. He informed me that at present, he couldn't return to his own place as it was far too dangerous. He was in a very excited mood. He said they had been doing some reconnaissance and had nicked some important supplies for the upcoming mission. I was in hysterics, but to shut me up, he gave a number of kisses and prattled on and on about how much he loved me. Before I could say anything in response, he put his finger to my lips and disappeared again into the same darkness from whence he had come. Such was our life; one lived in intense bursts, amidst long and increasingly frequent blackouts.

Before he had left, I managed to catch a glimpse of the film-wrapped tattoo on his arm. It read "*Ultima Cumaei venit iam carminis aetas*" *(Now comes the final era of the Sibyl's song)*. When he saw my wide-eyed stare, he mumbled something in passing about how all the senior members of the Ota Benga society had vowed to get one. He still wouldn't tell me anything about their activities or their whereabouts, but I was now certain of it. He had given himself over to some dark cult from which he couldn't rescue himself. I had visions of Tosca. I had visions of Lenore. I simply had visions of every potentially tragic opera we had seen at the Met together. The next morning, I was resolved. I finally decided I had to do something about it. I needed to go to the source. Determined and headstrong, I made a beeline over to the dog run and met that blinkered cow, Ms Light-Mind, and that gormless piece of work, Lord Hate-Good. Our conversation went as follows:

(Point blank) "What are you doing with John?"

"What are you talking about?"

"Look, I know you're doing something big and I want John out of it."

After looking at one another, those two twats merely laughed and smirked at me.

"Listen, if you don't tell me what you two are up to, I will go to the police?"

At this point, the neck-brace-wearing Light-Mind put her hands to her hips and curtly asked, "With what dear? The fact you can't keep track of your boyfriend? Instead of bothering with us, maybe you should try some makeup, or perhaps a little more between the sheets."

I could have hit that bitch right then and there. There was no doubt she was one catfight away from expending all her nine lives, but I relented. Instead, I stormed off home and decided to take some Zoloft to calm my nerves. Needless to say, I couldn't stop thinking of those two. In an effort to clear my head, I sunk two "mind erasers" (vodka, Kahlúa and tonic water on the rocks). I then agreed to meet with the Colonel and his new flavor of the month, Jenna. Incidentally, the Colonel had just purchased at auction a pair of Basquiats and couldn't stop talking about them. It was strange and somewhat disconcerting to see him before me so lucid and in rude health. The last I'd heard, he'd been holed up in his loft for three entire days, subsisting on little more than coke, prostitutes and Rammstein. Originally, our ways had been parted by the practical fact that in his latest manifestation as a cultish-type Peter Pan, he refused to go out and make the kids fly before two in the morning. Furthermore, his staunch requirement for getting out of bed (given by way of decree to his now numerous followers) was that he was on at least two or three guest lists. It was indeed good to see him still alive (which meant sadly I had won my bet with John). To top it all off, it appeared that throughout the chaos, he had even managed to enrich himself by a couple more million. In his own words, the "algorithms were working" despite the onset of the "crisis". If fact, he was hoping for an even bigger fall in the global markets as he was making a killing. Given his recent acquisitions, he was generally in high spirits, and despite years of hard living, he had successfully arrived to his mid-30s in a Dorian Gray-like fashion. In his usual course, he wanted us to follow him to Red Hook, where his layer *cum* party promoter friend was throwing a house party. Once there, we all sat in the living room and talked about doing drugs for want of actually having them. Personally, I wasn't saying much. I just sat there drinking white wine. At present, a seemingly endless version of The Orb's *Little Fluffy Clouds* played on and on. On the walls, projected in strange loops, where scenes from *Star Blazers*, *G-Force*, and other early

Japanimation cartoons. Bored of watching these, I turned my attention to a dizzy Asian girl who was shuttling between couch and kitchen, checking the trays of ketamine that cooked in the oven. She was going on in an incomprehensible manner about her two daughters (who had evidently learned to scale kitchen cabinets at a very young age in order to secure food and water for themselves) and her "loser" husband, who was currently at home babysitting (evidently, he was "barely" capable of pulling in "high-five figures", which was "not even a subsistence wage in this town").

Oblivious to his surroundings and in a completely matter of fact way, the Colonel was warbling loudly into Hiroko's ear, "When I go to the Matzoball, these JAPs ("Jewish-American-Princesses") – and I mean, the fake ones, not like you, little rice burners, are all over me. These ones go like a train and will put any Catholic girl to shame. Upper Eastside princesses, all locked up too long studying the Talmud. Yeah, you should probably go too, but these goody Jew boys won't marry you or bring you home to momma. They will take you on the side, but why not have some fun? They'll spend. They'll spend lots. I'll guarantee you'll see every place in Manhattan worth seeing, but their momma's living room. So, yes, you will see a lot of real JAPs there. The fake JAPs don't like it, but everyone wants a way in. People think three fourths of Goldman Sachs management will be there, but they're so deluded and soiled. Only place being Jewish is sexy. God save them."

At this point, Pharaoh walked in. Pharaoh was an exceptionally large and exceptionally good-looking black guy who used to be a linebacker at Stanford. He now worked as a structured derivatives trader and part-time fashion model. The Colonel immediately piped up more volubly, "Hey Pharaoh. Wanna go to the Matzoball? They would love you. We could even get you a *kippah*. Better yet, one of those Tutankhamun headdresses. All those fake JAPs would be like, 'Pharaoh, Pharaoh, come save me.' It would be so ironic as to be biblical."

My mind was evidently elsewhere (as usual these days), and I couldn't take much of the usual routine anymore. These people suddenly seemed like wasters to me. Clever wasters with nothing to do but waste whatever part of themselves someone else hadn't found a way to use up. For some reason, I had the dumb idea to go back to John's flat. I just had too many things in my head that were left unsaid. I quickly regretted my decision. We had another proper shouting match that night. John was blitzed and could barely stand. For the first time, I looked at him and he had such an anger in his eyes. He looked as if he were a hyena, ready to pounce upon an isolated wildebeest. In the coldest of voices he said, "Why did you go speak to Lord Hate-Good? You threatened him with the police, didn't you? What the hell were you thinking?"

"John, listen to me, please. I don't know what you're into these days but these people are changing you. Look at you. You're not the same person anymore. You drink by yourself. You're always a bit narky. You barely talk to me. What is going on? Can't you see that I care about you? Why are you doing this to yourself?"

John merely growled under his breath:

"He who makes a beast of himself gets rid of the pain of being a man."

Even in these moments, John couldn't avoid some form of literary reference. Not being in the best of moods myself, I snapped back, "Oh, for fuck's sake. Why are you doing this to us?"

"Us? Us? What us?"

"You know, John, sometimes, I just don't get you. It's like you have multiple personalities or something. Sometimes you are the most beautiful person I want to spend my entire life with, and at others, you're a sheer monster…"

"I am what my circumstances made me. Nothing else."

Again, I tried to stop him from leaving and he pushed me against the wall and struck me for the third time in the face. I broke down and started crying. John merely stood there and left the flat without saying anything. This was three times in as many months. Shinkirō was right. Something needed to change. I was furious at him. I tried my best to put myself in the right mood to sever all ties, but I couldn't do it just then. As an alternative and more subtle way of getting back at him, I decided I would cut my hair as short as his. It was indeed my long locks that he'd loved so much, and he swore he'd kill me if I ever cut them. With my new buzz, I began practicing to myself before the mirror, "John, this is it… John, we need to talk… John, get ready to meet your maker."

It so happened that during one of my practice sessions, John called me on my house line, just as I was singing some deep breakup music into my hairbrush, whilst staging my coup. I was finally ready, resolute and resolved to do it. Before I knew what was happening, my mouth began forming the words that were being pushed down the line in short, electrical bursts of static:

"John… John…"

"Yes."

"John, we need…"

"Yes."

"John… what do you want?"

It was clear what he wanted. He knew he owned me an apology (a big one) and invited me out of sheer guiltiness to the Brodsky and Utkin show. With a bouquet of roses (decorated thorns I never really liked) and a promise to talk things over, he won a brief reprieve. Once at the show, he pandered to my staged silence, caressing the nape of my neck as we walked from picture to picture with a set of Loris eyes. Before the *Villa Claustrophobia ("A House with an Atrium is similar to a Reserved Man wholly plunged into the endless space of his Inner World – of his Inner Court")*, he proffered the tiniest of intrigues with an understatement even the English could be proud of.

"So I guess you're wondering what I've been up to?" No, not the slightest, dear.

Unfortunately, instead of delivering the goods, he started to tell me some pointless story about a pianist he had recently met in a coffee shop:

"So I met this wonderfully crazy girl..."

Not the first thing a woman wants to hear when she's supposedly heading toward some form of rapprochement for past sins of the partner.

"She was a real talent."

I bet she was. Shark womb born.

"Supposedly could rehearse *Gaspard de la nuit* blindfolded. She could even play all of Weber's stuff from memory and with a Lisztian cigar between her fingers: a real specimen. I wish you were there. She had these NBA-sized hands. Having turned down Julliard to go to a much smaller, more specialized conservatory, she started to freak out. She just couldn't take the constant pressure. In the end, they had to kick her out once they discovered she was putting razor blades between the keys of the conservatory pianos so that when her schoolmates started to play..."

"Ouch! So what does she do now?"

"Oh, it all ended on a bad note. Anyway, I think she finished up turning to competitive sky diving."

One thing I will say for John, his sense of humor, even in the blackest of moments, never changed. Maybe that was one of those things that I loved so much about him. John had clearly sussed it out that the best way to keep a woman around was to play on her insecurities, and I was a veritable theme park in this regard. There was a predictable pattern: bad treatment on his part, following by fusillades of apology and puppy dog-like behavior. Unfortunately, whilst the former was waxing, the latter was clearly on the wane. I guess, no matter how bad your dog is, you never throw him out. It seemed my role in life was to give shelter to all the unwanted mutts of the world.

So time passes...

A strange, polar wind had entered the city, unannounced. It wove the vacated streets like a biblical wraith, passing door to door, heeding only those that bore the mark of significant sacrifice. I was happy to be outdoors. I remember that last, chilly walk along the promenade, when we looked over at a spectral version of Manhattan, whose sinking silhouette resembled the superstructure of a ghostly dreadnaught. Suddenly deserted of people, it had become our Mary Celeste, captained by some maniac Dutchman, foreboding doom. The last few months didn't seem to exist at all and the people who populated them simply disappeared in a dark drisk. The island had indeed become John's battleship, but it was fast becoming my shipwreck. I already felt submerged.

Sod's law: given my recent reticence, John had for the most part, unfairly dubbed me an "Ice Queen". However, he was right in at least one sense. Indeed, that February would be, for me, the skeleton track down which I slid under the weight of my own body, jarred again and again by the sudden curves and scrapes that seemed to come out of nowhere. I felt I had nothing else to show for our year and change together. The only thing that remained for me to grasp for dear life was the very thing that carried me down that dark, frozen tube to nowhere.

Somewhere, thousands of miles away, perhaps somewhere near Kyoto, I knew there was the other end of this long, dismal night. I went to Zulfikar's house and asked him if he knew anything about what John was up to, and he mentioned something about a large protest. That John was under a lot of pressure to get things right. As he was explaining these things to me, I received a text message from Shinkirō. It merely read:

"Come quickly. The world is at an end."

When I arrived at his Greenwich Village flat, I found Shinkirō crying his little eyes out, angry that his boyfriend had broken up with him. His fist was clenched inside a velvet glove, the color of scarlet. He was a mess and, by this point, had already been taking a lot of drugs, mostly ketamine and ecstasy. Now we feared he was doing even worse. He assured me that he had listened to Judy Garland's *I Wish you Love* constantly for the last four hours. He saw this routine as the only cure for his present malady. Over the next week, he would listen to the song another 657 times. Once he calmed down, he finally told me what had happened. How and when the world ended was recorded thus:

"Shinkirō, I loved you like I loved the first notes of the theme from *Love Story*. Beautiful, but one day, when the spell is broken, you realize you have to grow up and that the world isn't all gallery openings and de la Renta gowns..."

Sobbing, Shinkirō continued, "I can't believe he compared me to the theme from *Love Story*. And it's such an awful piece of music!"

The thing about Shinkirō, no one ever knew where he got his money from. All we did know was that he used to work at the Balenciaga store in Soho and had taken a number of design courses at the Fashion Institute, planning to work his way up the fashion ladder. There were rumors that his mother was a very important figure in haute couture circles and was on the board of trustees at the Guggenheim. Despite all this, she supposedly refused to acknowledge her son's homosexuality and the two were on terrible terms. Less was known of his father, but it was suspected he had, at some point, had associations with the Pana-

Wave Laboratory cult (a suspicion Shinkirō tried mercilessly to suppress). This cult had the distinction of worshiping a bearded seal named Tama Chan. It was, however, a definite fact that Shinkirō wore only the most expensive clothes. In his mind, he wore everything worth wearing: Maison Margiela, Dior, Yamamoto, vintage Yves St Laurent, de la Renta, Tom Ford by Tom Ford, Issey Miyake, and sometimes (on occasional "bad" days), Gaultier. For him, this jumble represented beatified names that, to me, might as well have been those of dead saints. While Shinkirō frequently hung out with a bunch of hollow-cheeked male catwalk models, he was adamant that would never date "within the industry", preferring I-bankers with big wallets. His boyfriend was actually a middle-aged M&A specialist of Lebanese descent, who would often consult a fortuneteller in Chelsea. My weekend ritual with Shinkirō had long ago settled into Sunday shopping at the East Village Sunrise Mart and afterward, eating at the takoyaki restaurant on 9th street. We'd then spend hours at his flat, looking through vintage catalogues of dresses for which he had a photographic memory. Sometimes, we'd watch parts of *Hiroshima, Mon Amour*, his all-time favorite movie, from which he could recite every line from memory. At present, I was considered his favorite "fag hag", and I never understood his great interest in me, given I knew nothing about fashion and had a pretty boring life, especially when compared to his own. Indeed, juxtaposed against his over the top persona, I saw myself as having all the personality of a wet flannel. Nonetheless, he said he liked me for my "innocence", and averred that given I was blonde and "sort of clueless", he needed to take me under his wing. Most of all, he enjoyed to excess our "makeup sessions" (amazing as he often wore more than me). He did, after all, show me how to apply shadow and foundation in proper proportion ("never too heavy on the ochers, dear, it doesn't suit your eye color and makes you look like your wearing some kinda New Jersey tan"). He frequently commented on my "pristine palate", a "surprisingly flawless" skin, for which I must have had the angels to thank. He said this was all the more surprising, taking into account my Scottish heritage, which provided me with what he kindly referred to as "infinite disadvantages".

Why am I telling you all this? It's because at that time, Shinkirō had also called me over to divulge a number of details about John's activities, the sum of which he darkly referred to as "a secret for which I could be killed if I told you". Unfortunately, before he could tell me anything of substance, he'd passed out, tears still enameling his eyes. He'd wake up hours later, his lashes plastered shut with the gold dust of dried tears. Seeing me beside him, he began speaking again as if in mid-sentence, having forgotten any reference to John's secret and instead, began dismantling, hem by shoddy hem, Gautier's latest collection. He then proceeded without break to spark up over his new favorite book, Vian's *L'Écume des jours*, a scripted daydream in which he saw in himself the figure of Chloe. "I just love flowers. They make me well." Air kiss. Air kiss. More than anything, he didn't want to be alone…

"I feel so clammy inside. So violated. I opened up my world to him and he plundered it."

Another shot at tea and sympathy at Dean & Deluca then we would take our separate ways. "Ciao. Ciao." I wouldn't see him for weeks afterward.

I went home by myself, feeling I needed someone to speak to. Not wanted to disturb anyone with my problems, I reluctantly phoned up Zulfikar, who had the greatest patience with me, bless him. He mentioned that John had briefly passed by his flat the previous night. Rumly, instead of knocking or coming inside, he merely stood outside his door for what must have been 10 minutes. The next day, Zulfikar found emblazoned on his door a single word: "Apollyon".

Fig 54. "Shinkirō"

# 13

Departures are never easy. As humans, as seekers, as uneasy pilgrims, we tend to focus on the purely physical elements of any journey, the rather pedestrian course of events that occurs between two arbitrary points on any given plane. Seldom, do we ever focus on the real journey, the journey of the heart, the mind. The pilgrim mind is that of an escapist, the alien mind of self-exile. And what of this peculiar beast of fantasy, this roughened pilgrim, this fantastical bird that can only soar on the pied wings of its own fiction? Seldom do we ever regard the pilgrim mind for the pilgrim mind is always striving toward a place at which it can never arrive. Indeed, the pilgrim mind inhabits the realm beyond insanity. For while the insane man believes in that which isn't real, the pilgrim declines to believe in that which is. America, my America, is nothing if not the product of a pilgrim mind.

For whatever reason, Paul's heart was tied by a string to one of the birches in his backyard. Nonetheless, he began to board up the house. First the windows, then the door, which like the rest of the house, had been stuffed full of bundled rags to keep the drafts out. No matter how much Willow stamped her feet and crossed her arms, he wouldn't allow her to help him, understanding now the direness of her present condition. The house was an old one and was held up by some mysterious force that no one wanted to probe, lest the entire thing collapse in a poof of unceremonious smoke. Next to the house was a ramshackle network of interconnected sheds, constructed for the most part of old wood and corrugated steel. Over the years, it had expanded and had become like a second home, the principal one's integrity being questioned increasingly by the

143

autumnal winds. Like clockwork, each October and November, strange new alcoves and recesses announced themselves to the outside world. The interior became like something reflected in a convex mirror, a phantasmagoria of oblique angles and radiuses.

Paul had conceived all of his sons during his few prolonged stays in Georgia. Almost four decades ago, he had come back to bury his father and ended up remaining for a couple of years. In the meantime, he'd gotten a local Cherokee girl pregnant. He and the girl never really got along for more than a few weeks at a time, so he usually went back out west until finally, he wouldn't see his boys for a number of years. The two were fine that way until the girl got sick and died without much in the way of warning. Paul was thus forced to return home and attempt to be some sort of father to his three sons. At first, the arrangement didn't work and the boys were resentful, having only seen their father a few times their entire lives. By that time, they were almost adults and really strangers to Paul. Nonetheless, they all looked the spitting image of one another (all of course except Brice, who lacked the sturdiness and vigor of the other two). Unfortunately, just when things were starting to go well, the oldest, Josiah, was killed in an alcohol-induced car accident. This caused things for the remaining two brothers to spiral out of control. Bishop, used somewhat to living in the dappled shade of his older brother, went and joined the military, leaving Brice, Willow's sire, alone with his own prodigal father. The two really didn't get along, but Paul tried to find a way to love him. He saw his son was in pain and had the same sickness that Josiah had: alcoholism. Brice had been dating his high-school sweetheart for a number of years, and the day after Bishop's mobilization, a week after his high-school graduation, he proposed to Jayna, Willow's eventual mother. From the very beginning, it was an unfortunate situation. Within a matter of weeks, Jayna was being ambushed by second thoughts about the relationship, and it soon became quite clear she hadn't been exactly faithful to him. She was a focused woman and frighteningly intelligent. A bit of a *wunderkind*, she had taught herself Greek, Latin and advanced calculus by the eighth grade (remarkable, considering she had skipped both the sixth and seventh grades). Her intelligence was noted in some of the local papers and she even managed an appearance on a nationally-broadcasted quiz show. She had always been an *enfant terrible* and was raised by a single father, who distinguished himself as a Brookhaven physicist and suspected homosexual. An arrogant man of Greek descent (Zephyros by name), he wore brash tartan suits and brandished a Wildean bearing and wit in all the wrong places. Not afraid to call a spade a spade, he was fond of pointing out other people's stupidity and wasn't exactly shy about flaunting his relative wealth, amidst the wayside purlieus. Furthermore, he openly flouted conventions and had purportedly come to this hinterland to flee the repercussions of a hushed up and rather indelicate affair he had had with a male undergraduate. Zephyros died when Jayna was very young, under rather suspicious circumstances. Some say he was found dead and beaten in a ditch with his pants down around his ankles, while others maintained he had overdosed in a similar ditch on barbiturates and heartbreak. One version of the story went that a mob of adolescent boys had found him messing around with a local farmhand and had decided to take both the law and his exposed corpus into their own hands. Strangely, his death seemed to have very little ostensible emotional effect on Jayna. The day-old adolescent merely cut her hair short and began dressing in a boy's two-piece suit. Adorned with nothing but a red carnation, she wore that jet-black suit every day for a year to the day. Soon after, Jayna was raised by the widowed sister whom her father had made his harried trip down from

New Jersey to live with. Unfortunately for Jayna, Roxana was left to wade at the rather shallower end of the family gene pool. Nonetheless, she was moral to a fault and worked three jobs in order to pay back her dead husband's gambling debts, while securing Jayna's sullen existence as a latchkey kid.

While very committed to making something of herself, Jayna – and perhaps as a direct result of her obvious precocity – also had a heightened predilection for experimenting with sex and illicit drugs, which one child psychologist would refer to in his notes as a "dangerous fascination with the taboo". Strangely, that very same psychologist (a married man in his mid-40s) was forced to flee the town soon after taking Jayna on as a patient. It was very clear she needed a way to rebel against all the inanity that surrounded her. She didn't really have much in the way of family and while she was clearly attracted to significantly older men, she somehow stuck to Brice, probably because she thought she could manipulate him. It was the only relationship she had had with someone of her own decade. Even at the tender age of 14, she enjoyed discovering her increasing power over men twice her age. Taking after her father, she was very open about this fact, which obviously didn't sit well with many local residents, who saw in her the equivalent of a perverse Second Coming. In fact, at least part of the reason she was with Brice was that after the child psychologist, she was under constant embargo, and no other man would take her. Nonetheless, it was apparent that she had managed a number of other secretive relationships with older men. Jayna could be spiteful and vengeful. In fact, she told Brice on several occasions that she had slept with other men just to make him angry. She would taunt him until he beat her because of it. Strangely, she seemed to enjoy Brice's rather light hand, at least at first. It was indeed a curious relationship. She never saw much in Brice and frankly, thought he was stupid and a coward. It was also rumored that she had thrown herself at his older and infinitely more promising brother, Bishop, with no success. But though many wouldn't have given her credit for it, there was a miniscule bit of something that attracted her to Brice, and she stayed with him through his two tours in Afghanistan. No doubt, she had always slept with men who weren't as bright as she was, and she made sure they knew it. If nothing else, this tactic allowed her to keep enough distance for herself so that she was allowed the small space she needed for her schoolwork. Ultimately, she wanted to make a man of Brice and he couldn't do without her. She had long known she could manipulate men; now she wanted to mold them. It was partly the reason he joined the army. Not only to live up to his brother, Josiah, but to prove to Jayna that he was a man.

Finally, once everything was locked up, Paul got in his pickup and made ready to leave. He had a tough time forcing Willow to get into the truck and finally, had to carry her under his arm, kicking and screaming. Once there, it took him a great deal of further effort to keep her inside the vehicle He finally resorted to tying her hands with a small rope. Evidently, she didn't feel safe leaving the house anymore and hated the idea of their traveling a great distance from it. She had gotten used to the idea that the only place she was safe was inside their home. Not knowing whether or not he would even be able to find Jayna, he refrained from making Willow aware of the goal of their journey, lest he disappointed her later. He had considered taking a Greyhound bus, but decided against it, due to both his fear of being unable to pinpoint Jayna's exact whereabouts and his deathly dread of Willow's condition being detected somewhere on a crowded bus. Though her swell was barely detectable, there was always the off chance that there was a doctor or a particularly curious old lady with better eyes than his. Thus, Paul would later visit deserted diners or vacant Denny's, forcing Willow to wear a heavy coat, even while inside. Little did he suspect that this only served to make his activities more suspicious. Nevertheless, the bump was so much bigger for him than it was to her innocent eyes, which had little idea of what was going on. Every day, the bump expanded twofold in poor Paul's worrisome eyes.

The drive from Georgia had only two rather unfortunate events (which will be reported in due time), neither of which had any long-term consequences for either party in question. They managed to do everything in two days, with Paul driving almost constantly. Paul didn't have much of a plan once he arrived to New York, as he wasn't even sure he had Jayna's current address. He would just have to put the pieces together once he arrived. Metaphorically speaking, the highway was their dried riverbed, a path of discovery not usually allowed to their wayward souls. Willow hadn't ever been outside the small world of their little backwater, and she was fascinated by an entirely new world, witnessed for the most part through a cracked and dirty windshield. Indeed, she experienced her first true sensation of freedom, the amputation of a shriveled and useless past in order to make way for the more muscular limbs of a better future. Though she couldn't have realized it at the time, it was a similar theme to that which ran throughout the entire current of the American story: the fundamental desire to plunder a possible future in order to cast down the shadows of an impoverished past. America, in all its wide expanse, gave one the freedom to dream, the freedom that only comes when one realizes the past has no more claim on a person than the future. So it was that the great Paul Bunyan, the one she learned about in school and whose identity she hadn't entirely separated from the man sitting next to her, carved for himself the lakes, the canyons, the rivers, and made an America into his own image. Indeed, his America is everyone's America, a story always on the first page. Willow was now finding her own story being written in the rolling hills, the dancing telephone wires, the leaping pine trees, and the brown, lazy rivers that snaked underneath her eyes. Indeed, she began to realize she had taken the first step into her future, the first step into a new life.

# 14

*Cephalovertens semperambulatus*

- *The Central American Whintosser is certainly a unique animal and unlike any other. It was discovered in the littoral ranges of California in 1906. In terms of appearance, it "seems to be constructed for the purpose of passing through unusual experiences. Its head is fastened to its body by a swivel neck; so is its short, tapering tail; and both can be spun around at the rate of a hundred revolutions a minute. The body is long and triangular, with three complete sets of legs." According to local lore, there is little that can kill a Whintosser, especially when it begins to spin and scream in rage. In fact, the only way to kill the animal is to "poke it into a flume pipe so that all its feet strike the surface, when it immediately starts to walk in three different directions at once and tears itself all apart."*

The Central American Whintosser

Grandpappy, was epileptic.

He sometimes had seizures. He told me what to do when he had one. First, I would put a shirt in his mouth and a pillow under his head. Then I closed my eyes and stuck fingers in my ears. Them danged seizures used to scare the living wits out of me. I asked him what happened during them seizures. He said he didn't know but that he used to see God. He said his body moved around like that 'cause he was filled with the Holy Spirit. I told him then I never wanted to see God. He said that was wrong.

I had never been in a motel before. Motels is really nice because they put chocolate on your pillow and they have blow-driers so you can dry your hair really fast. They have TV with many more channels than we have at home, and showers that make hot water come down like rain. I would like to live in a motel one day. I didn't want to leave home 'cause now the Fearsome Critters got no one, but now I don't want to go back. I want to keep driving all across the country. For dinner, me and Grandpappy went to Denny's and had a country fried steak. I ate a whole one myself and even had a banana split. Grandpappy made me wear my coat the whole time and I was so hot, I was sweating like it was middle of summer. We went to Waffle House for breakfast , and I ate loads of bacon with maple syrup and butter on top. Grandpappy said he was feeling wrong inside all morning. When we was back in the room, that's when it happened. Grandpappy got to shaking something mighty. He was flapping around like a catfish at the bottom of a fishing boat. I put the shirt in his mouth and held his head until he quieted down. After three minutes, his breathing started to slow until he almost wasn't breathing at all. After the seizure, he would normally have to sleep a long time. It had been almost a year since he had his last seizure. He liked it when I kissed him while he was sleeping. He said it made him feel all better after the seizure.

The next day, we was on the road again and I started to think about the Hidebehind and what he'd do without me. I was scared Shane and them boys would get to him and sit on him like they sat on me. I didn't want them to hurt the Hidebehind like they hurt me inside. When we was driving, I kept thinking about the Hidebehind and I decided I wanted to go back home and pick him up. I wrote it down in my book and asked Grandpappy where we was going, and all he said was we was going "somewheres". Grandpappy wouldn't tell me nothing no more. He just kept saying, "You'll see. It's a surprise." I wrote down that I didn't want to go nowhere unless I knew where we was going. Grandpappy kept on saying, "You'll see. You'll see." But I didn't want to go no more so I started making noises and hitting the dashboard like I was having a seizure myself. He didn't like that and he finally told me we was going to New York, so I would quiet down. I wrote down that I didn't want to go to New York. He asked me why I didn't want to go to New York. I told him because we was going to see my momma. He was surprised and said "Don't you want to see your mammy?"

I shook my head.

He said "Why you don't want to see your momma no more?"

I wrote down, "Because she is a whore."

He became angry again and asked, "Who told you that? What did I tell you about listening to other people? Your momma is no whore. You mommy is a doctor and she needs to fix you."

I wrote down, "Why I need fixing?"

He told me, "Listen, Willow, it don't matter why. All you need to know is that you need fixing and there ain't no two ways about it. Now sit back and stop your whining."

I grew so mad that I started up again like a raccoon with rabies. I was making all kinds of racket and started to bang on the windows and scream something mighty. I made more racket than fireworks on the 4th of July. I rolled down the windows and started screaming, but the wind took my voice away. Then I tried to open the truck door and Grandpappy, he tried to grab me. He yelled at me and then he hit me square in the face with his hard hand. I was crying and trying to open the door, and that made him drive off the freeway. When he stopped at the side of the road I opened the door and ran as fast as I could into the woods and across a large field. Grandpappy was mad as hornets and chased me the entire way as he was yelling after me. He had a bad heart and asthma so he couldn't chase me very far.

When he finally caught up to me, I was sitting down in the middle of an empty crop field. I was too tired to go any further and it was getting dark. I didn't know where I was and I became scared. I didn't used to be such a fraidy cat all the time. I didn't want to but I began to cry. When he saw me crying, he got down on his knees next to me. I could see the tears start coming out of his eyes. He started to cry and moan too. He gave me a big bear hug so hard I was lost inside that great beard of his. It was the first time I'd ever seen him cry and it scared me. He cried so much, I thought he was having another seizure. Then he took my small hands in his giant ones. He looked at me with his magic eye and said "You don't deserve none of this. I am a beast and I treated you like one. Can you ever forgive me, Willow? Can you ever? Forgive me for everything I done to you 'cause I really done wrong by you. I ain't no real father to you and I should've been."

I held his head as he sobbed and I signed to him that he shouldn't cry as he was the best darn Grandpappy I done ever knowed of. The best in the whole wide world. We was like that a long time. We was like peas in a pod again. When he stood up, he looked like a giant. He was taller than any of the trees in the forest. He could have cried the whole Chattahoochee out of his eyes, but now he wasn't crying no more and wiped his tears on his red lumberjack shirt. I felt as cold as a witch's tit, but nothing ever made him cold.

Grandpappy had brought his guitar with us and he'd play me songs sometimes at night. When we got back to the truck, we sat in the trunk and he played for me at the side of the road. He played my favorite song, *Sunflower River Blues*. He said a man wrote it, by the name of Blind Joe Death. I asked him with my hands if my momma would recognize me when she saw me. He said she was sure she would. I asked him if it was better if I wasn't born 'cause I wouldn't need all this fixing. He began to cry again.

"It's not you, Willow, that needs fixing, it's me. God done broke me."

# 15

Oh, Spirits bright, grant our fickle souls
Communion, grant us, Souls, our former John
For whom at twelve I'll turn a trick or two
With sage, with quartz, a ring of sprinkled salt.
I'll wait for him to cow the candle's glow
And in lively gloom, I'll press him hear
Till a cowrie's shell might bound us both.
Oh, bring not spirits charged with ill intent
Nor call to bear an evil clash of words.
We seek not darksome lore nor crooked signs,
But knowledge of that one demented spring
That stood apart from all before or after;
To know his mind that made a needle's eye
Wide enough to bear a camel's toe
And chanced this loveless scribe eternity…

"ALL FEELING LEFT ME AND THE SEASON TOOK ITS
PLACE"

Indeed, I was halfway through my ugly woman phase. I'd
been told that as an old man, one has these phantasies about
young, slatternly women, but here, I nevertheless indulged one
of my few precocities. Ah, the glories of "Fat Girl Spring": the
Marchtide in New York, when only the fleshiest girls can begin
to wear their skirts short. Women that you would have never
considered before, all of a sudden become ripe fruit. Aged tiger,
out of his season, teeth like mountains ground to glens, you
fantasize her, a homely girl on the subway, you see her naked
next to a smoldering ashtray and imagine she could love you,

please you in a way no other woman has, allow you the truly unexpected and the untrammelled (which in the right period of old age, can be a pleasure in itself). Only then can one separate the purely physical from the purely aesthetic. How a woman physically pleases you has nothing to do with her aesthetic merit. On the contrary, her beauty is an utter distraction, in a way, a complete detraction. What pleases you is how she communicates with you physically (the "I am fucking an ugly woman" moment that turns you on to no end). You want to discover her dirty, little secret, her cryptic coyness that doesn't notice you as you leer at her endlessly, endlessly... you think yourself in possession of a treasure no one else has ever claimed. Are you doing her a favor, letting her finally blossom as a rose might from its spikey tube? Men are rarely allowed to indulge their vanities and thus, any reasonable, young thing can and will flatter an old man into anything. So, alas, with a temple Apollo waxing inside us, can we also ask ourselves if it is also vanity to think that all dance partners are beautiful in their own way: the bald, the fat, the mentally crippled? So what is it about ugly women that flatters old age (is it not that they too reach full bloom at a later stage)? What is it about the years slipping by under a bridge that frees you to discover the true appreciation of pleasures passing by? In some small way, I loved them all: the desperately ugly, the emotionally handicapped, all the sheer castaways of this earth, I embraced them all. Oh, that beautiful parade! That holy phantasmagoria! In this carnival hall of mirrors, they were for me but the distorted reflections of Felicity, the one true beauty that existed amongst us.

"U DESERVED SUM HAPPINESS THE SMILES LOST ON ME"

*O Fortuna! Velut luna stau variabilis, semper crescis aut dieresis,* etc. etc. Presently, as I fetishize these days gone by, it all seems to have occurred only hours ago. Am I wrong or has a small bit of delusion, perhaps even insanity, crept into my brain? Wasn't it just yesterday that you and Felicity had been engaging in some heavy petting on my couch, still feeling the after effects of a leftover pill of ecstasy? I remember so clearly listening to Alice Coltrane's *World Galaxy* as the "roll" climaxed, our visions now soundtracked to her passage through *Satchidananda*. My diapered walls (half-century-old amaranthine, mottled by flecks of gold) became a feast for the eyes, enlivened as they were by a warm, red ray of afternoon sunburst. Two "doves" split three ways. The sylphs, tired of dancing on hypodermic needle heads, had gathered around us all that mazy, hazy afternoon. You, ready to explore her romantic chasm, and Felicity, atop your chest, supine and regal with her head tilted back, seemed on the verge of crying out for her demon lover. Oh that human form! *Oh wondrous machine!* All seemed ready to detonate when alas, the proverbial Person from Porlock reared his ugly head. That, tasteless, gray man and his ilk, who even once got the better of Monsieur Fermat, needed to check at that very instant our neglected gas meter. And thus, our shared moment was wrecked. Even as my own thick pants were breathing, I was, alas, robbed of this voyeuristic pleasure by an overabundance of hot air.

## "I STILL CRAVE. THE CRAVING HERE IS A TREE SHADOW BREAKING ACROSS THE RUIN OF A STONE TEMPLE, A WEED BLOOMING IN ANOTHER SHATTERED SIDEWALK TO NOWHERE"

It was only a month later that poor Felicity (her blood now on a low boil) would shed hot tears into your heatless lap. She was convinced of your holding secrets from her and she was right, as you were then deeply entwined within the machinations of the Ota Benga society. Our Casta Diva would later confront me, almost desperate, asking me if I knew anything and I, alas, had to put her off your trail by telling her you were planning a protest at City Hall. I suspect that she only half-believed it, and I truly regretted lying to her (the full consequences of my actions would only be discovered later). Indeed, I felt compromised, and even then, my loyalties to you outweighed my pity for her. She was indeed in a sorry state of dyspepsia. Mustering some deep access of guilt, I suggested we go for a night out to take her mind off the evil tidings that surrounded her. After much arm-twisting, she begrudgingly agreed. It wasn't long before our magic rug touched down in Soho, where we spent a couple of hours playing pool with Alessio, Billy Rubino and the "Bad Lieutenant", a former beat officer from Chicago, who resembled nothing else if not an overgrown *Peanuts* character. The Bad Lieutenant had to walk around on crutches, a pretense to hide a rather sordid affair involving a hydraulic battering ram and a lawsuit. This criminal cop was another bosom buddy of Alessio. Alessio's father was a made and minted Italian from Svorzinda. A man of no good repute, he once had the misfortune of turning up dead, face-down in a swimming pool. Like the Colonel, Alessio was the only other member of our circle capable of carrying an entourage. These gray beings followed him like a pack of dire wolves because, if nothing else, Alessio was a ladykiller. One must mention in passing that his obvious charms had failed on Felicity (thank God) after repeated efforts.

Referring to himself as a "sexual explorer" (a veritable Magellan of the Muff), Alessio had an almost felonious perversity, one that had taken him to the various fleshpots of the planet: he moved in a logarithmic fashion across the Killing Kitty parties of London, the KitKatClub in Berlin, Disturbathons in Dallas, and even to the Hungry Duck in Moscow. It wasn't clear where exactly his sexual escapades began or ended (phylum, order or family). In usual form, he was presently accoutered with a Russian "bombshell," a sallow thing with stringy, blonde hair, fake "Hindenberg" tits, and what seemed to me like collapsed veins. Her reason for existence? A simple case of Hanlon's razor: she had purportedly introduced Alessio to a one-time engagement with Krokodil. Rather tritely, Alessio would always list amongst his dreams in life the finding of co-ed therapy sessions for sexual addiction. The predictable volley of snorts and sniggers would ensue (unfortunately, from the same people each time). At one point of the proceedings, he handed me wad-fulls of money and begged me to provide some distraction for his crew, as he was scheduled to attend a "blue regatta orgy" where they wouldn't be welcomed. What, may I ask, was a "blue regatta orgy"?

"Oh, you don't know? Shit. It's where everybody drops a tab of X, paints themselves blue, and when a gong is struck, makes their way into one big bed and mimics the waves of the sea."

Sorry I asked. It was only couple of vodka tonics later that Alessio leaned on me with a heavy heart, confiding to me as he had with no one else. "Truly, I'm done with women. Too much money and time. I'm off to Mount Athos. I'm gonna be a monk." New York has its casualties. He was ultimately, true to his word.

In the meantime, you and Felicity had been avoiding one another until we had a "surprise" reunion 30 minutes later, when you arrived at my electronic beckoning. We settled into our usual corner of discontentment. Presently, our poor tribe was augmented by a triad of suddenly arrived escorts. John, rather drunk and abruptly voluminous, began speaking to a pair of them, going into reveries over Bach's violin *Chaconne* (something that one of them interpreted to be a form of designer drug). Felicity tried to steer you clear, but you kept talking and drafting lines of coke on a low table until your nose bled a sickly orange. It was a measure of her spiritual torque that she no longer recognized your emotional axes as being aligned, but still felt the need to help you out of these rather sticky situations. Hydra-headed, like a high gothic cathedral, you began to present more monsters than angels. A predictable course ensued, when your coked-up tongue managed to offend one of the pros and she took her two "friends" with her out of the room. Felicity again attempted to stop you doing more damage to yourself, but you also managed to send her away crying... an all-too-common occurrence in these latter days.

Previously, we had adapted as much as we could to your strange moods and fits of anger, putting them down to stress at work or the changeableness of the artistic temperament. It was all becoming a bit much for all of us involved, all of us who had hoped to ride upon your coattails. The creaking carousel of days and weeks passed and passed in what became a monotonous series of minor tortures until it all rained down from on high in the form of a communiqué from Lord Hate-Good and his proverbial Star Chamber. I will never forget the day I saw that note on your desk in his unmistakable script:

AYE, THE TIME IS NIGH AND THE GREAT WORK
MUST COMMENCE – BRETHREN HEED THE CALL
ALL MUST ASSEMBLE FOR THE GREAT RELEASE
THE EYE OF TRUTH FINALLY SHINES UPON US
THE GENERATIONS ARE WAITING FOR US
TO RAISE ARMS – A NEW AGE BEGINS TODAY
NOVUS ORDO SECLORUM – DOWN WITH APOLLYON

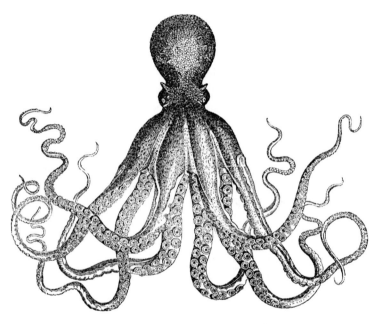

Fig. 77 "Novus ordo seclorum"

# 16

"Don't sit there, that's a wino bench," screamed an old man to a rather frightened Willow.

"Probably got needles coming out of it. If they see you sittin' on that bench, they gonna want it back."

Across the street, there came an eruption of indistinct activity: next to a cinematic oil-drum brimmed with fire, two unruly junkies that Ayn Rand could have written were fighting over a filthy blanket. The battle continued apace until one stabbed the other and ran off victorious with the torn item.

Paul and Willow were suddenly trapped in a world they never would have imagined existed.

After getting lost a number of times, they had ended up nowhere else but a "no-go" zone in the South Bronx. Predictably, they were low on gasoline and it was by a strange sort of magic that the truck rolled on, according to an invisible impulse. An hour earlier, at a busy intersection, they had endured their first real New York experience when they encountered an elderly black woman dressed entirely in garbage bags. At the time, she was making her slow way across the street, pushing four carts of nonsense ahead of her. Paul tried to give her the coat off his back, but she spat at him, mumbling something through her jack-o'-lantern teeth about the radio transmissions being particularly bad that night. Her head was wrapped in tinfoil to prevent unwanted microwaves from entering her mind. How the world was going to end, only she knew. Her eyes were those of a zealot. She had immediately put Paul down as one of the many demons that filled her ideographic world. It was clear that if they didn't leave, she would soon call down her counter-magic.

When Paul finally arrived at the address he was given, he was confronted with a very large man, lying passed out on the road, his face pressed into the pavement. A number of people were presently walking on the sidewalk. The more considerate ones merely shuffled around him without paying him much attention. Those in a less generous mood gave forth a volley of sudden kicks when the mutual rhythm of their footfalls had been rudely interrupted. When Paul tried to help the man and inquire into his condition, someone on a sidewalk stoop shouted at him:

"What the fuck you doin', man? Can't you see he's trying to sleep? Ain't no police or ambulance gonna come around here no hows. Best just leave him alone. If he's dead, nothin' nobody can do. They got someone who'll come round and pick him up. These junkies sometimes do that just to convince people to give them some more money."

Paul, not knowing any better, listened to the man and reluctantly went up the stairs of an old brownstone to ring the bell. This most recent incident with the "junkie" was just another confirmation of the wisdom that had instructed his life-long avoidance of large cities. It wasn't long before he could hear someone turning the deadbolts behind the gray portal. Once the door was cracked, Paul was confronted with a rather attractive, young black woman of lighter hue. Her hair was bundled in a hairnet, under which there was a herringbone hemorrhage of pastels: pink, blue and yellow rollers. Balancing an infant in one arm, she began unlatching the chain. With some effort, she finally managed to pry the door open. Without so much as a greeting, she looked over Paul's shoulder and immediately started shouting at the unconscious body, "Ah, hell no. That dead beat is at it again. Right in front of my house too. Don't he know I have kids. Iverson, get that bucket of water so I can wake this nigga up."

Flummoxed, Paul was at a loss as to what to say.

"What you gonna do? Just stand there and stare at me or are you gonna say somethin'."

"Well, mam, I was hoping you could help me out with somethin' as I'm looking for someone named Jayna Bunyan who lives in this here house."

"Ain't no one here who goes by that name. You got the wrong house."

"But it's written on the letter here, you see."

Paul pulled a crumpled piece of paper out of his pocket and showed it to the girl.

"I don't know nothin' about that... let me ask somebody."

After a series of shouts up a set of darkened stairs, an old, heavyset woman finally emerged from the hallway and asked what all the commotion was about. She was an impressive woman who carried herself with the utmost dignity. She wore a large, colorful *gele* on her head and was dressed in an equally colorful Nigerian *buba*. When Paul repeated his question, the elderly woman told him that Jayna had left too many years ago to remember, but that he need not fear as she might still have her address somewhere in one of her drawers. With welcoming gestures, she invited Paul into the dark, blue-lit abode and soon offered him tea and biscuits, but he declined, saying he couldn't stay long. The kindly lady was absolutely entranced by Willow, as were the younger woman's two children.

"Ain't you a quiet one? What? Cat got your tongue or are you just shy? Don't worry, you're not going to come to any harm around here."

After fumbling around a hopeless pile of papers for what must have been 15 minutes, she finally handed Paul another old crumpled piece of paper.

"See, I still got it. I'm sure Monique never thought I could have found it. Anyway, I don't know if it's still good, but it's all I have. Nice girl. Real nice girl. Good for her for getting out.

People behave like animals around here and they keep locking our boys up in cages. If you find her, tell her Dressella says hello."

Two hours later, at 1a.m., Paul was illegally parking his claptrap Ford on Greene Street. Above that vacant lane, one flight of stairs up from Hell's Hundred Acres, a great, throbbing enigma awaited him. For the second time, he found himself knocking on a door behind which he hadn't the faintest idea of what to expect.

When Jayna finally opened the door, all she could say was, "Oh God."

Without saying another word, she brushed inside the weary travelers, leading them through the black maze that preceded her living room. The apartment was immense. In fact, it was an entire series of immensities. More than anything else, it appeared somewhat reminiscent of a compartmented cow stomach, a cluttered vacuum that rather ingested one than invited one in. Fifty years ago, it had been little more than an old factory sweatshop. But somewhere in the last two decades, it had been converted into a loft space and afterward, into a convoluted series of partitioned rooms, some of which were separated by no more than pieces of bed linen. Even more recently, the apartment had transformed itself into a sort of lifeless menagerie, populated by a wilderness of leathery palms and stuffed animals that included, amongst other things, a crocodile, two wolves, innumerous parrots, several exotic birds, the larger cats, a fox, a black panther, an infant zebra, a quarter of a moose, half of an antelope, three armadillos, a golden-crowned bat, and even a Kodiak bear. To the post-apocalyptic eye, it appeared as if an entire section of Noah's ark had been marooned in her room. If nothing else, it represented an impressive shrine to taxidermy, one which smelled like the insides of an emptied formaldehyde bottle. It was a place where time was frozen, preserved as if in smudged layers of sedimentary rock. Perhaps the biggest surprise in all this was the mere fact of there being no animals that had actually made it alive.

Once they had exited the small foyer and entered the main room, Willow was absolutely entranced and seemed to care less about the mother she had barely glimpsed and hadn't yet been introduced to. The living room was certainly the largest living space she had ever been inside. It was two stories in height and was walled by a combination of plasterboard, large piles of boxes and various other odd assortments. Part of the loft contained a second story, the part where Jayna's bedroom resided. In the back of the apartment, there were enormous windows, running the entire length of the apartment along two perpendiculars. As Willow strolled past the glassy-eyed corpses, it wouldn't take her long before she tried to spot many of the creatures of her imagination, the Fearsome Critters. Some were clearly the products of a rogue taxidermy, like the Wolpertinger that perched menacingly atop one of the shelves.

Once Jayna had arrived to the set of windows at the very back of the loft, she suddenly paused and turned around to face Paul and Willow. She was a woman of average height and wore a rather garish bed robe of yellow silk. Her hair was died auburn and she had a number of large red bracelets on both wrists. As regards Paul and Willow, she could only manage a shocked stare, not knowing exactly what to say. It was a strange tableaux. Paul and Willow stood at one side of the room while Jayna menaced at the other. The 20 feet between them might as well have been 20 miles. Neither party said a single word to the other for what must have been five minutes. Jayna was in obvious anguish as she peered curiously at Willow, not believing her eyes and the obvious similarities in their appearance. Finally, Paul, without moving and without taking his eyes off Jayna, said, "Willow, this is your momma."

Jayna hadn't been able to take her rather frightened-looking eyes off Willow, even as she began to open her mouth toward Paul. Her response was quick and somewhat of an utter wobble:

"Listen, Paul, I don't know what business you have doin' here, but you know damn well that you shouldn't have come and showed your face like this unannounced. We had an agreement. You know... you know damn well that ain't..."

"Listen, Jayna... let's let bygones be bygones and put all that nasty stuff behind us. She needs you. She needs a doctor. She's... she's..."

Paul walked across the room and whispered something into Jayna's ear. Jayna immediately put two trembling hands to her mouth and doubled over, almost falling to the floor. She was clearly fighting for air.

"Dear God, what? How the... But that isn't even possible. She's... she's too young."

"It ain't no lie..."

"You... you are some kinda monster. Oh my God. This... this is your doing?"

"No... no... it ain't. I promise. Some boys... I'll tell you later..."

Jayna, her eyes already red with tears, walked straight across the room and slapped Paul hard in the face.

"Give me one reason I shouldn't call the police right now. How... how the hell could you let something like this happen to her? She's just a child. I couldn't trust you then and I sure as hell can't trust you now. I've been such a fool. I can't believe it, I've been such a fool."

As Jayna kept repeating the words over and over again, Paul just hung his head in utter shame. Jayna then rushed at him for a second time and tried to hit him again and again until Willow put herself between the two in an attempt to stop the fighting. With Paul not giving an ounce of resistance and Willow making her own set of frightful noises, Jayna fell to the ground in utter exhaustion and began sobbing.

"How could you? How could you? And I wasn't there to stop it."

She could no longer look at Willow, though she felt she wanted to grab her up in her arms. She had even reached out to her in mere motherly instinct, but quickly recoiled in fear as if she might somehow pass an awful leprosy to the girl. Paul then knelt to her level and tried to comfort her.

"Listen… I know I ain't been a good… good guardian to her. That's for sure. But I promise you, I ain't done this. You know I would never… of all the things, I wouldn't do this to her. Please, believe me. You know I would do anything to protect that girl. It hurts me to the death just knowin' I haven't. You gotta believe me."

"Why the hell should I?"

"Listen, if you don't then she is gonna come out the worst of everyone. You gotta help her. Now I told you, I didn't do this. I mean, you ever knowed me to lie?"

Jayna thought it over and after a short pause, she gave out a low, guttural growl.

"You are an evil man, but you are no liar."

"Yes, let's put that aside for now. She… she needs a doctor, this moment. You gonna take care of her?"

"You ain't changed a bit you old, drunk, stupid fool. You still don't get it, do you? Even if I wanted to help her, I can't. I ain't no doctor, I'm a veterinarian."

At first, Paul stood up in wall-eyed shock. He then paced the floor a couple of times, after which a desperate light flickered in the deep recesses of one of his eyes.

"Well, what difference does it make? All animals is 'bout the same in that sense."

"What? Are you out of your mind? You think I could deliver this... this thing here in my living room? She's at least got..."

There was a pause as Paul hung his head and looked down at his shoes, holding his hat in his hands. Suddenly, Jayna stood up again and walked over to him. Willow was clutching his leg in fear as Paul patted her dark curls in an effort to calm her soft sobbing. Meanwhile, Jayna's face turned from one of crimson-hued pain to one of pale disbelief.

"Wait... wha— No, you didn't come here to ask me to deliver this... you came here... Oh my God. I can't believe it. What, you think I'm going to go at her with some Ergotrate and a dirty clothes hanger? Is that what you brought her up here for?"

"Well..."

"How long has it been?"

"Not exactly sure. Four months more or less. Not really sure."

"Four months! Not really sure! Aw hell... that's too late. You can't... you can't, it's too late now to do much of anything, even Misopro— What the hell, Paul? I thought you were a religious man. You used to come down on me hard with all your religious thunder and now..."

"I still don't think it's right to kill no... but this, God brought this evil on us. This is an abomination."

"An abomination?"

"C'mon, Jayna, you know this is your flesh and blood and I know from years that it ain't no way to grow up."

"It may be my blood, but you can't possibly ask me to do this after what happened. This is crazy, even by your standards."

By this time, Jayna was again sobbing furiously.

"How can I? How could you? Why? This ain't right. Why did you come back here, dammit?"

"I had no choice... I tried to send you letters but..."

"I'm sorry, but you guys can't stay here. It took me five years to get settled and this ain't even my place. David will be back in a few days. And what if she remembers? You... you have to leave. I sent you the money, now why do you have to... you shouldn't have come. You really shouldn't have come..."

"We ain't got no place to stay."

"I'll give you some money. You can find a motel."

"C'mon. The little girl's tired. It's almost two in the mornin'. We been lookin' for your place all day. Can't you just let us stay the night?"

After seeing Willow's red eyes and her tired head lolling about her shoulders, Jayna finally relented. At present, she put them both up in a makeshift room made of plasterboard and some curtain hangings. Later that night, once Paul had put Willow to sleep, he returned to the living room to reengage Jayna. A fraught three hours ensued, one in which they spent every minute shouting at one another. Willow, unable to sleep in the strange room, and thinking there really was something wrong with her, spent the next two hours in fear, clutching her stuffed rabbits, KK and Kiko. Behind the curtains, she could make out the animated figures of Paul and Jayna as they wove into a kind of demonic shadow play. The curtains seethed with angry whispers, which sounded to her like the corybantic hiss of striking cobras.

"I told you never to come here. Do you realize what your son did to me? What you did to me? I can never forgive myself for what I did either..."

"Look, we all know it was... Anyway, she don't know what happened. You know, I never said nothin' all those years, and people were suspicious of you leavin' when you did. Fortunately, they knowed he was always going out in the woods by himself and they remember that time he near drownded, all drunk as he usually was. When I ask her about it, she just shakes her head. What happened, happened. We can't change it no more than we can change the weather. You were never meant for the life there. You were better than all of us."

"Don't give me any of your preachin'. It was you that caused all of this. You. Without you, none of this would have ever happened."

"You know what the war did to him. I was just trying to protect my son. I was trying to protect both of you."

"Protect!? Protect!?"

The terrible hiss continued until Willow finally fell asleep and troubled dreams replaced the miserable shadow show.

For most of the next afternoon, an uneasy silence reigned across the apartment. It was a rainy day. Willow spent the entirety of it inside her makeshift room, reading her books and writing in her journal. She deliberately waited until it became dark to explore the shiftless menagerie that haunted her wakeful eyes with at least a hundred different varieties of animals. Indeed, she wanted to scare herself, something she enjoyed at various times growing up in the woods, where peril was never far away, especially if one was looking for it. Whether it was climbing a tree, jumping a creek, or bouldering across a steep ridge, she had to prove to herself that she was strong; strong enough to make her grandfather proud of her, strong enough to take care of herself once her Grandpappy couldn't. Besides the animals, one strange habit that her mother entertained was her constant playing of music throughout the house. Music that seemed perfectly suited to every climate of the mind. At night, the music was strange and enchanting, and included selections from Les Baxter's *Ritual of the Savage* and Martin Denny's *Exotica* (names that Willow made her mother write down). It made her feel that she was in a jungle somewhere in South America during a hot summer's night (something beautifully elicited in her surviving diaries and confirming that something of her mother's own childhood precociousness had worn off on her).

She had managed to bring along her cherished lipstick and imagined her curiously absent mother wearing it, together with a rich satin dress. Furthermore, she imagined herself leaving a fancy ball to explore the jungle outside the grounds of a strange, vine-covered palace. In the background, she could hear Offenbach's *Barcarolle*, paired together with Boccherini's *Musica notturna delle strade di Madrid* (these again are written in the marginalia by another more delicate hand*)*. She was entranced by the rampant bear, the passant jaguar, several volant birds and a few sejant rodents. She even dared to brush her hands over numerous snakes, fish, deer, foxes, and owls; she felt she could never really possess them, understand them, unless she touched them. The eyes all possessed the same glassy, earnest look that Paul's own false eye betrayed. She asked her mother what the name of each animal was, but Jayna seemed almost horrified by the poor, little creature, and could barely manage speaking to her. In total, Paul and Willow spent about three days at Jayna's apartment until she could no longer overcome the awkwardness of having Willow around. Indeed, she spent most of the time trying to hide from her. Every morning, her eyes were swollen and red with tears, which she tried unsuccessfully to hide; every night, Paul and her, like *Ra* and *Apep*, continued their nocturnal contest after Willow went to sleep. Even over the course of the three days, Jayna renewed her hard drinking, even reprising her habitual chain-smoking for good measure. She almost trembled in sheer fright every time Willow attempted to sit next to her. Finally, one morning, Willow heard them talking behind doors.

"Listen, you have to go. Today. Now. Dave will be back in a couple of hours."

"What will we do with the... the pregnancy?"

"We've been over this a million times... abortion is far too dangerous. Younger girls have had..."

"But they is gonna know something happened. What if they take her?"

"Listen, there is DNA and all that today. I don't pretend you will understand, but they can't link you to her unless, of course, you..."

"No..."

"Well this needs to be monitored. I know people and I can get her in for regular appointments, but that will have to wait for later. I will let you know where and when. For now, find someplace... anonymous... out of the way. I have an address..."

"Why can't we stay here? It's workin' ok, ain't it? After all, it's your daughter... it's blood."

"Stop there. Just stop. Dave would never accept this and he doesn't know anything about my past. I'm just not... not ready for this. I cannot let her continue to see me like this. I will come find you. I just need time to work things out. Can't you at least get that through that thick skull of yours?"

"Ok... but... we don't know this place. The city, I'm not..."

"Just find this address. You managed to find me here, so you won't have problems finding this place. You have my number. We'll work the rest out later. For now, I just need some space..."

"Ok, but for how long? How..."

"Listen, you have money, right? No... wait."

She went back into her upstairs room and came back with a purse, from which she took out about a hundred dollars.

"Here, take this. It's all I have... and my credit card number. This is the pin."

And that was it. In a matter of minutes, Willow and Paul were unceremoniously hurried out of the apartment. At the door, Willow gave her mom the lipstick she had brought. The look in her mother's eyes would haunt her for years to come, especially as she was destined to see her mother only once more. When Paul and her got back into the pickup, Willow put both her hands atop her stomach in a gesture of warm embrace. Then, like two frightened birds, a pair of tiny sparrows ascended into the darkened sky of Paul's face, where they shaped the following question on Willow's behalf:

"Am I gonna be a mommy now too?"

# 17

Dear John,

I realize I will never send this letter to you, but I feel I must write it nonetheless, for both our sakes.

First off, I want to tell you how much I appreciate your having shown me excerpts from Willow's diary and your "Guide". I am terribly touched by your desire to tell this young, unfortunate girl's story. I did suggest some changes: like bringing more to the fore Paul's motivations. Perhaps also avoiding overly complex sentence structures and the constant insertion of yourself into the story through the sometimes overwhelming flood of sarcastic commentary. But then, it dawned on me; the awful realization of why it was you had placed yourself inside her story in the first place. Ultimately, you had no choice. Unfortunately, for us, it appears my realization has come far too late to be of any real help to either of us.

It all started with that incident on the couch, an event that I still feel terrible about. I certainly didn't understand you then, and I thought perhaps that you may just have had some difficulty in communicating with me sexually, that maybe there was something about me that physically repulsed you. But, now, I realize the horrible truth behind it all and I feel absolutely gutted.

Seeking some form of confirmation for my suspicions, I went back and re-read some of your earliest letters and in one of them, I found the line:

"If I was stronger, I could have stopped it. I wish I were stronger!"

This was all the confirmation I needed to finally come to grips with the fact that you must have been there at the time of Willow's rape. In fact, I understand now that you were actually one of the boys accompanying Shane: the last, nameless one who had been forced into that frightful incident. It made me cry just to think about all the dreadful guilt you must have carried around inside you for all these years. What an appalling burden to have had on your back. It literally crushed me just thinking about it.

I admit, my first reflex was one of sheer trepidation and horror, imagining that you might be capable of such atrocities. Then I thought more about it: you, the youngest, the frailest boy, were forced into witnessing and even participating in that heinous act. How it must have destroyed you and your faith in humankind. I do realize this guilt is probably something you can never entirely rid yourself from. However, I also appreciate the fact that the "Guide" is as much your story as it is Willow's. If nothing else (and I hope I can say this without too much presumption), I see the "Guide" as your own attempt at trying to come to terms with (perhaps even forgive yourself for) one more unspeakable sin that has occurred on this earth.

As a slight aside, I did read the book of Nietzsche you sent to me. I did it, purely in an honest attempt to better understand your ferocious anger and boundless bitterness. Despite all else, I found myself reading one passage over and over again and couldn't help thinking of you:

> "From the fight with wild beasts returned he home: but even yet a wild beast gazeth out of his seriousness an unconquered wild beast! As a tiger doth he ever stand, on the point of springing; but I do not like those strained souls; ungracious is my taste towards all those self-engrossed ones."

John, I beg you in any way I can, please don't turn yourself into a beast. You were born in the wild but you _are not_ an animal. I think even you have to recognize that Nietzsche ultimately went crazy because he too was a slave to his own passions. He died of syphilis and probably was nothing more than a vile, angry man, disappointed with life because he could not find someone who loved him. You, John, instead, have someone who loves you...me.

If there was any doubt, I too have forgiven you (or should I better say, accepted you) for what happened in the past, and I'm sure Willow will have as well. I keep telling myself the obvious truth: that sometimes, our choices have been made for us and we have to live with them. I understand this revisionist moralizing doesn't help (and is probably the best reason for my not sending this letter), but I do think that what has happened to you was equivalently harsh, as if you were the one who was raped (but without the same access to self-pity). I know you would never admit that to yourself, but despite your thinking me some sort of spoiled, pitying creature, I do indeed pity you, even if I am in no position to. I am incredibly sorry on your behalf (something you would, no doubt, never allow me). You deserve a better life than this, a better inheritance. And I, for one, love you more than I ever have.

Ever thine,
Your constant,
Felicity

# 18

aturday night answering machine messages (untypically prevalent)...

None of them from John...

1. "Hello Felicity, where are you? Me and the Brits are goin' out "on the pull" or however it is you guys say it? Here's another one: we'll be hoovering plenty of Charlie too if you want to get involved later? Am I taking the piss, luv? Where are you? Haven't seen you in weeks. Your favorite goomba, Alessio."

2. "Hello. Have you been in a recent car accident? According to our records... BEEP."

3. "Wa' gwan, girlie? I haven't see you for mad time now, yo. Ya not gwan holla at a bruver na more. It's me, Skoolie D. We gonna check out some trip hop, old school, broken beats, dub kinda shit goin' on tonight down in the L.E.S. Will try again later. Holla!"

4. "Hey, Felicity, get your crotch down here. We are... shit, sorry, gotta go."

5. "Hey, this is Shinkirō. I know you haven't heard from me in a while, but..."

I almost ran to the phone, attempting to catch Shinkirō before he'd gotten off the line. It took me another couple of seconds for it to register that the message was probably left hours if not days ago.

I was truly at my wits' end. I missed John. No, I <u>REALLY</u> missed him, which pained me doubly as I saw myself becoming nothing but a clingy, little limpet.

That was it.

I decided right then and there to take Shinkirō's advice. I decided I was gonna to be mean. <u>Real mean!</u> For a change, I was going to have what he had always referred to as "attitude". Yes, indeed. I was going to strike out and become my own warrior. And how would I achieve it? Of course, I needed to instantiate my own set of ground rules. A series of steps that would ensure I achieved the panacea of the Self-Love Independent Warrior State.

So what were these steps to enlightenment?

Step 1: to achieving the Self-Love Independent Warrior State: walk out of the flat.

Right, easy enough.

Step 2: Don't fear the light. Get yourself onto the pavement, dear, the hard roads. Washington Square Park.

Great job. Now what?

First, look past the angry street magician, that miserable Spock who ventures all his bad tricks with a scowl on his face. Indeed, how could a self-respecting magician of his ilk ever maintain any sense of dignity? The rabbit never came out of the hat, the handkerchief never out of the ear, the right card was never guessed and when it was, the attitude didn't change. He couldn't make a Tootsie Roll disappear, much less my loneliness.

Right.

Keep on down the hard road. Walk on past the two fat, lesbian blobs: round-faced emoticons the blokes back home would have definitely dubbed double-baggers. "Those lot and their Cadillac-sized arses. Grim mingers!" They wink. They wink.

Doing just fine.

Step 3  to achieving the Self-Love Independent Warrior State:
Storm the castle. Claim your territory.

Righto! I wanted space, enough to crowd John right out of
existence. Keep ahead! Keep ahead! Ahoy! Ahoy!

Step 4: Stay focused. Forget John. Focus on anything but him.

Ah, yes, can't you tell I'm making this up as I go along? I'm just
out joy riding on a concentrated wave of pure Felicity? Nah, I'm
just being <u>MEAN</u>!

Let us take a pause to ask some questions from the audience:

"Felicity, dear", the reader may justifiably ask, "what are
these golden, glorious tribes that surround you, this delectable
fauna? Furthermore, what are these angry, aggressive sounds
crowding around you on all sides? Can't you embrace them? Try
to make them your own?"

The popping and locking of break-dancers: the float, the
freeze, the simulated glide.

*No Warrior, let 'em just sod off!*

The fist-pump of pointless posers, pins in their faces,
perpetually falling off their skateboards, perpetually impressing
no one, not even themselves.

*No Warrior, let 'em just sod off!*

The trashcan bangers, the spray-paint taggers, the Upper
East Side braggers.

*No Warrior, let 'em just sod off!*

All these things I normally walked by without ever noticing, I
was now inviting into my head. Why? <u>BECAUSE, I WANTED TO
MAKE MYSELF OPEN TO ANYTHING AND EVERYTHING,
ALL AT THE SAME TIME.</u>

*Warrior! Warrior! Listen. Let 'em just sod off! Sod the hell off!*

Step 5 to achieving the Self-Love Independent Warrior State:
Don't question anything.

And especially don't ask yourself the following:
What the hell was any of this for anyway? Why did I ever let myself remain in this heartless, heatless jungle? What fix was I looking for and what the hell's left for me now? Why the fuck isn't John here to save me?

Step 6: Move on.
Step 7: Ah...

How many more steps? Am I even close to achieving the Self-Love Independent Warrior State?
*Felicity, dear, what kind of Self-Love Independent Warrior are you? Back to steps 5 and 6, immediately!*
Step 8 to achieving the Self-Love Independent Warrior State: Disk clean, defrag, mind erase. Have some fun, Warrior!
Splendid, let's do this right: two gin and tonics, one cosmo and a pink thing with a white Japanese umbrella. Done.
Right. I really dug my high heels in on Step 8! All this just to collapse a few blocks away in a less than warrior-like fashion. And so, there I was again, stuck in a small West Side bar. Indeed, one I had never visited before and never will again.

Fig 15. "Crazy Dancing Bird"

It was a small establishment, lit entirely by red Christmas lights, strewn over every stable thing in the entire room. Woebegone Warrior, I spent the next three hours in earnest conversation with a man I'd never met before. My Samaritan heart, collector of strays, was attempting to convince this middle-aged man not to leave his wife. Eventually, our muddled figures were joined by another pair of drunken Scots (supposedly his best friends and now mine). A few more rounds of Jäger/whiskey and they all joined in chorus to sing for my benefit and eventual glory:

*Green grow the rashes, O;*
*Green grow the rashes, O...*
*Her prentice han' she try'd on man,*
*An' then she made the lasses, O.*

Once I'd given away my Scottish descent, I never paid for another drink. Unfortunately, I became so blitzed, I fell off the barstool and into the lap of the man whose marriage I'd was trying to save. It became immediately clear that he would have to take me back to my flat in a taxi. When we arrived there (and much to his shock), I gave him the sloppiest of French kisses and stumbled back into my vacant flat. It all made so much sense to me at the time that I had to laugh. Indeed, New York is everything and nothing all at the same time. My flat was just another one of the many contradictions encountered here: too small to entertain, too large not to make me feel the lack of having someone else.

Next day, I woke up finding I didn't even come close to achieving a Self-Love Independent Warrior-like state. I decided to take some of the leftover pharmahuasca capsules I'd kept hidden under my pillow (proverbially). Impatient for the effects to work, I took the opportunity to visit the Natural History Museum where John and I went on our first official date. Foolishly, I wanted to try to recapture some of our earlier, happier days.

I waited in line for what seemed to be hours. It was just enough time for the pharmahuasca to lay claim to my brain. Once at the desk, I was already beginning to have trouble with communication. A very patient lady working at the register was attempting desperately to make me understand that I needed to purchase a ticket for a certain price. Unfortunately, in my happy generosity, I was attempting to give her three times the amount because I couldn't be bothered to count. In any regard, I didn't understand why she wouldn't accept my sudden charity. All I wanted after all was to get on the proper "guest list". After a great deal of confused back and forth, I simply left all the money at the register and ran into the museum hall, hoping she or another bouncer wouldn't pursue me.

Once inside, I made the usual beeline for the Hall of Mammals. The museum was incredibly crowded, even for a weekend. At first, it seemed to me as if the people around me were trying to address me, but their sped-up mouths were clearly not moving at the same rate the words were gathering around my person. Furthermore, in my present cloud of unknowing, I couldn't really understand anything that was being said. I struggled even with the simplest of concepts, which all seemed to possess a hidden, double meeting, their inferences humorously twisted back on themselves like Mobius strips. It didn't even dawn on me that these words weren't even addressed to me at all. With all the buzzing around me, I felt like I was in the middle of a hive.

After a long fit of getting lost, I finally found myself again in the welcomed darkness that hove between the numerous, honey-filled dioramas. Strangely, both the lack of light and the familiar surroundings made me feel safer. That was, of course, until one of the Alaskan brown bears, who was standing on his hind legs, began to speak to me:

"Felicity," he ventured, with a considerable air of urbane politeness, his voice resonant like that of a provincial deity or a shopping mall genie. At first, I thought the voice might have come from the people directly behind me, but their mouths weren't moving in my direction and they paid me no heed.

"Yes," I gave out with some suspicion.

"You know who I am, don't you?"

"Well, according to the placard, you're a bear, aren't you?"

"No, not exactly."

"Well then, I'm not exactly sure who you are, but I am quite sure you shouldn't be talking."

"Listen, Felicity. Listen to me. You have, of course, neglected me a long time. Look at yourself. Do you really think that you've chosen the path of righteousness? Furthermore, are you really quite as willing as you seem to perish for your sins? It's been such a long time since we've spoken to one another that I feel the need to remind you of certain things. For instance, to beware of Apollyon, lest he cast down and destroy your soul."

It was then that I began questioning myself quite feebly, fortunately, in little more than a whisper. "Apollyon? But... this is simply ridiculous. How can he talk anyway? I must have taken too many of those dots. This surely isn't happening, is it?"

Then I heard a crude "*hruff*" behind me, which induced me to swivel round. And there, I encountered not one but two mountain goats addressing me from atop a frozen ledge of snow:

"If that a pearl may in a toad's head dwell, and may be found too in an oyster shell."

At this point, the considerately quiet Pronghorn also jumped into the fray: "Are you not afraid of Apollyon?"

The mountain goats then responded in my place: "These beasts range in the night for their prey, and if they should meet with me in the dark, how should I shift them? How should I escape being by them torn in pieces?"

By this time, I was becoming more than a little afraid and apprehensive. I decided to ignore their voices, but I couldn't make them stop. I became terrified that someone would notice my strange behavior and perhaps report me to the authorities. I started to back away from the dioramas into the center of the room. Underneath my breath, I whispered to myself, "Why are you doing this to me?"

Once more, I felt like crying. I knew I was finally cracking up this time. However, the moose, with its glassy eyes, looked straight at me:

"I see the dirt of the Slough of Despond is upon thee: but that slough is the beginning of the sorrows that do attend those that go on in that way."

Stop talking to me. Just stop it, I cried inside my head.

The bear then spoke up again. "Are you not seeing it? Don't you get it at all? You are saying all this, not us."

It was definitely time I tried another method. Indeed, I thought it certain that the people around me had finally discovered my secret insanity. In a fright, I shuttled past the remaining dioramas. To the outside world, I gave off the forced smile of a lunatic. I thought the best thing for me at present was to prevent myself from becoming unhappy or upset. If nothing else, I needed positive reinforcement. To think bad thoughts would just make everything worse. After all, I didn't want to break down in such a public place. As the anxiety continued to feed on itself, I whispered thus from the echo chamber of my own head, "See, everything is fine. It's funny. This is a joke and I'm laughing, see?"

Before I could fully exit the room, the pronghorn bade me stay: "You see, Felicity, some things are of that nature as to make one's fancy chuckle, while his heart doth ache."

I couldn't take it. I needed to escape these animals. There was no other way out of it. I ran as fast as I could up a couple flights of stairs to the second floor, where I found myself amongst an entire pack of zebras, who seemed really quite chatty and eager to speak. As I blasted past them, I heard one call back, "Hey, where are you going so fast?"

The lions also protested: "How rude!"

I then hung a quick left and found myself in a smallish room, relatively bereft of people. You couldn't imagine my relief. I was finally safe in the African culture hall (or so I thought). No sooner had I caught my breath than the seashell-encrusted Egungun dancer started shaking and the Gelede figure with his gun looked towards me quite upset. Within seconds, I became sure the Mende man, with his black bullet-shaped head, was Death himself. They were all looking at me the wrong way and I knew for certain what was about to happen. A man stood before me with dark skin and white stars painted on his flesh. He had hollows for eyes and a voided mouth, through which he started to speak. It was as if a dark plasma radiated from his body and wove around him in an expanding halo of evilness. Frighteningly, he even had the voice of Lord Hate-Good,

"You fool. You weak, little fool. You think you can oppose me? You think you can take John away from me"

I turned away in horror and fled the room, almost bumping into another of the displays. When I finally decided it was safe enough to look around me, I saw Ota Benga, the Mbuti prisoner himself, still encased in a glass display box, amidst a jade-colored forest. A mere four feet tall, he was using a child's bow to shoot an arrow up into an unwitnessable distance. I pressed my face against the glass and pleaded with him.

"Why have they locked you up," I queried quite audibly. "Why don't they let you free?"

Whether it was through pure rudeness or whether it was perhaps the combined fault of glass and an unbreakable concentration that forbade my words from reaching him, I didn't know, but he kept his back turned to me, granting me nothing in the way of polite recognition. At this point, given I had been so popular amongst all the animals (who clearly wanted to be my friend), I decided I was not going to be ignored. I thus began to beat on the glass and address him by name. It wasn't long before the people surrounding me started to stare and move their small children away as if I were Lamia herself. Time to go. As I ran past a few more dioramas, I began to feel like I was on an adult ride at Epcot. Not knowing where to go next, I hung a left into the cul-de-sac of the Hall of Asian Peoples. There, the dark-skinned Ainu woman took her turn at chiding me with her black, tattooed lips,

"Why did you leave John alone like that? You can still save him."

Enough, I kept running upstairs and blew past the third floor, where I knew the African mammals were just waiting to strike up a conversation. Even those cute, little, furry things, corsairs of the heart, I didn't dare pause for. I ended up on the fourth floor, where I found myself amidst sunshine and light. Release. I already felt freer at the surface. Like a weight of water had been lifted off my shoulders. I tried to walk calmly through the petrified forest of fossils, the gigantic skeletons that slowly roamed the museum floor. Unfortunately, they too were speaking to me with the voice of John:

"When I die, I will blame you. You could have prevented this."

Alas, there was no escape, even here. As I ran frantically through the remaining fossils, the bones began to move with more violent motions, which especially freaked me out. There really was no way out of this. Finally, in a brief moment of clarity,

I decided that I needed to find the Hall of Minerals. Rocks can't talk, right? It was the only way.

In desperation, I took the elevator all the way down to the first floor. By this point, I was almost hyperventilating. A woman in the elevator looked at my flushed face and asked me if I was ok. When the elevator doors finally opened, I made a break for the farthest back corner of the museum. Attempting to close my eyes as I ran, I ended up bumping into a number of people. With a whoosh and a slide, I finally arrived at the Hall of Minerals. I had never been so happy to see a bunch of rocks in my entire life. I sat in there for a full 30 minutes until I could calm myself down. It took me 15 more until I was finally at a point where I was able to go home. It's safe to say that I now know what it's like to have a bad trip. I kept myself indoors for the next two days and dared not show up at the animal shelter for at least as many more.

We hadn't seen or heard from Shinkirō for weeks. I'd tried calling him several times, but his ancient StarTAC went straight to voicemail. Finally, it emerged through the wire that he had actually tried to kill himself by cutting his wrists. When that didn't work, he had moved on to sleeping pills. Radio silence for weeks afterward. Then, out of nowhere, I suddenly received a call from him, only to discover that he had been magically resuscitated, returned in one piece to our mortal coil, and by all accounts, he was surprisingly happy. He invited John, Zulfikar and myself over to his place for tea. There he sat, in his Japanese-designed living room, wearing a jet-black *gakuran*, listening to a mix of Harrison's *La Koro Sutro* and Crumb's *Ancient Voices of Children*. The bandages from his wrists had just been removed and he bore a pair of tiny brown scars. He seemed almost in an altered state, disturbingly cheerful and content with himself, as some are who emerge from a stint in rehab. For ourselves, we were so afraid of breaking this crystalline state of calm equilibrium, we could barely speak. He already seemed a stranger to us, a relic from an ice age we could no longer access. He didn't say much, asked us about how things were going in our lives. Apologized for being out of contact, and mentioned some obscure story he'd heard about a couple we knew who'd just separated due to "lesbian bed death". He then said he'd decided to rid himself of all his old friends, only keeping those around him who possessed a "positive energy". "Otherwise," he added, "I've gone a bit *hikikomori*." During a brief gap in the conversation, Shinkirō and I both looked down and almost simultaneously noticed the small, bookmarked copy of Kōbō Abe's *Suna no onna*. Oddly, it was a book I had actually read in translation, one that concerned a hapless schoolteacher who gets thrown into a desert pit and is forced with Sisyphean regularity to dig himself out of an hourglass, daily overturned. Strangely, when he saw that I had noticed it, he quickly tucked it into a corner of the couch behind his back. A moment of slight awkwardness ensued and almost in reflex, he suggested he wanted to show us something. He then went into another room and came back carrying a most mysterious object before him, cupping it in both his hands like a newborn baby. Suddenly, he stopped in the middle of the room, smiling, but not saying anything. What was it in his hands but a *Kintsukuroi* vase. It was the first I'd ever seen. It was a beautiful and no doubt very expensive representation of an ancient Japanese art form that took shattered objects like vases or cups and fused the pieces together using gold as a bonding agent. It was such a delicate thing, but nonetheless, possessed a sense of strength and utter integrity. By the look of love on Shinkirō's face, it seemed clear that this priceless piece signified everything that had occurred in his life over the last few weeks. Shinkirō proceeded to tell us that this magnificent technique was a physical manifestation of the Japanese philosophy of *wabi-sabi*, one in which a person embraces the flawed or imperfect. Indeed, it is the very flaws inherent in the object that eventually turn it into a thing of great beauty. That was you too, John, our little *Kintsukuroi* vase. Sadly, in a matter of weeks, both John and Shinkirō would be dead. But, ironically, of all the people, it was Shinkirō who managed that loneliest of all deaths, the dreaded *kodokushi* of which he always said he was afraid.

# 19

editations on a crazy-man death, caught between two
worlds

| | |
|---|---|
| cold bodies | lukewarm bodies |
| unseen amidst the | irradiated by the televised |
| ultramarine glow | glow |
| of earth, already ghosts | of emerald oceans |
| of the infrared | seeking a destination spot |
| | |
| cold bodies | lukewarm bodies |
| in which a greater peace | pallid after intercourse |
| has entered | speechless after the jargon |
| strewn in lines | of unrest |
| | |
| cold bodies | lukewarm bodies |
| once simulated targets | ordained for honest work |
| now simulate | another fascinating step |
| | awaits |
| another functioning sleep | their culture of fulfillment |
| | |
| cold bodies | lukewarm bodies |
| exiles of our earth | exiles of our earth |
| enmeshed under | enmeshed under |
| a bloody carapace of sky | a sky of blue and white |
| | |
| cold bodies | lukewarm bodies |
| awaiting a barber | aware of their borders |

their fingernails
grown long, unruly

aware of occupation
aware of...

cold bodies
ignore the natural rules of
transubstantiation, seem
lighter as they recoil from
light

lukewarm bodies
enormous, bulbous, obscene,
orotund, curvaceous,
 big-boned, full of life

cold bodies
bulldozed over in the night
two angels carry each
between many pairs of wings

lukewarm bodies
by apposite inflection
assume the proper posture
to ensure posterity

cold bodies
100 kilograms
170 kilograms
192 kilograms

lukewarm bodies
2,000 yen
80,000 yen
150,000 yen

cold bodies
foreshortened for the camera

still have beautiful skin
more and more alive every
day

lukewarm bodies
have their development
arrested:
beaten, bruised, bludgeoned,
healed, adored, resurrected

cold bodies
quivering falsely
robbed of personal effects
better that way

lukewarm bodies
stymied, bituminous, clog
the rivers, push the
flotation device

cold bodies              lukewarm bodies
are touching             seldom touch
awake again              never awaken
from sleep               from sleep

# 20

After leaving Jayna's apartment, Paul and Willow drove straight to the address they had been given; a series of coded letters that foretold nothing more than a three-story, colonial-style house in New Rochelle. A Caribbean family occupied the upstairs floor, while the downstairs was to be left to them. Jayna chose the relatively out of the way location because she knew the city would prove too much for Paul, and furthermore, that the suburban backdrop would not only ease the transition, but ease Paul's anxiety about prying eyes. Located not more than a 15-minute walk from the Mount Vernon railroad station, the wooden house stood in quiet anonymity behind a pair of old oaks. Throughout the year, its gray mass was orbited by a constellation of stray cats. Indeed, the next-door neighbor was an animal hoarder and kept at least 12 felines at all times. During the night, one could see their shadowy forms flit about, prowling the moonlight arcs and lending their air of mystery to the dull polyhedrons of reflected light. There was of course some trouble with the ASPCA, who were regularly called to pick up and destroy these marauding creatures. However, these sleek Egyptians were more clever than most, blessed as they were with a sixth sense. By some strange magic, before the dawn would break, they were transported to the moon via the hieroglyph of Ra.

On certain nights, these spellbound cats would mate-call in a matter frightening to all who heard it. On February 24th, 12 days after their arrival, Willow's diary contained the following entry:

*In the room, I heard a loud scream and I jumped outta bed and asked my Grandpappy what it was, and he*

*said, "Don't worry none and go back to sleep." I
kept asking him and asking him and he said, "Listen
Willow, it's just an old Wampus cat." And I tol' him
that ain't no good because when you hear a Wampus
cat cry, that means someone is gonna die in three
days, true to my soul. He wasn't having any of it and
told me to shut up and don't mind them none.*

It was only a couple days later that Paul left the house to meet with
the specialist Jayna had suggested. This particular specialist was
known for one thing alone, his complete and uncircumstantial
discreteness. Under no condition did Paul want to leave Willow
by herself, however, the doctor insisted that the initial meeting
be without her as he wanted to assess for himself the above-
boardness of everything. Although Paul didn't feel good about
it, he knew Willow could be trusted to stay indoors and out of
harm's way. It took a lot of doing, but Paul finally managed to
convince her to let him out of her sight. Fortunately, despite his
great discomfort, she had struck up a relationship with the three
children upstairs. Indeed, she felt safer, as long as she heard the
soft patter of their footsteps above her. For his part, Paul had
long grown used to the hazards of raising a mute child in the
wilderness, and insisted she wear her lime-green whistle. As
soon as he left the house, she cast it back into their luggage, it
being for her a cripple's aid.

Given the downpour outside, Willow had no trouble
remaining within doors. After a short break in the weather,
she caught the creak of the front door and ran toward what
she thought to be her grandfather. Though she knew he wasn't
expected for at least another couple hours, she thought he might
have arrived early. Imagine her shock when she found Mr
Miles, the next-door neighbor, standing in the narrow vestibule,
drenched in rain. Willow had always found him to be a strange

man and didn't exactly feel comfortable around him, especially given the way he stared at her. On the rare occasions she left the house with Paul, he had often asked her if she wanted to pet whichever one of his cats he had about him. He had even been so bold as to offer her candy or perhaps a small toy. In a handful of instances, Willow had been surprised to find him peeking through a dirty window or hiding under a hedge through which she had just passed. He had all too quickly figured out from the upstairs neighbors that she couldn't talk and would always greet her with a garish smile or a soft hello when she walked past. Indeed, what made the present occasion so startling was that it was the first time he had been completely alone in her presence. He was clearly nervous and stood looking around himself as if he were being harried by a leopard that could lead out at any point. After a couple of minutes, he finally managed to ask her in a faint whisper where her Grandpappy was. She wrote on her small chalkboard that he had gone to find a doctor for her. He then asked if she was sick. She wrote she didn't know but she felt ok. At this point, a queer glint suddenly flashed into Mr. Miles' eyes. He proceeded to tell her that he was in fact a doctor and asked her if she wanted to know for sure whether she was sick or not. She shook her head and became increasingly uncertain of what to do. Mr Miles tried to assuage her and patted her on the head, asking her if she had ever been to a doctor before. She nodded her head. He then asked her if she knew what doctors did when they examined their patients. She nodded her head again. He then purred a sickly "goooood" and asked her to remove her shirt so he could listen to her chest. She had wanted to ask him where his stethoscope was but quickly realized she didn't know how to spell it. Instead, she merely stuck her fingers in her ears and then moving them toward her chest, formed a circle in front of her heart. At first, Mr Miles was puzzled by her strange gesture, but after a few more attempts, he finally realized what she was after.

"Oh, my stethoscope. You want to know where my stethoscope is?"

Willow nodded.

"Smart girl. Well, I don't need it because I can just use my ears, dear. I'm like one of those cats you see at my house. I have super-good hearing."

Willow was uncertain, but he assured her that everything would be ok and that he wouldn't have to touch her. Despite her wariness, she proceeded to take off her shirt, afraid Mr Miles might get angry with her in the same way Shane did. After all, she was used to taking her shirt of in the forest and saw nothing really wrong with it, as long as he didn't touch her. This was an adult after all. Once she had removed her shirt, Mr Miles sat on his knees and smiled in wonder before her. He then asked her to take off her pants, as he would have to check to see if she had any black spots that could turn into large warts. Again, she was unsure, but didn't know what to do. Her eyes were deep wells of mistrust. She tried not to be afraid. She had no choice and did what he said, removing her pants while keeping on her underwear. At this point, Mr Miles began to act strangely. He began to squirm and at times seemed to be fidgeting with something inside his pants. The look on his face certainly made her uncomfortable, especially as he seemed to have increasing trouble breathing. In a horrible way, it reminded her of the way Shane behaved when he sat on top of her. Nonetheless, Mr Miles asked her to remove her underwear, his fierce eyes now locked upon her frail frame. He added that he would have to snap some pictures so he could take them to the hospital, where the nurses would run the proper tests for her invisible black spots. Willow, now feeling something was definitely wrong, was virtually trembling before him. However, she was afraid to do anything else than what she was told. He was too near her and she felt unusually vulnerable amidst these strange surroundings. With nothing else to do, she froze and couldn't bear moving. When Mr Miles told her for a second time in a much sterner voice to remove her underwear, she finally complied, at which point Mr. Miles croaked, "Yesssss. Yesssss. That's right. That's a good girl. You are my blessssing. My blesssssing. Take them off slowly."

Almost excited enough to forget his caution, he began to regret the fact that he hadn't actually brought a camera. He couldn't believe his bad luck and was working out a way in his mind to best advantage the situation.

"Listen, Willow. You know you can't ever tell your father about this, right? Otherwise, he will be very, very upset with you and never forgive you. I will also have to report it to the police that he left you here alone unless you keep this our little secret, you hear? He would go to prison, you understand?"

Willow nodded, almost wanting to cry.

"Goood little girl. You are my blessing. I will wash your toes for you."

By this point, Mr Miles was crawling on the floor like a wild animal, his lascivious smile becoming more obscene by the second. Doglike, he began to pant heavily, his tongue practically lolling out of his mouth. Willow didn't understand his strange fascination with her small body and had hoped that he would put an end to this strange kind of game. Unflappable, he crawled across the floor until he was close enough to touch her. He then began to stretch out one of his trembling hands toward her chest in slow motion. However, just as he was about to put his fingers to her skin, Willow stomped down hard on his remaining hand, which had flattened itself on the floor. Immediately, Mr Miles gave out a stifled cry and shook his pained fingers in the air.

"Goddamn you, you little shit."

He wanted so bad to shout but he knew he couldn't. He merely clutched his hand in pain while cursing her under his breath. Just as he was about to take by force what he couldn't by persuasion, he heard a shout come down from above.

"Hey. A wha' gwan? Willow, dat you down da? Evryting ok down de, gurl? Your grandfadda tol mi ta keep good eye on you, ya know? Lil' Miss Bunyan?"

His shouts met with no response.

"Oh yeah, what am I tinkin'. Me is so forgetful, I forgot ya can't talk none. Not a squeak. Don' trouble ya self none. Me com down de."

At this point, Mr Miles and Willow both panicked. She grabbed her clothes while he ran out the door, throwing all caution to the wind. By the time Mr Farrow got down the stairs, Willow had already run in to the bathroom where she was shivering and struggling to put her clothes back on.

"Miss Bunyan? Miss Bunyan? Ya so quiet, gurl. A wha' gwaan? Was da someone in 'ere? Me taut me 'eard da fron' door… Miss Bunyan?"

Willow, finally dressed, ran out of the bathroom and tried to look as normal and unaffected as she could.

"Dere's you ah. A wha' gwaan? Ya had me all worried, ya know? Fi sure, dis ain't the safes' neighbahood and me know ya is not from des parts, but frum down Sout sa ya nuh know. But listen, gurl, ya need to learn to lock da door. Dem tief will come in 'ere an' mash up da place. Mash it up completely. Me done seen it before. Jus' de udda day, me saw it lef completely unlock. But, da neighba dere, bless him, usually sits on dat porch dere all day and him sees all the comings and goings round 'ere. Him, good man, dere. Very quiet and him keep to himself. Anyway, ya hungry, gurl? Look like ya belly starv. We gwaan go eat now upstair. Come tink of it, yo' grandfadda's been gawn a long time, ya know. Taut him shuld be back by now. Me lose track a da time fi sure."

Willow shook her head.

"Ok. Ya shure ya ain't hungry none?"

Willow shook her head again.

"Ok. Me will save some curry goat fu ya jus in case. Ya never had no curry goat nor aki and sal fish? No? Course not. Well, ya will die for it fi sure. Ok. Me leev ya alone now den and me come and check on ya laata. Rememba ta lock da door doe, alright? Don' wan' nobody come 'ere an' mash up the place, right? Good."

Once Mr Farrow had left, Willow felt an initial sense of relief. Then, as she began to reflect on what had just occurred, she sensed a great void open up inside of her, a vastness, which she knew had no end and which she couldn't recall experiencing before or since. For the very first time, she felt an insurmountable sensation of shame, even guilt. It was to be her first bitter taste of adulthood, her first true contact with a fallen nature, one which she knew had existed within her even before she was born. The hot tears trembled at the rims of her now restless eyes. As she fell to the floor, she began to recall those painful cries, the screams that had once surrounded her as she lay on that forest floor. She knew the sound she was hearing. It was the sound of the entire forest as it cried out in heartfelt lamentation. She remembered the zigzag of empty treetops, she remembered the smell of dead leaves, she remembered the way two dark birds of prey made their inexorable flight across a mackerel sky. She knew nothing would ever stop them. She remembered everything, the crawling of ants, the whirring note of bees, the quick mechanical motions the flies made as they stuck their funnels into her de-virginized blood. *Natura naturans*: nature was taking its deliberate course. So much so, she felt that nature cry out inside of her, a hopeless rebellion against the aged, dire wolf that gnawed at her tiny bones. Changes were indeed occurring inside of her, changes she couldn't yet fully appreciate. With no way to stop them, she started to pray, knowing full well it was too late for anyone to save her. She would never be young again. The jaws of nature had opened up inside of her and would devour her whole.

For a child, nothing is more traumatic than the discovery of that most fundamental horror, the horror that nature exists without morals. The horror was apprehended. It had bridged the cosmic gap, the gap in her mind between what those boys had done to her and what this disgusting man had evidently wanted of her. As the screams continued to mount inside her head, she decided for once that she wanted to fight back, to drown out all those angry noises. She wanted for once to speak and give a name to the horror mounting within her chest. If nothing else, she wanted to ask Paul the reasons why all these awful things were happening to her. Why it was that seemingly, everyone around her wanted to hurt her and make her feel like she wasn't strong, that she wasn't worth the dirt under her feet. She wanted to ask him why she needed fixing and why she still had nightmares about her mother's eyes. She also wanted to understand what had happened to her father. About why that old, dying wolf had made her bleed from the inside. All these questions that burned inside her head were now scorching the trembling tip of her unpracticed tongue. She knew all the words, the exact ones she wanted to say, but still couldn't say them. She only had to wait for Paul to arrive home before she could make the required sounds. She practiced several times before a mirror and even enjoyed mouthing the most important one to herself, the four-letter word she had only ever remembered writing down on birthdays or before she went to sleep. She wanted to tell him she loved him, that she never wanted to be away from him again. She wanted to hear herself say it. She finally felt she could speak, not as a child, but as a fully-formed person. She knew she could do it. All she had to do was wait.

But, unfortunately, all the waiting in the world wouldn't have helped, as Paul was never to return that night. As it goes in stories of this kind, Willow's words would die inside her, much in the same way that Paul was dying on an anonymous street not more than four blocks away. She never really understood exactly what had happened to him. All she was told was that on the way home, he was stopped by a gang of men who would attempt to mug him. By nature, Paul fought back. And as is normal in these cases, instinct fought with instinct until they beat him unconscious. He wouldn't die immediately, but lived another three days, never to wake again. She would never get to say goodbye.

Willow would only see Jayna once again, when she came with a distant aunt to pick her up. This same woman was to take Willow and raise her somewhere in upstate New York. It was a very quick affair. Her mother, still unable to face her daughter, sobbed uncontrollably as Willow was huddled into a black SUV and driven away. Years later, just before she went to college, her aunt gave her the following letter from Paul:

dear willow,

i was never a man of many words. never really went to school much. but given i could never tell you this in person, in case something happened to me, i wanted to make sure you knew the story between me and your momma. most of all, i wanted you to understand who your father really was. let the lord god forgive me for how i'm putting these words down on paper, but what is done is done.

let me start by telling you about when you was born. you was born not long after brice went into the military. he was a man that definitely should never have gone to no war. he was a sensitive sort. he had a certain way about him, a certain way of doing things. he was a different sort of kid. deep down, he was a good man, but troubled. he worshiped the ground that his brothers walked on. he wanted to be like them. they was all good at sports. the girls liked them. they was strong, but brice was none of those things. bishop took to the bottle and ended up killing himself in a car accident. it almost killed me when he passed. he was a beautiful boy and every one liked him, especially brice. bishop was like a father to him, so while his death hit both of them hard, for brice, it was double. after his death, josiah went to the military. left alone, brice got mixed up in the wrong crowd. he started drinking like bishop and doing all sorts a things. lord, willow, i pray you never pick up a bottle 'cause it runs in the family. anyway, when his mom died, i came back from california. i tried to take care of all my sons. it was tough going at first, but we reached an understanding of each other. all except me and brice. we never did quite see eye to eye. he was a good seven years younger than his older brother and still at the age where he resented me not being around. his mom begged me several times to come back and straighten him out. like me, he didn't seem to have much for words, but he had something about him that told me he never felt at peace with himself. he had a sadness hanging over him. when he was old enough, he followed his brother off to the military. a few years later, both of them would be sent to afghanistan to be part of operation enduring freedom. josiah wasn't lucky and when brice heard he'd been killed in kandahar, something deep down inside of him broke. he wasn't far off from being discharged, but then, he became a reckless man. he didn't care about his life no more and put himself in all kinds of danger.

let me tell you a story about brice. when he came back on leave and saw you for the first time, he never wanted to put you down after that. he became a changed man. it was the first time i'd ever seen him really happy. every night, he put you to bed and every day, he'd carry you around in his arms everywhere he went.

205

it pained him so much to have to go back to active duty. it was the first time he really had anything in his life to live for. if he hadn't a gone back for that last tour in afghanistan, i truly think everything would have been different. no one will ever know what happened to him out there, but honest to god, it was that last tour that destroyed his head. when he come back, he wasn't even a shadow of the same man that left. both brice, your mother and i all had a hard time and we took to the bottle too. we used to fight. fight each other like father and son are not supposed to. he wasn't treating your mom too well either, but it wasn't his fault. we tried to get help for him, to talk to him, but nothing seemed to get through. it got to the point i couldn't take it no more.

well, your mom and brice kept fighting until one night, a terrible accident happened. a terrible accident that was nobody's fault but my own. because of this accident, your father lost his life and your momma thought she shouldn't be with you no more. she never stopped loving you though. not for one minute. she would always write these letters and make sure you was ok. she sent money all regular, much more than we needed.

she hoped one day, she would be ready to be like a real parent to you again, the way i wasn't to my sons. she wasn't ready yet, but she promised me if you ever did speak again, she would come visit, first thing.

when you read this, i hope you will have it in your heart to forgive us all. lord, help me for having put another of sons under. if nothing else, please remember that we all loved you, we just never quite loved ourselves enough to be able to show it. i hope you understand.

your grandpappy,

paul

# 21

I have to admit it.

Really, I do.

Looking back at these pages, it sometimes seems as if I am writing this _____ (whatever noun you may want to insert for this confused tangle of words) to myself. At times, I feel so in touch with you that I am convinced we are one and the same. At others, when I read your writing, you seem to me like a sphinx, one that a thousand years of burning suns couldn't render any less inscrutable. I was always taken by Felicity's theory of love, one that represented a complete melding of spirits. In most cases, when I touch the planchette to our beloved board, I know we are once again in unison, you and I. However, nothing exceeds the tripartite joy of my sharing the Mystic Hand with our dear Felicity, for it is then that I feel most a third set of fingers guiding us through a swarm of words no one of us could ever have uttered alone. They came at first like cryptic secrets shared and understood by us only.

"SO WE WULD IN WALK IN PAIRS OF 3 ALWAYS WONDERING WHO THE SPEECHLESS ONE WAS"

Then, more confident. More assured. After a while, once we got the gist of it, we came to understand you in ways we hadn't even when you were alive. It is quite literally a haunting experience attempting to finish your work, to be for you, something of a ghostwriter.

"U FLATTR ME 2 THINK U CULD DIE 4 ME AS FELICITY ONCE DID"

Although we were close for just a little while, I think our strands will never really part.

No, never shall we part…

No, never shall we forget...

Time lapse – a single night's sky, a bubble chamber streaked with the ripples of planets, airplanes, and shooting stars – all the luminous things of this uranographic world. You have ventured too far from our cozy, little campfire into a wilderness from which no light can return. Indeed, I remember the day Voyager 1 left behind our little garden of light. Amazingly, the news saddened me more than I could have ever accounted for. Maybe because it made me think of myself, fifty years into the future as an elderly man of no family, my ancient dog nosing its way out of earshot, until fate makes it play amongst those garden shades; indeed, neither I nor my little version of Titus will ever know the exact moment when our reason for existence might simply disappear. I can only ascertain from this that there is a distance in this universe from which the simple sharing of "I love yous" would take longer than a lifetime. Why all this existential curiosity? No doubt, it was this that caused me to start my turns upon the board. I did it, knowing full well that there was still something that both of us desperately needed to say, because words meant more to us than life (indeed, they were the very proof of our existence). Perhaps, I just needed a real conversation with myself. Alas, those of us left ventured each day to find the transit of your daylight star, the twin of the *Sidus Iulium*, which in 44 BC, was seen all the way from Rome to Chang'an. So enraptured were we within your limitless afterglow that there remains no doubt that your dust tail will burn brightest in any sky we care to look up to.

"LET THE SURFACE OF EVRY SEA BARE THE CIPHER OF MY NAME"

Having no doubt buttered you up, I must now discuss, against my wish, that ugly period, when you, John, were persuaded, no, in fact, convinced that Felicity and I were having a relationship behind your back. At first, the casualties were rather minor:

those of us unlucky enough to surround you would often catch the shrapnel of your cantankerous, but rather lightweight persiflage. Then it became worse. Much, much worse. One faints at the ugliness of your trigonometric suspicions that put us both at perpendiculars, due entirely to the untoward implication of a phantom hypotenuse you accused her and I of sharing. Admittedly, Felicity got the worst of it, but there were indeed, public outbursts, at random, usually when you were less than yourself. One particularly bad experience occurred at a Murray Hill restaurant, where you started shouting atop a table to a stunned audience:

"Why is it that the only people you think you can trust can best strangle you with a length of your own rope?"

Another day, another evacuation. Days later, you officially began your Reign of Terror, stalking both Felicity and I, day and night, leaving us handwritten notes in odd places:

*I know what you're up to.*

*Et tu, Brute?*

*Real estate just went up in the Second Circle... You might try the Eight.*

*If backstabbing were an Olympic sport...*

To the point, it became frightening. And we, your close circle, became little more than inmates of your selfish little Panopticon, one in which you installed yourself at its most miserable core. Indeed, I too hated you then, not for anything you had done to me, but for how you treated Felicity, especially as I...

"FURGIVE. MAKE ME SPEEK NO MORE. EYE SUFFR 2 SEE. THE EYES R WICKED HERE"

After more than a week of this, it came to the point where I felt obliged to prove my loyalty to you (a proof you ultimately secured by implicating me further into the Ota Benga society). It was around this time that according to one of Lord Hate-Good's more unreasonable requests, the Ota Benga society began communicating in Glagolitic (Linear B proving too difficult to adapt, and Glagolitic being, in your estimation, "infinitely more beautiful on the page"). With great difficulty, these notes were translated with the aid of photocopied versions of Angelo Rocca's *Bibliotheca Apostolica*. A weak cypher, but nonetheless, suitable for present circumstances. Admirably, it didn't take Lord Hate-Good or yourself long to figure out how I could be of use to the society. Due to the fact I worked for the city's permitting division, it was determined I should be brought into your little cabal. Indeed, you had waged your bout of psychological warfare well, and I wonder to this day if it was not ornately planned. I was, no doubt, your device.

"U HEAR MORE THAN I CAN EVR SAY U SEE MOR THAN I CAN EVER SHOW"

After helping you to determine some key information, it was decided I should be taken one dark morning to The Land of Beulah (in actuality, the code name for the mysterious and barely accessible North Brother Island where the society's parent organization had their headquarters). It was there that my commitment to the cause would be probed to its fullest extent. Indeed, I was to be forced across my own Rubicund. A date was set, a fortnight hence, from whence at the witching hour, I would be smuggled into the back of an anonymous, white van.

\* \* \*

D-day. Zero hour. For 45 minutes, our moving cell threaded what little traffic there was between Alphabet City and our final destination. I would be jostled and thrown across all 10 feet of dissolving space. And there I was, happy, little me, second-guessing my choice in friends, sitting handcuffed, blindfolded, amidst hushed voices and ski-masked recriminations.

In the early hours of the morning, we finally arrived at some anonymous industrial park. Within seconds, I was guided to a leaden piece of shore, where a small boat and perhaps even Charon awaited us (his owed obol was nothing more than my misgiving, which stuck in my throat like a rusty piece of metal). After awaiting our proper signal (given via a child's walkie-talkie), we set off before a crazed Aurora could blush at our pettiness. At that hour, the violet air was still rank with the smell of ozone, interspersed occasionally with dieseled jets of cold breeze. Trees combed the air like the raw nerves of invisible hands. Just before the sky turned platinum, the horizon was that of an old planetarium, its simulated light possessed of a certain tincture of twilight, only dispersed just before the show begins, right before the room darkens to the low purr of its double-domed star projector. And here, the harrowing experience truly began, as we sailed through the Hell Gate (a particularly treacherous stretch of the East River), which squirmed beneath the weight of our hull like some black, prelapsarian tar. We spent a quiet hour adrift without anyone speaking, my captors' faces and identities still hidden from me. Finally, on the surface of the river, the sun's arc lamp shuddered as we jerked our way free from the cold, greenish grasp of invisible fingers. Behind us, the city seemed to rise weightlessly, like a gray cloud of smog. We had reached the other shore and in the distance somewhere, those fleshless hands were still waving.

We would eventually walk toward what I would later determine was the Riverside Hospital – an old shrew of a building, it had become a cold, sunless place, despite its being increasingly dispossessed by each year of any shade of interior space. It was there that we would spend the night, awaiting a darkness under which we could safely return across the strait. In the rising light, we could see tufts of juicy vine, the xanthic outlines of old buildings, half submerged and drowned in a sea of kudzu. Inside these dead walls, famished even of echoes, it was clear that Time had been seduced by the spark of city lights and departed long ago, never to return. Careless Time left behind, amongst other things, this haunted chapel, cracked open like an egg, left entirely to the worshipful service of a shivering brethren of birds. What was certain was that this was a place out of bounds and equally outside of time. In the last century, it had been little more than a warehouse to cold store the sufferers of smallpox, eventually expanding to house all manner of infectious diseases. As I passed through those vacant spaces, I felt an electric thrill. Call me sentimental, but it enlivened me to see the books still on the library shelves, the standing rows of chairs arrayed within a modest theatre, a lost kitchen, my heart's pale green jewel, one more article Time's absence rendered into something more than mere tumbledown; to me, it all seemed like the quiet aftermath of a neutron bomb. In fact, I half expected to see the shadows of former inhabitants imprinted upon the gaping walls.

We had to be extremely quiet and no light was allowed until we'd entered the secret enclosure, the holiest of holies, the inner sanctum. Unnecessarily, a sackcloth hood was put over my head as I was led through the furthest maze of this unflinching underworld:

"NEVUR WILL I LEEVE THIS ISLAND. DEATH SURROUNDS ME MY BLOOD IS POISON"

When my feet finally stopped, I was sat down in a chair, at which point the hood was removed from my head. Three minutes later, a pair of comic-book thugs tied my torso inside a harness and hoisted me toward the ceiling with a rusty chain. The room was completely dark except for a single spotlight, which they thereafter extinguished. I spent another 20 minutes in isolation until a single, red blade of light leapt towards me across the floor, cutting me off from darkness. That's when Igor came in.

Igor was a short, stubby Russian, dressed in gray camouflage pants and a black t-shirt. He also wore a camouflage hat the same color as his pants. In his hand, he carried what looked to be a bowie knife. He walked straight up to me without saying a word. He then took out a rather high chair, on which he stood to reach my eye level. As he stood before me, he peered deeply into my eyes with a look of sheer malice, one that made me almost lose control of bodily functions. He then looked me up and down and, with a smirk, waved the knife in front of my face like a wand. After these threatening displays, he spoke in what appeared to be a heavy Russian accent; his manner of pronouncing English words seemed nothing if not a deliberate act of vandalism.

"In all honesty, we would prefer to use practiced methods to get what we want from you. If we had our way, we would normally default to the Reid technique of non-invasive interrogation and torture, but as it stands, this is subject to trademark so we have to resort to more primitive and brutal methods. I hope you can understand. Don't take it personally, we certainly don't. You take torture personally, it becomes sloppy, unprofessional. But, I'm getting ahead of myself. Fortunately, today is your lucky day because in the last few months, we sort of came up with our own magic formula that we also hope to market one day. So, of course, before we begin, we need you to sign this itsy-bitsy, little NDA."

It was a great shock to me when Igor actually walked over to a metal desk and returned with a clipboard and a piece of paper.

"This is of course so that we don't lose our potential patent. You are American so I am sure you understand this?"

Still in shock, I nodded my head and, without thinking, I took the pad and quickly signed the paper without reading the fine print.

"Oh yes, and initial and date here. I always forget."

I put my signature on the blank that remained.

"So, let's begin. What is your name? Oh yes, Zulfikar. Yes, Zulfikar, actually, our methods are really quite simple and very effective. I'm surprised no one has patented it before. You see, we have this little studio over there and once we take you in, we are going to take some pictures of you naked with a bunch of gay boys, animals, etcetera, etcetera. We have millions of servers in Russia and access to all kinds of social media sites. You get the idea, of course. We can make you disappear or make you known everywhere, whichever we choose. We can put your face on a billion screens with the flip of a switch. In this country and in Russia, you hate gay boys so much that it's enough to convince any man to say either nothing or everything, whichever we choose. In the worst case, like if the man is already a gay boy himself, we use props. We have these really realistic dolls that look just like real children. It's all very sick and twisted, but we are professionals here."

It was all too strange to be believed. At this point, I really wondered whether I was being put on a form of *Candid Camera*. It was the only thing that prevented me from taking any of this very seriously.

"If we are ready to begin, Yuri is our photographer. Yuri! Can you come over here and bring camera?"

A strange-looking man with round, impossibly thick glasses came in through the same door Igor had. Meanwhile, a reprise of the two comic-book thugs took me down from the ceiling and out of the metal harness. I was beginning to feel slightly more comfortable until they began frog-marching me over to the studio, where I could discern, through dirty windows, the various implements and stage props Igor had mentioned. It appeared Igor had been serious the entire time and that this really was going to happen. In front of us, there were a couple of studio assistants scurrying around the largish studio, making the necessary arrangements for our shoot. For my part, I felt the dim stirrings of a panic attack. It goes without saying that I was quite a bit more than pleased when John suddenly walked into the room and cast a wink of aspersion in my direction. After a salute and a few cursory handshakes, he whispered something into Igor's ear. What I learned later was that he and Lord Hate-Good had essentially vouched for me, allowing me to avoid all the aforementioned indiscretions with little more than a promise. Once I was "in", Igor's attitude towards me completely changed. At once, he became the most bosom of companions, gushing smiles like a vacuum salesman. In short order and unprompted, he proceeded to tell me all kinds of minor secrets about the inner workings of disparate anarchic cells, of which the Ota Benga society was just one:

"Hey Zulf – can I call you Zulf – you ever seen those birdwatchers near Kerbs Boathouse in Central Park? You know, the ones with the telescopes and binoculars who look like they are doing nothing interesting. They look like normal people, right? No, those sonofabitches are completely out of their minds. They are super-radicalized crypto-anarchists. They even scare the hell outta me. I wouldn't be caught dead in a room alone with one of those sonofabitches. Goes to show, we've got eyes everywhere."

After a few more revelations of the salacious sort, we all started drinking vodka and he (along with several other Russians) became the most red-faced, jolly Russian you could ever meet. Once I was stood next to him, I discovered that he was a man of only five foot seven, but had massive, Popeye-like forearms with large, scary tattoos (one of which was a naked woman he could make dance by flexing and unflexing his forearms). After these rather ridiculous entertainments, he told me the story of one Piotr (known officially as Piotr the Pointless), who worked for them and was able to generate millions of dollars a year in gross profit by selling dead peasants' insurance to the Bahamian Military.

"I didn't even know the Bahamas had an army."

"Oh yes, and they are quite active. They are even deployed overseas for all kinds of operations. They are very successful at forming cordons. Supposedly some of the best, most disciplined cordons you'll ever see."

Surprisingly, the local cells had made an enormous amount of money out of this scam; enough to furnish the participating generals with some sizeable kickbacks.

"We've tried with a few other small governments and we are currently working on the US military, who seem really intrigued."

I watched Igor as he paced the floor in a childlike fashion, his eyes flooding with unalloyed excitement.

"You see, because when the soldiers die, that's when the profits really kick in. In fact, you don't even need them to die, you just make up a bunch of names, put some weights and pillows in a black casket, cover it with a US flag and declare another one dead. A few poor, and sometimes imaginary, families make some money, the generals and insurance executives make buckets of money, and we just recycle the slush funds over and over again, skimming a little off the top each time. It's beautiful."

I nodded my vague agreement.

"He got the idea from a book, he says. Piotr has always got his head in these books, you know. He is always reading Pushkin and those old, boring Russian novels. How could we know it would make us so much money? And the best thing of all, it's easier than drugs, prostitutes, or extortion. In any case, the entire thing is above board and supported by many governments. You see, here in New York, we don't play in the usual rackets. We leave that to the mob and the petty gangs. We are different, you see. We are professional. We use our heads."

Once it was understood that I had been thoroughly vetted, I was invited into a "workshop" session. It so happened that a regional conference was going on at the time, and there were a number of minor delegates there. In the workshop session I was allowed to attend, I was given the impression of large goings-on without much in the way of detail. We were all given name badges with our codenames written on them (mine, for some reason, was "Man Spanker"). Just as in a real corporation, we were split into breakout groups for team-building and brainstorming exercises. Here was an entire parallel galaxy of nightshift workers, security guards, office cleaners, illegal gangsters, reserve bank employees – in other words, all the things that coalesce to form a city within a city, a state within a state; all those things that an average Sunday tourist would never even know existed. These were the people that managed the various public works, the deployment of police forces, and in a certain individual case, oversaw the petty details of quantitative easing: an entire network of non-entities, intent on one thing, the overthrow of government and society as we know it. There were numerous hints that this gray society had infiltrated the very highest corridors of power via a secret army of paid politicians and corporate rent boys, not revealed by name. Upcoming meetings at Bilderberg were alluded to, alongside purported hacks of block chain systems that would, within a matter of days, unleash a series of ghostly payments that, under the right conditions, could only but bring forth the demise of a number of central banks. It became increasingly clear by the way they addressed one another that most of these people had rarely met, and were primarily acquainted through the Dark Web. When rare face to face meetings were absolutely required, this, it appears, was one of their many meeting places. I was told that if I ever spoke a word, they could implicate me in any number of unfortunate doings. I was even required to bring a passport (which was duly copied) and I soon began to regret that I got mixed up in these affairs. Lord Hate-Good, I discovered, was merely the nucleus of a very minor cell in a much larger organism, the enormity of which none of those present even knew. One thing I did discover for certain was that the plan (whatever it was) was moving ahead and would be completed in a very short space of time.

At some point, the conversation turned to my work at the Department for Planning, which set off a virtual electrical storm in Piotr's head. There was a general agreement that I could help with providing detailed blueprints and the exact timing of certain events. Ultimately, I proved to be of only limited help for what they wanted to achieve, but it was enough to secure their trust and longer-term consideration.

"EYE WUS WICKED ZULF IS TRU BLOOD CARE 4 HIM"

The meetings ended on a high note and I was duly shuttled back to Manhattan. When I finally arrived at my apartment, I was surprised to find Felicity there. She had something important to tell me. Something that floored me more than anything else I had seen or heard that day.

# 22

Codebreaker: Felicity

Mission: To stop John at all costs

Result: I almost stopped it. Almost...

Because John, usually careful, became sloppy at times. Here I was, the prying wife, digging out affairs inside of waste bins. Served him right. After all, it was he who accused me of numerous false affairs in the recent past.

How did it all begin?

The first clue: Waste bin. Piece of paper on which was scribbled "Nihilist Cipher".

Nihilist who? This little piece of information was the prime mover to my recent activities: one that impelled me to take a "sabbatical" from the shelter and remain holed up for days in the New York Library.

Who were these shadowy Nihilists?

It turns out that the Nihilists were a bunch of anti-tsarists, who used specialized ciphers during the 1880s to organize various terrorist plots. They were originally inspired by the ideology of Mikhail Bakunin and Sergey Nechayev, whose *Catechism of a Revolutionary* I knew John had read with great enthusiasm. This Sergey must have been quite a pleasant fellow indeed, and perhaps overly coddled by his mother, as he was clearly the type who would have provided her (had she lived) with a sappy card each and every Mother's Day. Nonetheless, it was quite clear that John had, for the last few weeks, taken to heart one of Sergey's many pearls of wisdom, particularly in the form of his sixth catechism:

> "Tyrannical toward himself, he (the revolutionary) must be tyrannical toward others. All the gentle and enervating sentiments of kinship, love, friendship, gratitude, and even honor, must be suppressed in him and give place to the cold and single-minded passion for revolution."

John was also particularly fond of Bakunin's maxim of "permanent revolution", quoting it endlessly:

> "If you took the most ardent revolutionary, vested him in absolute power, within a year, he would be worse than the Tsar himself."

On a separate piece of paper, fished out of John's pocket, I found what I would later discover to be a 5x5 Polybius Square:

|   | 1 | 2 | 3 | 4 | 5 |
|---|---|---|---|---|---|
| 1 | U | N | IJ | T | E |
| 2 | D | S | A | O | F |
| 3 | M | R | C | B | G |
| 4 | H | K | L | P | Q |
| 5 | V | W | X | Y | Z |

Keyword: United States of America

Clever. Yes.

Then codes on several random bits of paper found in John's flat could be deciphered at will.

Code: 14 41 15 14 13 31 15 13 12 12 13 35 41

Translation: "The time is nigh"

Code: 55 24 24 42 15 15 44 15 32 22 13 12 44 43 23 33 15

Translation: "Zookeepers in place"

Code: 43 13 24 12 14 23 31 15 32 24 12 24 11 32 22 13 21 15

Translation: "Lion-tamer on our side"

Sussed. After a while, it became second nature.

Given a few more messages, I would have had the entire thing cracked. I kept up a regular search in his trouser pockets and waste bins, in the hopes of finding the missing pieces to the puzzle. It all became rather exhilarating, as I didn't feel so helpless anymore. I felt I had finally found a way to help him and secure for him a better future.

Then there were the codes I wasn't prepared to break...

Though by that point, our relationship was something between medieval torture and methadone withdrawal, we managed to keep some semblance of a bond together. However, it wasn't long until I made my most shocking discovery, one which I should have at least half expected. While I was looking for some old stockings of my own (that was at least the excuse I gave myself), I dared peek into his closet safe, which was curiously and rather surprisingly unlocked. Fortunately, his recent mental state had allowed him a number of oversights. When I opened the said safe, I found an enormous number of pill bottles, carrying labels in a private language of their own:

First, the normal: Remeron, Lexapro, Venlafaxine, Savella, Cymbalta, Luvox.

Then, the less: Androstenedione, 4-androstenediol, 5-androstenediol, 19-androstenediol, 19-norandrostenediol.

And then, the completely out there: testosterone.

Testosterone? Charm me with the magic of a switch, indeed! Unsurprisingly, I decided to confront John about it immediately. At the time, he was sitting on the floor cross-legged, with a large pair of noise-cancelling headphones, listening to a vinyl of *Ascenseur pour l'échafaud.* Titus was away, yapping in the background.

I shoved a random selection of bottles into his face and demanded he tell me what they were for. In a surprisingly calm manner, he took off his headphones, looked up at me and in a measured voice, said, "So what? Nice to see your back to your snooping again."

"So what!? These pills... they are for depression and testosterone. What... what would you be taking that for?"

At this point, John gave me a wide grin, looking at me knowingly.

"C'mon, Felicity, you're a big girl. Tell me you don't know."

"John, frankly, at this moment, I have no idea what I do and don't know. I mean, I don't even know who or, more importantly, WHAT you are."

There, the circuit breaker popped. John, zero to sixty, grew more angry than I had ever seen him before. He stood up and looked at me with his eyes boiling. He then turned around, walked out of the room, slamming the door behind him. Determined not to cry, I followed him outside and down the stairs. He had descended toward the basement floor where there was a small laundry room. Once there, he turned on me with a sudden fury. In the coldest of voices, he said, "Tell me, are you ashamed of what you are? Tell me you didn't know the truth the entire time."

I had to admit, I had always had suspicions. Suspicions that had advanced to the verge of certainty during the last few weeks. To my surprise, I couldn't give him an immediate response. I thought it strange I was so stunned and caught off-guard by the question. Perhaps I had always known, but didn't want to admit to myself something that would have amounted to as much a statement about myself as it would have about him.

Lamely, I told him "no" and asked him the same question. He didn't answer. Neither of us clearly knew what to say so he just blurted, "What would your dad say about all this?"

I told him I didn't care. I then asked him why he was hiding himself.

"Hiding? Hiding in plain sight. Don't say I tricked you 'cause I didn't. You knew what you were getting into the entire time. From the very moment we said go, didn't you? I knew you were playing along and I was playing along with your playing along, and it all got ridiculous, didn't it? It's part of the reason you put up with all that abuse, isn't it? I wanted you to admit it first, even despite that whole ugly scene on the couch, but the thing is, you proved weaker than even I thought you were. And guess what, I know the other half of why you held on so long. You want to know what it is? It was because YOU wanted ME to betray our little, open secret so that you could fault ME for utterly deluding you? Isn't it?"

"John, why do you always want to turn this all back on me and give me abuse?"

"Give you abuse? Give you abuse?"

"Look, by now, I know that when you uncoil your tongue, you don't stop. Please, don't be mean. We should be talking about this, not arguing. I don't want to argue anymore."

Seeing the softness in my eyes, John relented and we decided to return upstairs for a walk around the block. Unfortunately, neither of us really knew how to begin the conversation.

After a couple of silent trips around the building, I asked him if he really believed he was a man. Did he really believe he was born a boy?

"Oh God. You're not going to go there, are you? You're not going to go all Judith Butler on me, are you? You know, we have a model for everything nowadays. I may be second-stage Kübler-Ross or third-stage Kelley-Conner. What do you think? Do they even have something for trannies?"

"As usual, John, I have no idea what you are talking about."

"You know: Denial, Anger, Bargaining… blah, blah, blah."

"No, I actually don't know, but… but what I do know is that I still love you, no matter what. I don't really care about this."

"This what?"

"You know, this. You really being a girl and all."

Taking out a cigarette, John gave me a dismissive smirk.

"Why, John? Why do we have to lie to each other as much as we do to ourselves? Can we finally take the masks off for a change?"

While saying this, I took his hand and tried to kiss him. Before we had realized it, we were already at Tompkins Square Park, where there were some boys playing next to the dog run, which was the true beginning of all of our problems.

We sat together on a rain-dampened bench. Though I kept prodding him, John clearly wasn't prepared to say anything. At a certain point, he seemed on the verge of crying himself, but instead, he threw down his cigarette and kissed me on the lips.

It was the closest I had felt to him for a long, long time. It made it all worth it, the weeks of aborted bliss, all the terrible abuse, the stabbing pain of regret. Even then, I wanted to hold on to this moment with him forever. As we got up to leave, the boys yelled after us, "Carpet munchers!"

Not paying much attention, we walked away with each of our arms around the other's shoulders. Once we had left the park, John addressed me in a somewhat conspiratorial tone.

"Tell me something…"

"Yes?"

"Why are trannies considered mentally healthy but pedos are considered deviant?"

"Well, because it's obvious."

"Why?"

"Because pedos prey on innocent children who don't have a choice, and transsexuals, well…"

"Prey upon themselves."

"No, that's not what I meant. I mean they were the victim of the body they were born into."

"You and your victims again. I told you about this…"

"John, you are a victim… struggling with who you are."

"I am no victim. I'm just whatever I decide to become. This world needs changing. Everything needs changing: you, me, everything. Great works are afoot, I tell you. You will see. Great works. You haven't seen anything yet."

"What do you mean, John?"

"This city will never be the same again."

"What is it you have planned, John? You're starting to scare me again."

"Felicity, if you really love me, you won't ask. Maybe in another life, you could be mine. All I can say is John will have to disappear for a while and someone else will replace him."

"What?"

"Smile Felicity… since you've cut your hair, maybe, you'll let me be the girl for a change. Just kiss me goodnight and don't ask any more questions."

# 23

Strange occurrences of late: glasses falling off the table without any prompting, doors slamming, books disappearing; it can only be a version of your *spukhafte Fernwirkung*. All these "accidents" were timed according to the flux and reflux of your visitation. It seems after all that in telling this tale I have, alas, disturbed your final rest. Even over the last week, your transmissions have become noticeably more stifled, more petulant:

"LEEV ME B"

Days after, you wouldn't speak to us at all, and after several all-night vigils, we thought our bridge to the other world had been sundered forever.

"SET A MAN 2 WATCH ALL NIGHT 4 I AM THE ANIMAL OF 3 SKINS"

Perhaps we were too insistent on the board (we were, after all, naught but pimpled tyros in these occult sciences), perhaps there were too many visitors you would rather not hear from. Perhaps in our eagerness to find out more about Willow and how her story ended, we had offended you. Tell us, John, had we trespassed on your eternal peace far too much? Crossed an Acheron we shouldn't have crossed? Even now, the smell of Damascus rose litters the place. Along with it, stinking nightshade, woodbine, and mandrake root. In fact, the entire contents of Hecuba's black cabinet were suggested to appease you (it turns out Ms Bat-Eyes really was a witch after all). On several occasions, we tried to use some of her counter-magic, her own brand of an apotropaic hex. We read spells from the Egyptian *Book of the Dead*, consulted the Urim and Thummim, conjured the Witch of Endor. We did everything, in fact, but stopped just short of animal sacrifice (which, needless to say, would have to have been limited to a tofu-based ersatz).

For an entire month, you seemed intent on scaring our guest away. Ms Light-Mind practically fled the place as the wind started to shudder. Indeed, your use of the pathetic fallacy (the storm winds, the thunder, the general mood) gives an inkling of the scene I am now about to describe, the setting matching the reality of where your relationship with Felicity had come. Somehow, I can still imagine you and Felicity on the grassy slope of Wave Hill with a Giorgione background of windswept trees. I recall without regret one of the last few happy times we shared together. Friends had long ago wondered if your relationship with Felicity had begun to wobble and, probing Felicity myself, she responded with a stained smile. "John and I are like Cheerios. All holes." My interpretation of what she said was completely different than what was intended at the time.

"AT END OF TIME EVEN IN OUR FUGITIVE CARESS FELCITY AND I WILL FUSE AGEN"

And so, finally, we come to that fateful 4th of July where the fireworks finally fizzled. Essentially, the only creative plot that an uninspired group of anarchists could come up with was a midnight raid on the city's two zoos and a large, visiting circus. The intention of all this was to smuggle out the more intelligent animals and release them into the wild. At some point after your disappearance, I found in your apartment the following text, which was later lost for unknown and rather mysterious reasons:

## LORD HATE-GOOD'S GUIDE TO BUILDING
## AN EXPLOSIVE DEVICE

Introduction – A few pointers for the would-be bomb maker

1.  A bomb is like a child. One must nurture it and fashion it to purpose.
2.  Each bomb serves a purpose and there are many different types. From pipe and petrol bombs to electromagnetic and flour bombs.
3.  One must ask oneself. What do you want your bomb to do? What do you want it to accomplish? To impress, inspire awe and worship? To send a message or merely cause destruction?
4.  A bomb is a representation of you. If your bomb fails or sputters, so do you.
5.  Study your target and know everything about it. Your bomb will not act in isolation. Remember that.

It continued on for pages with such drivel. Furthermore, there were a number of detailed schematics and instructions on how to build otherwise primitive explosive devices. I discovered later that you and a German IT professional, working for the UN, were assigned the task of putting together, amongst other things, the detonation devices.

A month before the fateful day, it was announced in the papers, plastered on placards all over the city, that the Ringling Brothers were in town. Lord Hate-Good sent out a simple Glagolitic intermediary to gather his myrmidons:

THE TIME IS NIGH

Though Felicity continued to question me (even at times, threatening me with the immediate and irreparable loss of her friendship), I couldn't tell her anything about John's secret doings, pretending ignorance in most cases. Her eyebeams could have melted me. On those occasions, how I could hear her heart sing, the blood throbbing within her like a plucked chord:

*Tempra tu de' cori ardenti*
*Tempra ancora lo zelo audace,*

Had she a chorus, had she an orchestra, what would she beg of him? What would she have asked me to tell him?

*Ah, riedi ancora qual eri allora,*
*quando il cor ti diedi allora,*
*ah, riedi a me.*

But it was not to be and Felicity and I began to part in smoldering silences, both knowing the truth that inevitably would divide us until the end of time. Everything she needed me to say was exactly everything I couldn't. It was only through our séances that she finally and definitely learned of my many deceptions. In the final hour, our bond too was eventually extinguished. If, dearest Felicity, we do meet again, I would forever beg your forgiveness for a sin an eternity couldn't wash away.

The plan had actually been years in the making: it was the minimum required time to get a suitable coterie of fifth columnists installed on the farther side of the zoos' enclosures. On the contrary, the tactical portion of maneuvers took shape quite quickly. Indeed, the overarching strategy took the apposite form of a mythical creature: that of the Lernaean Hydra (which was, incidentally, the code name John gave to the mission, as a loving reference to a gilded page in his most beloved bestiary). When the time came, this unassailable monster would ruthlessly stick a single frothing head inside the door of the Bronx Zoo, another at a similar establishment in Central Park, and a slithering third at the Ringling Brothers and Barnum Bailey Circus (at that time, being deployed in the rather dejected-looking environs of the Barclays Center).

John had been assigned to the most dangerous and symbolic part of the project. From the beginning, it was the part of the mission perhaps most likely to fail, as it focused on the large and comparably intractable Bronx Zoo, the historical prison of Ota Benga himself. However, being as independent as he was, John had his own peculiar interest in this section of the project. He proposed a number of rather risky innovations, which had been shouted down at an early stage by none other than Lord Hate-Good himself. Needless to say, John's ego would broach no resistance and his stubbornness, combined with a deep gash in his ego, meant he would never truly abandon what he felt was his own true mission, the one which would eventually inspire an internal mutiny against his own better judgment.

Ultimately, John's singular goal was always to rescue an okapi, that rarest and most mysterious of all animals, which must have caused a gleam in the Creator's eye. It was a schizophrenic's waking dream of a zebra, a giraffe and a horse all mixed into one. For reasons unclear at the time, it was the animal John was most obsessed by and the animal that ultimately led to the downfall of the entire mission. The original plan was that once they had broken into the zoo, they would proceed to open a number of predetermined enclosures and attempt to lead the more friendly animals toward a flock of awaiting vans (the unfriendly ones would of course be sedated and carried in little Cushmans). Once the vans had successfully driven off, it would be bombs galore: an attention-grabbing stunt meant to frighten to flight the remaining animals, all of whose enclosures had now been opened. The vans themselves would be driven to various points of New York State, where the sedated animals would be released into the wilds, regardless of whether the habitat suited them or not (in John and Lord Hate-Good's collective minds, it was a mere *casus belli* to instantiate the first wave of fractious anarchy). John's orders were to concentrate on the symbolically most important part of the zoo, the Congo Gorilla forest. Not only was Ota Benga from the Congo, but the gorillas were thought of as being the most prized (and therefore, the most unjustly imprisoned) members of the Bronx Zoo. This portion of the zoo that held the gorillas was nestled in its southwest corner, conveniently situated near the Southern Boulevard gate, which provided for an easy getaway (really, it's amazing how few people expect a zoo will be robbed and correspondingly, how few precautions are made against it). Fortunately, for John's purposes, the okapi were kept in the same enclosure as the gorillas. While it was assumed that John would assist the six others to sedate and transport the family of gorillas, John, on the contrary, decided he would splinter off and, with the aid of a tranquilizer gun, trap an okapi. His first signs of insurrection occurred while he was finishing off his bombs. He stood in deep thought next to another of his comrades at arms, who had begun carving on the glass of the gorilla enclosure (to be reported widely later):

*Iam redit et Virgo, redeunt Saturnnia regna,*

Fig 24. "Okapi"

*Iam nove progenies caelo demittitur alto.*

John told his rather short-sighted and carbuncular mission lieutenant, "I'm going for the okapi."

"What? You know you're not supposed to. The gorillas are just being sedated now. We haven't got much time."

"Don't worry. The bombs are all set. Will only take me a minute. It will all be fine, trust me."

All too famous last words. The plot would ultimately fail miserably. Indeed, while John was away, his remaining charges had enormous difficulties lifting the sleeping gorilla babies onto the turf tricksters. Furthermore, one of the larger gorillas began to regain consciousness quicker than expected. Ominously, it turned out they had neglected to bring enough sedative and with John off with what remained, there was nothing else to be done. The angry female gorilla started wreaking havoc, forcing her would-be liberators to flee. John hadn't heard the shouting, but when he came back (unsuccessfully without the okapi), he witnessed a mad scene: the female gorilla was making the most frightful noise and running around with what she perceived to be her dead baby. The others had left the enclosure but were now afraid for John's safety. Behind glass, they signaled him toward the enclosure's exit, which the mother was now guarding anxiously, while the father began twitching from his own induced coma. John was temporarily paralyzed and had little idea of what to do. His first thought was to flee, but then the angry mother had other ideas and started charging at him. John knew he had only one opportunity to save himself. I'm told that during the frightful instant, he was stolid as an oak. Just as the gorilla was within a 20-foot distance, John coolly raised the tranquilizer gun and using the skills he had practiced so many times in the Manhattan firing range, shot her squarely in the chest. The animal, seeing the dart protruding from its left breast, suddenly lost its rage and became strangely pensive. The shot had entered not too far away from where she was cradling her daughter. Fortunately for John, it was also at that point that the mother gorilla noticed that her child was still writhing in the slowish manner of sleepers still troubled by dreams. At this point, the gorilla slowly sat down and nestled her daughter until she too fell asleep. John was saved. After a nail-biting 10-minute wait, he was able to approach the enclosure door. By now, it was far too late to rescue the operation and John and his cohort had to abandon their mission, as the time-bombs would soon count down their final digits. They all ran toward the vans and drove off hurriedly through the night. Fortunately, despite all the failings, no one got caught.

John was forced to go into hiding, and despite the fact they managed to keep an elephant-tamer in captivity for a week and scare the living wits out of him, nothing much else happened. And so, after months of careful planning, the entire mission was reduced to utter failure. Indeed, it was only the circus crew who were somewhat successful, which meant that a few lucky New Yorkers woke up to a pair of giraffes, one elephant, two monkeys and a sea lion all lounging about Central Park's River Cafe, all to their respective want, doing backstrokes in the lake, pulling the pigtails of little girls, or lazily grazing on Sheep's Meadow. However, much to Lord Hate-Good's grave disappointment, there were no lions, no tigers or bears to really make anyone afraid. Hardly the "greatest show on earth", much less the beginnings of a world revolution. Indeed, out of all the missions, the Central Park Zoo operation was the worst failure of them all: the Offsidesmen were tipped off, most of the people involved there were arrested, and Lord Hate-Good, as the leader of the operation, was ironically one of the few to have gotten away scot-free.

# 24

Dear John,

Just a quick note.

I was told I should not attempt to contact you under any circumstances, but should rather relay messages to you via Zulfikar. I received your note today, slipped under the door. I also heard from Zulf, what little he knew about the failed attempt by the Ota Benga society. He said they were threatening him and that he had no choice but to do as they said. I am truly horrified. The news is all over the papers. I hope they aren't threatening you too. My fingers are trembling as I write this.

Tell me, why would you ever do something so stupid and ridiculous? I can't tell you how much I hate you for it and at the same time, I hope you are safe. For some idiotic reason, I can't quite fathom, I do still love you. Please, call me if you can.

By the way, I also read the poem you included, the Mother of Miscarriage, and now, after all this time, I understand the truth I've always known about Willow.

# 25

The Mother of Miscarriage

Spiny bubble, dangerous
in your element, porcu-
pine of the undersea
clothed in nettles
like some sex toy
a true product of
your environment
eons and eons ago
says a loud voice not
unlike that that spoke
to Moses and Abraham
you first flexed beneath
the Flood, where Noah
was counting the birds
of the air, the beast of
the earth. Had he known
anything of you, one
crowned in thorns, built
by tedious assembly
as if by the iron mind
of the Holy Inquisition?
Animal of the unloved,
Angel of the unresolved
most fearful when you
where most feared, how
slander plagued you, how
like the great desert sun.

Where you truly wronged?
Where you
merely full of hot air?
Poisonous as death adders?
Where you
trying to be dangerous,
*Achtung!*
you who knew this sun
would one day set
*Achtung!*
you who never slept and
would rise from oblivion
*Achtung!*
to one day teach us fools
*Achtung!*
to approach your proximity
*Achtung!*
somewhat unafraid...


**How they Build The Blow Fish**


It wasn't under the grease and sweat
Of the Industrial Machine Or
Under the Rigid Light of the Clean Room
That You were Made
The Miracle of many Hosannas
The Red Light of the Femme District
Gears and Cogs, Transistors and LEDs
Prayer Wheel and Recursive Loop
Yet you were a Created Thing
Flawless in Design The Great Architect
Who holds the Blueprint saw Beauty
In your Dreadnought Exoskeleton

He was German and grew Up
In a QUIET village near Hamburg
He entered the Polytechnic at 18
Learning Prefabrication and Mech
He read the *Great Gatsby* in Translation
HE put you in a Great Cauldron
And Drew you out HOT
Sat you on a Sanitary Table
And there You Sat like a Nervous Dream
In a Goose-Feathered Pillow
Steaming from the previous Night
You Were the Answer to All
His Prayers and He Saw you
And Knew You as His Own
He loved You but you Spurned Him
I am of No Creator, You Said
Put Me back In the Cauldron
And he Would not Unmake You

Fig 7. "Mother of Miscarriage"

# 26

Dear John,

Though I know you will never read this, I still feel I need to write it down.

I have heard the news of your passing only days ago. I shall not attend any funeral, even if there is one. I do not know, myself, if I am dead or alive any longer. Maybe both...

Slow learner, at least I've finally figured out that you and Willow are in fact the same person. Everything started coming together: the "magic eye", the Latin phrases "novus ordo seclorum"... how could I have missed it all? Of course, deep inside, I knew almost from the very beginning... that you were a muxe spirit. That I too was perhaps somewhat of one, but I could never accept it because I knew no one I ever cared about could either. I wanted to believe you were a boy (even THAT timid, nameless boy), so much so that for a time, I think I did. Our little couch scene was just one more petty attempt to alleviate my own cognitive dissonance and served only to make it worse.

Notwithstanding my own inner turmoil, I will never quite understand how you could have spent so many years denying yourself, splitting your personality into two, into three, into four parts? I suppose it must have run in the family. Your mother never recognized you so why should you. That you often used those horrible words - "faggots", "dikes", "trannies" - is all the evidence I need to know that you must have hated yourself.

While you presented as a man, you also presented as a lover, a revolutionary, indeed, you presented as a number of things, but I always wondered if even you, of all people, knew your true self, or whether in fact there were many Johns and that your whole confusion with life was how to figure out which one you actually were at any given time. Certainly, much of you was in every personality you selected, but, imagine me, being stuck in your hall of mirrors, futilely trying to separate the source from the reflection. In the end, they all in a sense have their own reality.

Zulfikar was kind enough to let me borrow some of Willow's/your diaries. I will always remember one particularly heartbreaking entry:

> "Sometimes, I wish I weren't a girl at all. I don't want to be weak. I want to have a voice like everyone else. I wish I was strong enough to speak. Them boys was right. Without a voice, I am nothing. I don't deserve to live."

So Tiresias, "throbbing between two lives", do you dare come back and reveal to me how this is all going to end, especially as you've so kindly left me behind? I can't tell you how much I hate you for leaving me alone, scared, and confused about everything in my life. Who should I be nowadays? Should I be your carpet-munching Orphea? Maybe I will listen to what you commanded in one of my last sessions on the ouija:

"DON'T B 2 GUD IN THE END WANT 2 SEE U SOONER THAN L8ER."

John, how can I say it? I miss you more than life. Maybe I too will follow you below. I already seem to be having wild imaginings...

Like the other day, I could have sworn I saw you and even chased you down into the subway, only to find you had melted into the crowd. These days, I seem to see glimpses of you everywhere. It's like I can't give you up. You still haunt me, John. I never believed in ghosts, but I do now.

# 27

An alchemist, they say, can turn lead into gold, but I fear I've done quite the opposite in my attempts to rescue your *Guide*. The elements have all been expended and we are left with the mere dross of a failed experiment, the insipid goop of a worthless wind egg. I am told on authority that even the periodic table must have an end, and so alas, even the universe and its mad demiurge, that poor, behind-the-scenes comedian, must also run out of material. Dear John, I still see your eyes flash in that dark Hall of Minerals: Iron, Lithium, Carbon, Iodine, Tantalum, Sulfur... all elements of your distress: mere representations of your will, your heartbreak, your humanity, your salt pillar of a past, your endless suffering and finally, your ultimate hell.

"WILO AND I R UNITED AGEN AS SHE IS THE FLAME OF MY OWN IMOLATION"

Let us recount now your last week with us. You now resembled nothing, if not the eternal Man of Sorrows, your moods as noxious and subject to the weather as quicksilver. It was a particularly cold October, described in the usual fashion: bare branches, spiraling wind, dead oak leaves, *Gretchen am Spinnrade*. Indeed, only the logarithmic passage of the days has managed to put all these paradigm shifts into their proper proportion, so that like Bruegel (a logarithmic scale painter himself), we see in its proper shade and dimension the pettiness of human struggle. Your hair disheveled, barely eating, you seldom came outside, and for good reason. You were having to lay low to avoid a once nameless authority that had, by that point, assembled itself into very specific acronyms: the NYPD, the FBI, and probably even the CIA. It is only now, with certain events having occurred, that I can even contemplate committing all this to paper. And what were these events? Ms Light-Mind, foolish cow, died a couple years later; Felicity, dear angel, moved back to England (visits time to time) with Titus, and Lord Hate-Good, never content, and having been arrested for assisting in yet another violent animal rights protest, felt a searing heat from the Offsidesmen. To his great credit, he finally decided to flee New York. It wouldn't surprise me if he one day faked his own death like other of his previous accomplices. As for my fate, I, a mere "attendant lord", hope this document will go some way in exonerating me from the present coil, otherwise, I shall see the inside of a prison cell soon enough. If someone else besides myself is reading this, it's probably unlikely that I've escaped my fate. Maybe a similar plea of insanity is all I've got.

Now, I only have to relate the very last time I or anyone else I know saw you.

It was the night of October 7th, 11:43. You came to my house to apprise me of your intention to visit your mother. To participate in what you referred to as some "good, old-fashioned Primal Therapy". Indeed, it was something you thought you had neglected far too long. I remember clearly the gray atmosphere: for at least a week, the strains of Bach's *Die letzten Leiden des Erlösers* had writhed constantly in your presence. Unfortunately, between that moment and this, you ultimately found infinity, leaving me, *contra fiat*, to close your great, parthenogenetic curse. Indeed, though Webster or Kyd might not have rated so well the body count, I have no doubt we all felt in full the loss of each soul that fell into the marginalia. Let the earth rest upon them lightly: John, Willow, Paul, Brice, Shinkiro and the rest... all now exiles of our Earth.

But I had long ago sainted you both: *Perpetuae et Felicitatis*

You are now her perpetual dream, while she endures as an eternal slave to your memory. For all of us that remain, the city has become an obstacle course of dead zones we can no longer access, as they invariably recall signs of your passage. It has become one more world reduced to mere geography. On the table, in my darkened apartment, one still finds, amongst many monuments of a shared past, dead azaleas the wind no longer bestirs; this formation you placed inside that red, plastic icosahedron, whose water evaporated so long ago, even as to evoke the barren surface of a distant, failed planet.

And even now, Felicity is convinced that she did espy you with her own eye. Felicity, so desperate to wish you back, is asking everyone she knows if they have also seen you. Poor thing, she has the appearance of the living dead and seems more and more part of your world by the day. Even at the board, I once felt her forehead: cold and confining as a crypt, even as she tried to raise the temper of your ghost, censuring you for leaving her alone. Pale angel, her eyes already filled with tomorrow's tears…

Oh, Pale Laodamia, after your brief exchange, please leap not into the flame.


"REMEMBR 2 MEDUSA ONCE BEAUTIFUL TWICE VIOLETED"


And you too would have hated anyone's pity, perhaps preferring to be your own sort of monster.


"DO NOT REFLECT U MUST DEFLECT ALL PITY 4 UR MONSTERS"


At least I know now that your body will finally find rest, cold as a seabed, pale as birch. There was a part of you in all of us. Eunuchoid, little seraphim, whose heart has been reduced to a smoke swirling across the oceans. Your memory sealed by the six-sided wing stroke of a collective memory... even now, I'm having a bit of trouble keeping it all together as sense has left me...

My thoughts fray...

My thoughts fray...

So now, we must return to our Eleusinian Mysteries: a couple of candles, a bright tear of rum mixed in a china bowl to allow our little planchette to weave the remainder of its tale. So one more deep intake of breath as the spirits of the netherworld gather sly as polecats, hovering over us, reminding us that our past is always with us. Like you, we surrendered all our dread of death...

"ORPHEO SHOWED DEATH A LYR AND I MAY 2"

For you, John, a stranded couplet is all I can muster...

The whispers wound him round and round
His soul aloft, his body underground

Everything in the end falls apart...

*The Guide* was ultimately the only sign of your final desquamation. Your problem was simple, John, you never thought yourself worthy of anybody's love, including your own, and you had to prove this to yourself over and over again. I know I could never truly understand how hard it must have been for you. Being one of that spoiled progeny of boomers, I was taught from an early age never to open the gate latch and venture far outside the safe garden of my childhood. We (as a generation) never wanted to grow up, but rather remain children of entitlement and pure fantasy. But you were different. Your childhood was piteously ripped away from you. In many ways, I think this forced you to live a life in reverse, one that ultimately led you on a pilgrimage to find the genesis of all your troubles. I guess, in some way, you've now given all us fools a good reason to finally grow up.

We spent weeks dealing with your passage. There were small weepy gatherings in dark apartments where no one really knew what to say or do. What Felicity had mourned most was the fact of not hearing your voice anymore, a thing she was unable to fully come to terms with. Fate is cruelest when it is nearest. Indeed, just when we started to get glimpses of your true identity, you deliberately took yourself away from us. After all, you had managed a neat, little card trick. You only presented certain faces, certain parts of your personality to certain people; other cards, you kept hidden, and only revealed them to those you thought might appreciate a particular one the most. In the end, no one saw the full deck. We had long accepted the disconcerting fact that though we might not know much about you as individuals, collectively, we could add different shades of perspective and, in so doing, put together a composite of the man. It was this simple realization that made me hit on the idea of the ouija. At first, the entire concept was treated with utter disdain (and I accused of poor taste), but it gradually gained currency, first with Miss Bat-Eyes, then with others, until Felicity (after seeing some of the written transcripts) agreed with great reluctance to give it a try. With Felicity, the shuttle was the most timid, but in time, the most moving. It was with her that you made one of your most poignant statements:

"HAPPY 2 HAV LUVED ONCE IN MY LIFE"

Even now, I sit, aching for your voice, but it doesn't always come. So I remain here in this empty room, surrounded by candles, trying to evoke your presence in other ways. The playlist on repeat:

1. Second movement of Wagenseil's *Concerto for Harp, 2 Violins and Cello*
2. Faure's *Prélude et fugue*
3. Górecki's third symphony
4. Albioni, *Adagio in G minor*
5. Strauss' *Four Last Songs*

And last, but not least:

6. Joy Division's *Atmosphere*

It was these songs that I often heard you play in your saddest of moods. I remember that very last, brief moment in your room. I had to smuggle you into your own building under heavy disguise (in retrospect, a needless precaution). At two in the morning, while you were collecting certain things, I stood engrossed in a single large print you had on your wall. One that I had never really contemplated before. It was what you referred to as Uccello's *Wilde Jagd*, or in layman's terms, the *Hunt in the Forest*. It was a painting you once told me represented "a strange and ultimately reductionist form of death". You wondered endlessly at those sleek greyhounds, the glassy-eyed horses mystified by the darkness, the curiously unseen prey and ultimately, the absurd conundrum posed by the painting itself: indeed, what thing could be captured (or even hunted for that matter) in the very blackness of night? As always, you had your answer. "If nothing else," you said, "this painting proves that the meaning of life will be hidden from us, even at the very end, that the picture is nothing more than life's mystery, blurred to its final vanishing point." Unfortunately, it was a vantage from which none of us could save you. Perhaps now, you have finally found your sought-after prey.

Last rites: before you left, you gave me various instructions, one of which included the delivery of a valedictory letter to Felicity. You also implored me to burn *The Guide*, as you couldn't bear to do it yourself. Call it a premonition, but despite my being unable to admit it to myself, I knew this was to be our last meeting. You were never good with goodbyes and wanted to make sure the whole thing seemed a casual departure, nothing so final as it proved to be. Nonetheless, I cried my eyes out in front of that painting, long after you left. Why? Because, amongst other things, though I never said anything, I'd lost a friend I had truly grown to love.

So now, I am left to close your book and by necessity, give you the last word:

> "I SEE MY FATHER I HAV BUREED AWAY HIS DARKNESS I ENTER THE ARENA AS IT FILLS WITH TEARS THE WILD BEASTS MOVE INWARD THREATEN I WAS STRIPPED NAKED AND BECAME A MAN MY NAME HAS BEEN TAKEN FRUM ME BORN IN VIOLENCE DIE IN VIOLENCE I AM DEVOURED FROM WITHIN NAM SIBYLLAM QUIDEM CUMIS EGO IPSE OCULIS MEIS VIDI IN AMPULLA PENDERE ET CUM ILI PUERI DICERENT SYBL WHAT DO U WANT RESPONDEBAT ILA I WANT 2 DIE BLOOD MY BLUD RUNS AND NEVER LETS ME LEEV MY BLUD POISONS I AM MOVING BACKWARD AS THE OARS THE MOTHER NIGHT HAS GIVEN ME SAIL INTO HER DARKNESS 2 U LET ME RETAIN MY NAME THE CARNELIAN WINGS THE NIGHT HAS GIVEN ME R LIKE OARS THE CITY HAS ITS CASUALTIES I MUST FIND MY NAME IS WRITEN DOWN SOMEWHERE BENEATH THE WILO THEY TORE ME APART FRUM THE INSIDE I BEAR

NO NAME LET ME PASS I WAS STRIPPED
NAKED MY KINGDOM COME THERE IS
LIFE AFTER THE GRAVE THERE IS A LIGHT
I BECAME A MAN ALL CRAVING ALL
CRAVING MY KINGDOM DESIRING I LOVED
ONCE I SEE MY FATHER AND HE DOES
NOT KNOW MY NAME I MUST BEAR HIS
SIGN MOTHER I MUST BEAR HER SIGN IT'S
IN MY NATURE THE WORLD IS A TURTLE
IT IS WADING THE NIGHT AND I AM A
CARNELIAN SCORPION UPON ITS BACK
I AM UPON ITS BACK I AM STRUCK DOWN
IN THE ARENA AND SO MY HAPPINESS I
AM MOVING IN DOWN A CORRIDOR LIT
FROM WITHIN I AM A WOMAN A WEEPING
WILO BY THE RIVER GOD I AM CLIMBING
INTO THE MOTHER NIGHT I AM 2 SEE MY
BLOOD RUINED LET ME PASS AS I HAVE NO
NAME NO DUST BEARS A NAME I AM 2 SEE
MY FATHER LET MY NAME REMAIN WITH
ME I DID LUV ONCE THE DAY IS COMING
AGEN I WILL SEE U AGEN CLIMB DOWN
THE NIGHT LIT FRUM WITHIN"

# 28

Dear Felicity,

How do you really begin a suicide note? Probably not like this...

First off, I just wanted to say how awfully sorry I am for the way I treated you. For all the things I put you through. As you can now fully see, I wasn t having an easy time of it, myself. Anyway...

I guess, ultimately, we were never meant to live long with each other. Given that what I fear most in life is the dreaded cliché, I m sorry to leave you with yet another... the infamous "by the time you read this..."

I m sorry if I ever tricked you into thinking I was something I wasn t. I realized you pretty much figured out I was a girl much earlier than you might have admitted it to yourself. Nonetheless, you went on with it, because I guess we might both have agreed that living with the illusion was better than living without it. Did it really matter much in the end anyway? If anything, we were honest in the one way that did matter... we cared deeply about each other and perhaps even loved one other. I know I loved you.

Given I had forced *The Guide* on you, I wanted to put a final period to Willow s (my) story.

I m sure you ve figured this all out by now, so please excuse my being redundant.

You see, I finally learned the full truth of my violent background. It took my angrily confronting Jayna at three in the morning to get her version of a story, one that perhaps compromised impartiality for the sake completeness. How many times I stood drunk and lachrymose in front of her apartment at ungodly hours, just building my courage and rage? How many times did I not go in or dare knock at her door? How many times I was left wondering whether or not she spent a single moment thinking about me and what I might or might not be doing? When I finally did knock on her door, revolver in hand, I wasn t surprised to find that nothing had changed in all those years. She still lived in that wild apartment amongst all the dead things of the earth.

The first thing I discovered from her (and which any child is so happy to discover) was that my "mother" had never wanted me. For obvious reasons, she desired a life outside of that confining backwater and a child would have merely gotten in her way. I also learned that Paul (dear "Grandpappy ") was the myth of a myth, a lie two times removed from any kind of truth. Maybe that s what makes the pain he left behind so difficult to place. Our little family tragedy all started when he came back from the wildernesses out West. After the three sons put their worn-out mother to rest,

Paul tried to corral these children (who were little more than strangers to him) into a wild approximation of a family. Unfortunately, just when the project showed some initial signs of success, Bishop was killed in a car accident. This forced everything to break apart again: Josiah went off to the military and Brice, in a moment of desperation, convinced my mother to marry him, threatening suicide otherwise. It was a fairly loveless marriage, but somehow worked for a time. Needless to say, the relationship quickly descended into its inexorable nightmare phase. After a number of relatively minor run-ins with the authorities and a ridiculous need to prove himself to Jayna, Brice followed his brother Josiah into the military. Three years later, they would send him, along with Josiah, to Afghanistan during the first Gulf War. When he came back for good, he was in absolute pieces. He had, of course, been diagnosed with post-war syndrome, but they (and in this case, I mean the government/army) couldn t or wouldn t do much to help him. Given the circumstances, it was inevitable that Brice would revisit his old habits and like the rest of his family (except of course Josiah), turned into a drunk.

Even before the war, Brice was unable to hold down a regular job and wasn t completely happy with Jayna traveling every day to go to college. He became increasingly resentful of her wanting to make something of herself and leave that podunk town, where her own father had been so tragically slaughtered. For anyone who saw them fight, it was obvious something had to break. Seeing all the signs, Paul became deathly afraid my mother would ultimately leave Brice, which would have had catastrophic consequences. Already prone to depression, Brice didn t seem to have much to live for and would sally forth into the deep woods for weeks at a time, with no one knowing whether he was dead or alive. Spineless Paul, now resigned to Jayna s immanent departure, got it into his head that the only way to keep her around was to get her pregnant. Fortunately, for his purposes, Jayna had also become increasingly unstable and had taken to the bottle. Within a matter of weeks, she found herself dropping out of college for a semester.

Curiously, when things began to go south, Paul took the side of Jayna over that of his own son. Indeed, he was incredibly supportive of her, a charm offensive that must have been near impossible for a man of his proclivities. It got to the point that she would run to his comforting arms whenever Brice would treat her badly. It started subtly at first, he would hold her hand, innocently kiss her forehead, until one night, he managed to get her so drunk, she was virtually unconscious. Like a hyena waiting in the bushes, he took full advantage of her temporary handicap: one of those reckless moods in which she would do almost anything to spite Brice. Rumors had already abounded about her sleeping around with other men. Furthermore, she had become more than wise to the fact that Paul had begun to caress her in a different manner than he had in the past. The embraces were now a tad too long, his hands wandered ever so slightly off the mark. At times, she teased herself, wondering how far could she take it. After all, she understood she lived in a world of base animals. What worst could she do? She took the whole thing with a devilish fascination and thought she could play one off the other, father against son. Although she wouldn t admit it to me or to herself, in all probability, she had intentionally seduced the old fool. Brice being gone (his long absences had of themselves begun to attract rumors of infidelity), Jayna was in a dangerous mood and tried with as much alcohol as she could to obliterate all the misery she had endured over the past few months. All she wanted was to feel like a woman again like a human being. Unfortunately, once she d started the machine, she couldn t stop the gears from grinding away and ultimately (and perhaps even predictably), she was left in a dark shed, crying after the experience. She would only realize later that Paul had finally achieved exactly what he intended the entire time. For once, she had been outsmarted by the old idiot.

A couple of months later, when she realized she was pregnant, she was completely distraught. Once Paul knew he had achieved his aim, he treated her in a completely different manner. She d considered an abortion, but Paul wouldn t let her out of the house and even sabotaged her car so she couldn t drive herself to town. In his view, that little child would straighten Brice out and no one had to know anything about his involvement at all. As for Jayna, there was nothing she could do. She was only 20 at the time, trying as hard as she could to make her slow way though pre-med. At the time, she thought the best solution was to get Brice out of the house and persuaded him to join the army. With him gone, she endured the pregnancy and Paul s cruel treatment throughout. Brice had sobered up and was immediately sent to Desert Shield to join his remaining brother. In fact, it was just after he left that he learned of her pregnancy. With him out of the way and the pregnancy advanced beyond return, she somehow convinced Paul to let her finish school at the local community college. A brief period of peace ensued, where Brice became so obsessed with me that a golden halo once again returned to their relationship. That was of course until that fateful last tour, from which he returned worse than ever. Already, in the middle of his second tour, he had gotten wind of Josiah s death. But as Paul would always say, two sons were ultimately lost to that war.

After being discharged and despite his now having what he thought to be his child, it didn t take Brice long to reinstate his pattern of domestic violence. Neither Jayna nor Paul

were exactly sure as to whether he had begun to
have suspicions about my parentage. Jayna, on
the one hand, suspected he might have. In any
regard, he began to beat her on a regular basis,
sometimes even in front of me. In one moment
of utter craziness, he d even pulled a gun on
her, thinking she was an Afghani militant.
It goes without saying that Jayna began to
fear for her own safety and hated to watch the
disintegration of a man she cared less and less
about, a man who resolved to do nothing but
drink all day. She finally got up the courage
to tell him that she had been accepted to
medical school and that she was going to take
me with her to New York. At first, he didn t say
much, but instead, went out on his usual run
to the town to get wasted. When he came back, he
was ready to commit to his normal demolition,
this time with a belt. We were all in the house
and I must have been screaming as even Paul
was woken out of one of his post-epileptic
comas. That s when it happened. Jayna, in an
effort to defend herself, went under the bed and
pulled out Brice s gun, and killed him right
then and there. He had been shot almost point
blank so that bits of his brains were sprayed
all over the room. She hadn t meant to kill him,
only to frighten him, but she was trembling so
much that when he lunged, her finger twitched
ever so lightly against that hair trigger.
It s the only thing I remember of the incident,
my mother slowly twisting her head towards
me. She took one look at me, realizing what

she had done. I can recall nothing else than
the frozen image of those banjo eyes, nothing
else of the gore and resultant drama. Memory
is a funny thing, especially in children. I
remember not one iota of how she stood there,
covered in his brains, how she then almost put
the gun to her own head. She only filled me
in on those details when I spoke to her last
night. She could do nothing else but run. You,
of course, know that we never saw her again
until that day we arrived at her doorstep.

Unsurprisingly, it was left to Paul, that
heartless man, to clean up all the mess. What
was going through his head the entire time, I
will never know. That inscrutable monster put
his son s dead body into the lake and tied it
down with a bunch of stones. He then spread
the news far and wide that Brice must have died
in an accident on one of the lakes. With three
sons now dead under tragic circumstances, no
one bothered to ask any questions. The body
was never recovered, but his overturned boat
was. For my own part, I didn t speak a word for
almost seven years. Post-traumatic syndrome
is what they called it (guess it must run in
the family). Months later, we learned that
Jayna had made her way up to New York, where
she worked as a waitress, paid her way through
veterinary school, and still somehow had
money enough to send back home. How she had
found the strength amidst all her weakness, I
will never know.

The great irony of everything is that I pretty much found my voice again right after my "Grandpappy" was killed. But not before, I put another part of myself to rest. When they finally told me what had happened to Grandpappy, it really bled me. Fortunately, it happened when I was all by myself out in the woods. At nine years old, I finally buried that wolf that had been eating me, eating Willow from the inside only to find there was nothing of her left. Only John and the scars of a tortured child remained. "Mother", never said nothing. In fact, before any of this was allowed to happen, my "mother", still unable to come to terms with her fear of my potential hatred, refused to take custody of me and pawned me off to a relative she had rediscovered upon arriving in New York. No excuse was given except that I had been through a lot and that I needed a more stable household. Perhaps for good measure, she even slipped some misoprostol into my breakfast milk without me knowing. In any case, a kind old, suburban woman fed me, took me to school, and made sure I wanted for nothing except a real family. Children, if nothing else, are extremely adaptable. It was only when I was an adolescent that John began to manifest himself. When that kind, old woman died not far away from my 16th birthday, I was completely free.

So there it is. Can you believe it? I probably belong on *The Jerry Springer* Show or in an anthropological museum as a representation of the most psychologically messed-up creature in human history, the gray-matter perversion of a mental okapi. Just think of it: the man who was supposed to be my father was killed by my mother and my real father, a product of pure evil, died before I knew who or what he was. You once told me not to make a beast of myself, but I was raised by nothing more than animals.

Whether I live or not, I will always remember a passage my dear "Grandpappy" once read to me from the Bible:

*"For that which befalls the sons of men befalls beasts; the same thing befalls them: as the one dies, so dies the other; yea, they have all one breath; so that a man has no advantage over a beast: for all is vanity."*

There is no doubt, I feel sick in my own skin. More sick than even I have ever felt before. The person I invested all my trust and love in was nothing more than a rapist, a liar, a potential pedophile, you name it. I honestly believe those protesters must have taken his humanity from him out there in that forest. The great Paul Bunyan, logging man, indeed. When they took his livelihood, they took his manhood too. That s why he was doing all those things to her and to me. And as for Jayna, no wonder she never wanted anything to do with me. How could she? How could she raise a daughter who had witnessed her murder what the daughter believed to be its father? How could she face again a child she had lied to about everything for several years? The money she sent back was her wage of guilt, her blood money. I can certainly understand why she rejected me and why I ultimately even rejected myself. I realize now that I am an abomination. Neither man nor woman, neither son nor daughter, I am without any place in this world. As the product of violence, it is only fit that my life ends in violence. Ultimately, in this world, we are all part of the wildlife.

I m not sure why I m telling you this, but you are really the only person I have ever loved. Perhaps, raised the way I was, I never knew how to love. I therefore loved like a beast and I apologize for that. But I did (in the only way I knew how) love you. If out of everything you think you now know about me, you can only believe one thing, I hope, at least, it is this.

Goodbye Felicity, please, I beg, remember something good of me...

CPSIA information can be obtained
at www.ICGtesting.com
Printed in the USA
LVOW12s1729020317

525947LV00004B/833/P

9 781911 079477